His hand slid up her arm and hauled her closer.

She held herself very still. He couldn't know, could he, that every tender place on her body was throbbing? And she refused to give him the satisfaction of knowing how well his deviltry worked.

"Go ahead, dollface," he said softly, his fingers caressing. "Say no."

It took everything she had to wrench away from him. "No. I will not fall for your chicanery again."

Magee blinked. "My 'chicanery'?"

"This game that you play. I think you're good at this thrill business. And that you enjoy how you can make me . . . respond."

"I guess that's something—being good at this thrill business." He crossed his arms over his chest. "But how come your response is my fault?"

"Because it's obvious you're doing something to mess me up. My head rules my hormones. My brain commands my body. The fact is, I have a short list of qualities that interest me in a man, and nothing about you, Magee, is on it."

By Christie Ridgway

THE THRILL OF IT ALL
DO NOT DISTURB
THEN COMES MARRIAGE
FIRST COMES LOVE
THIS PERFECT KISS
WISH YOU WERE HERE

CHRISTIE RIDGWAY

THE THRILL OF IT ALL

AVON BOOKS
An Imprint of HarperCollinsPublishers

This is a work of fiction. Names, characters, places, and incidents are products of the author's imagination or are used fictitiously and are not to be construed as real. Any resemblance to actual events, locales, organizations, or persons, living or dead, is entirely coincidental.

AVON BOOKS
An Imprint of HarperCollins*Publishers*
10 East 53rd Street
New York, New York 10022-5299

Copyright © 2004 by Christie Ridgway
ISBN: 0-06-050290-8
www.avonromance.com

First Avon Books paperback printing: November 2004

Avon Trademark Reg. U.S. Pat. Off. and in Other Countries, Marca Registrada, Hecho en U.S.A.
HarperCollins® is a registered trademark of HarperCollins Publishers Inc.

Printed in the U.S.A.

10 9 8 7 6 5 4 3 2 1

For the Hartley family—
Alan, Dana, Brandon, and Caelyn—
the perfect companions for our
Joshua Tree National Park adventure.
Thank you for being such great friends.

One

There was more dazzle in the Las Vegas ballroom than a convention of Crest White Strippers on a glitter factory tour. Ultraviolet smiles snapped on and off like flashbulbs, their beams catching in the diamond-drop chandeliers overhead and in the facets of the cut-crystal stemware on the snowy tablecloths. Celine's show at Caesar's Palace was dark that night, but Celine herself was still at work, her silver sequins winking as she slinked forward to double-airkiss the cheeks of the Home Shopping Network's CEO. Nearby, the canary-yellow jewel in J-Lo's cocktail ring—a simulated "Jem" from her own signature line—caught the light and bounced off the glasses of the QVC executive sitting beside her.

At the table reserved for GetTV—front and center, as GetTV had received the most nominations for the awards that honored the best in the shopping network and infomercial industry—no high-powered executive or high-salaried celebrity could distract Felicity Charm from the single most important figure in the room. Elegant, serene, and standing alone on a satin-skirted table atop the stage, the fourteen-inch statuette, nicknamed the "Joanie," commanded all Felicity's attention.

Her hand curled, as if already wrapping around the trophy's slick surface. The Joanie's gleaming fourteen-karat finish would pick up the matching threads in the white chiffon of her simple strapless evening dress, Felicity thought. Perfect. The crowning touch to the image she'd been shaping and polishing for the past sixteen years.

A silky southern accent snaked through the buzz of the crowd. "Don't you feel like a big ol' fake?"

"No." Felicity's gaze whipped left, clashing with the cool, calculating one of Andrea Rice, the co-worker seated next to her at the banquet table. To cover for her knee-jerk outburst, Felicity tempered her voice and worked up a half-smile. "I mean, uh . . . what?"

Andrea shrugged. "Oh, it's just me and my jitters. About now I start thinkin' how undeservin' I am or I start worryin' about givin' my acceptance speech while somethin' leafy green and the size of south Texas is stuck between my teeth."

Felicity hung on to her noncommittal smile. Not only wouldn't she let that four-letter word "fake" into her head, but she'd start cashiering at K mart before she imagined herself standing up in front of three thousand industry professionals—not to mention the TV viewers watching the awards ceremony live at home—with a Popeye-worthy portion of spinach wedged in the seam of her two front incisors.

Andrea waved a hand. "I can't imagine why I'm givin' it a li'l ol' thought. This might be my *seventh* nomination for Host of the Year and the *only* time you've been mentioned, but I'm just sure you'll win."

It wasn't lost on Felicity that the moment demanded she reciprocate, but it was all she could do to respond with another smile. Her stage crew had let her know that in the weeks since *Advertising Age* magazine had named her "America's Sweetheart of Sales," the other woman had been tirelessly campaigning the members of the Electronic Retail Association to vote for anyone *but* "Felicity Full-of-Herself," as Andrea liked to call her behind her back.

The chandeliers briefly flickered, signaling that the commercial break was almost over and sending Felicity's pulse rate soaring. As live close-ups of herself and the four other Host of the Year nominees popped onto the huge screens hanging over the stage, the man on her right, her producer, Drew Hartnett, leaned down to murmur into her ear.

"This is it," he said.

She smiled for the umpteenth time, as anxious to hide her nerves from him as she was to conceal them from everyone else. Drew always looked like her ideal man—but tonight! He wore a tuxedo like other men wore jeans and sweatsocks and his cultured bearing only made her more determined that any cracks in her poised, self-assured shell wouldn't show.

Drew deserved no less. They'd worked together the past two years with the tacit agreement that they were too busy with the transformation of GetTV to allow a romantic relationship to steal their focus, but with this year's success, she knew the time was ripe for that to change.

Winning the Joanie would prove Felicity good enough to win Drew, too.

The chandeliers dimmed, and then the emcee bounded back onto the stage. During the next few minutes, while the cameras retained live, tight shots on the others, the fifth screen displayed a canned segment about each nominee, complete with gushing voice-over and clips from their respective shows.

Felicity sat frozen, trying to look bright-eyed and attentive through the others' spotlights. Then it was her turn.

"In the past year at GetTV, Felicity Charm has turned our industry on its ear. Not content with the demographic targeted by QVC, HSN, Worldwide Shopping, and the infomercial retailers, Felicity speaks to—and more importantly sells to—her generation. *InStyle* magazine calls her the 'It Girl of Electronic Retail.'

"Maybe it's the products she presents—many that she selects herself—or the celebrities she convinces to appear with her, from Sarah Michelle Geller demonstrating moves from her *Buffed-Up* series of exercise DVDs to the rock band the Red Hot Chili Peppers offering up their special Red Hot Chili Pepper pasta sauce. Whatever the reason, there's an undeniable magic about Felicity that has twenty- and thirty-somethings tuning in."

Then they ran a clip from a recent show. Felicity saw herself admiring a more run-of-the-mill product—a set of 250-threadcount Egyptian cotton bedwear—"Boyfriends don't leave beds dressed in these sheets!"—and then she suggested to the at-home audience that the product also made great gifts for older relatives. Her Aunt Vi's book group—Classic Ladies Read the Classics—used them on every bed in their first and second homes, she told the audience, and her Uncle Billy's golf foursome swore sleeping on the smooth cotton had taken an average of six strokes off their golf score.

Her segment came to an end, there was a gratifying round of applause, and then it was time to announce the Host of the Year winner. Felicity's heart pumped fast and hard as a six-foot showgirl sashayed the envelope out to the emcee.

letmewin letmewin letmewin letmewin letmewin letmewin

Let me finally declare the reinvention of Felicity Charm complete.

One of Andrea's claw-tipped hands grabbed Felicity's and gave it a vicious squeeze. "Good luck," the other woman said.

"Good luck to you, too," Felicity replied, though she'd never believed in such a thing. To get what you wanted in life required smart choices and hard work.

The emcee dragged out the unsealing of the envelope. Finally he looked up. "And the Joanie goes to . . ."

Felicity tried breathing, but the air in the room had evaporated. A high note whined in her ears and she

wondered why the emcee was moving his mouth
without any sound coming out. She leaned forward.
What? Who?

The people around her erupted into movement.
She still couldn't hear a thing over that high-pitched
buzz, but heads were turning toward her and Drew's
hands were lifting her out of her chair. Then, finally,
the thunderous, glorious sound of applause burst into
her head.

She stared at Drew. "I won?"

He smiled. "Yes, yes. Now get up there."

She'd won! As she walked toward the stage, Felicity's gaze lifted to the golden, gleaming Joanie in the
emcee's hand.

That's mine, she thought. *No, that's me*. Gleaming,
golden, polished. Something special. Something to be
proud of. Her shoulders squared and she ascended the
steps and headed toward the podium, feeling as if she
grew an inch with each foot of stage she crossed.

The emcee held out the statuette and she reached
for it with both hands. As she looked out at the audience, all ten fingers tightened on its cool, solid
weight.

"I'm thrilled," she said into the microphone.

Nobody can take this away from me.

"There are so many people to thank. First and fore-
most, our wonderful viewers, who have so generously
taken me into their hearts."

And for that, I pledge never to disappoint them.

"The Hartnett family, who own GetTV, for giving

me the opportunity. Drew Hartnett, in particular, for being such an innovative producer."

As well as the man I now feel worthy of marrying.

"Then there's my teachers and professors, in particular those in the Communications Department at USC."

Though I won't forget Mrs. Myers, the principal at Desert Elementary, who taught me what it is to feel shame.

"My family."

The one I can now, finally, turn my back on. After all these years, the Joanie proved that she was no longer one of them. Like them.

"Thank you again, thank you all."

Applause thundered as she followed the showgirl away from the podium. In a daze of happiness backstage, she almost waved off the set of car keys the emcee rushed after her with. So intent on the Joanie, she'd forgotten the prize included a brand-new Thunderbird convertible.

Then, stepping over cables and stepping around the awards show crew, she spied a pay phone in a secluded corner. On impulse she headed for it, deciding to call the Charms then and there. Joanie in hand, she would make a clean break with them.

Aunt Vi answered on the first ring. "Hello?"

Despite the way she described her aunt to her viewers, it was no trouble at all for Felicity to picture the real Aunt Vi, wrapped in her usual ancient, snagged housecoat. No trouble at all to picture her with one of her seventeen or so cats on her lap. The *National En-quirer* would be open on the rickety kitchen table and the TV would be droning out one of the two stations that the cable-challenged citizens of the community of Half Palm managed to catch with a wire-hanger-enhanced pair of rabbit ears.

"It's Felicity, Aunt Vi, I—"

"Oh, wonderful! You got my message."

Her message? "No, Aunt Vi, I—"

"Oh? Well, it's about Ben."

Felicity could picture her cousin Ben, too, just one of the many no-good, no-account, never-make-a-thing-of-themselves Charms.

"I called because we need your help, Felicity. He's disappeared."

Her help? *Disappeared?*

Well, he wasn't the only one to have gone missing, Felicity thought, stifling a sudden urge to giggle. Because already, less than three sentences into the con-versation with Aunt Vi—*poof!*—the gleaming, golden Felicity had vanished. Gone. In her place stood the no-good, no-account, mosquito-bitten desert ratette she'd been told she was when she was eleven years old, and who she'd been struggling to remake since.

"Felicity? Are you there? Better yet, can you come here? Can you come home?"

Home? No, no! Half Palm wasn't home. Clutching the trophy tightly, Felicity struggled to remind herself of that. She wasn't anything like the others in her family, either; hadn't winning the Joanie proved that?

"Felicity, I'm worried. We need you here right away."

No. Next on her agenda was Drew. He'd insisted she take the next couple of weeks off and she wanted to use them to start working on that personal relationship with him.

"Felicity?"

Her heart thumped heavily. But she couldn't work on a personal relationship, she realized, not with Half Palm and the real Charms still hanging over her head. Not when, with one phone call, they thought to make her part of them again.

Before she could have Drew, she needed to get them out of her life. She needed to make them understand that she didn't belong in Half Palm and that she wasn't one of them anymore.

Michael Magee's number was up.

What a stinking waste, he thought, as a gleaming white convertible, its backside fishtailing, careened through the desert night straight for his Jeep. Being saved from taking the six-foot dirt nap on Denali had given him only eighteen more months of life—and taken away his best friend's.

Ah, well. It was final payment, he supposed, for his previous thirty-some years of good fortune.

But then instinct overcame resignation. Half-lifting from his seat, Magee stood on the brakes and aimed the Jeep for the flat sand at the side of the road. It was too late. Before he could clear the other car, it clipped his back bumper and set him spinning. One revolution—he saw the convertible on its own merry-go-round ride—and another.

Adrenaline kicked in, working its old black magic. His muscles steeled and his mind sharpened, honing to the ice-axe-edge clarity he'd discovered at fourteen when he'd taken a dare and tightroped a two-by-four twenty feet off the ground. Everything else fell away as fear took form and he stared into its eyes.

The Jeep made another revolution, this time skidding into soft sand and slowing him some. Then the other car slid back into his field of vision, its accidental path lining up once again for a head-on collision.

Magee's adrenaline spike plunged. *Well. This is it. This is really it.*

His eyes shut.

Impact was a stiff, brutal jolt. The explosion of breaking glass. But not the cataclysm he'd expected. He opened his eyes. It was dark—both pairs of headlights had shattered—but he could breathe and he could move.

What the hell. Apparently cheating death was becoming a habit with him.

Not your time to cark it, you lucky bastard.

Magee jerked, then looked quickly about him. But he was alone in the Jeep, of course. Simon's Aussie slang and gleeful Aussie voice was only a figment of Magee's imagination, probably a by-product of that brief deluge of adrenaline. It got him moving, though, out of the driver's seat and into the weedy sand.

Shit. The front bumpers of the two vehicles were

engaged in something resembling a passionate, near-permanent French kiss.

He glanced toward the other driver. "Hey, are you—"

"Okay" jammed in his throat. In the thin moonlight he could see the convertible's inflated airbag with a woman draped over it, not moving.

Felicity awoke to find herself flat on her back, her head pounding and her mouth dry. Not ready to open her eyes, she licked her lips and tried accounting for her grogginess. The only time she'd felt like this was after her first freshman dorm party and too many Dixie cups of Mountain-Dew-and-lime-sherbet wine cooler. At the thought, her heart started thumping in time with her head, and she groped along either side of herself, eyes still tightly shut. It seemed wiser that way.

The morning after the wine cooler wingding, she'd found herself in her single bed, fully clothed, but not alone. The couple sharing the mattress had never bothered to introduce themselves, though they'd dressed hastily enough after her startled good-morning shriek.

But this time there weren't any warm bodies beside her, nor any warm sheets, for that matter. Only sand. Cold sand?

Felicity let her eyelashes part. Dark night sky. A gazillion stars, like you only saw in the desert.

Desert. *Oh.*

She closed her eyes again as her head redoubled its Blue Man Group rhythm. She'd been in Vegas. Won the Joanie. Called Aunt Vi. With the keys to a brand-new Thunderbird convertible in her hands, she'd taken it into her now-aching head to immediately climb into the thing and hie off for Half Palm.

Memory returned in a series of snapshots. Speeding through the night. The car suddenly losing traction. The steering wheel wrenched out of her hands. Then . . . then . . . Nothing.

Until the cold sand, the dark night, the gazillion stars. *Oh, God.* She was alone in the dark in the desert, just her and the sand and— Her eyes shot open and she instinctively jackknifed to a sitting position, jerking arms and legs close to her chest as a ripple of goosebumps moved over her skin—every freaky, creepy, crawly, hairy, scary, multilegged nocturnal critter that called the night its own.

A man's voice sounded behind her. "You're back."

True to form, Felicity shrieked, her head whipping around. She stared at a pair of denim-covered kneecaps, then her gaze followed long legs upward as she took in the new throb at her temples, the new rasp in her throat, and—she blinked a couple of times just to be sure—the new man in her life.

"*You.*" Fear evaporated. "It's you."

The stranger's shoulders twitched, as if she'd spooked him. "Me?"

That's right, she thought, now confused. He *was* a stranger—someone she'd never seen before, and one of those dark, reckless-looking types she'd always been careful to shun. Yet . . .

Felicity put up a hand to hold her aching head, trying to make sense of this certain, deep-down recognition. "There's something . . . I . . ." What there was, was no way to explain it, she realized, embarrassed heat washing over her face. "You said, 'You're back.' I guess I, uh, thought you knew me."

Lame, but it was the only excuse her hazy brain provided.

It seemed to satisfy him, though, because he lowered to a crouch beside her. "I meant you're back with me. I've been waiting for you to open your eyes."

"What—" She broke off as she took in the sight over his shoulder. "My car." It was nose-to-nose with some sort of black, heavy metal vehicle that belonged at an Iron Maiden concert or in a Terminator movie. Worse, her once sleekly built automobile now had the profile of a pedigreed Pekingese. "*My new car.*"

"And my old one," the man added dryly.

Felicity's gaze moved back to his face, and her thoughts were derailed by another wave of that odd, undeniable familiarity. How *did* she know him? she wondered, attempting to sift through the muddle in her head. Had they met sometime before?

His face was lean, with high cheekbones and deep outdoorsy brackets around his mouth. A breeze stirred the ends of his tangle of black hair and she could swear she remembered them brushing against her cheek.

She shivered.

His already grim expression deepened. "You should lie back down." He reached out as if to help her, but she scooted away to avoid him.

That was odd, too, because she could swear she already knew his touch. Her mind might not be clear at the moment, but her mind's eye was 20/20. In it she could see his fingertips stroking her skin. Even now the ghost of their rasping caress seemed to linger on the vulnerable underside of her chin. Another shiver skittered over her flesh.

His dark eyes missed nothing. "Lie down," he commanded again.

"I'm okay." Or she would be, when she solved the puzzle. She'd feel more like herself once she could explain how she could know him and yet *not* know him at the same time.

Trying to come up with an answer, she continued to study his face. With his hard-edged features and overlong hair, he looked too uncivilized for someone she might have dated. Absolutely nothing like the urbane, blond-and-blue-eyed Drew, who she'd set her sights on not long after their first meeting—persuaded by everything about him, from his single-minded dedication to the job to the European way in which he held his fork.

By contrast, this man looked like the kind who would bite the hand that fed him.

Shivering again, she huddled beneath the leather jacket hanging over her shoulders, pulling the zippered edges closer together. Stroking its sleek softness absently, it dawned on her that while she was still in her evening dress the jacket wasn't hers. It must be his.

The thought pierced the fog in her head, and she finally noticed that his pale-colored dress shirt was streaked with black grease and ripped at one shoulder. Her eyes widened. "My God, what happened to *you*? Are you hurt?"

"I'm fine." He looked down at the ruined shirt. "This happened after the accident."

The accident. The fog cleared more and her gaze jumped to their cars, then back to him. "Oh, my God. I didn't, did I? Tell me I didn't hit you."

"No can do, dollface," he replied, shaking his head. "You hit me, all right, even though my car's gotta be the only thing bigger than yours within a thirty-five-mile radius."

Her jaw dropped. "But—but how could that be?" She didn't remember it.

His teeth flashed in something that wasn't a smile. "Karma. The way I figure it, you're my very own spit-wad of bad karma."

Felicity barely paid attention to the words, because he shifted, the moonlight now illuminating the dark stubble on his chin. She remembered watching the short bristles brush against her cheek as his mouth found hers and—

No! She put her hand to her head again. The accident must have knocked her wiring loose. "Nothing's making sense."

He grunted. "Take a few more minutes—but do me a favor by taking them lying down."

"*No*." Recalling her earlier fear, she pulled her skirt closer against her bent legs and scanned the deceptively quiet sand around her. If she hadn't felt too dizzy to stand, she'd be on her feet.

He raked back his hair in an impatient gesture. "Please. You hit your head, so you need to take it easy. I get that you're a little confused or scared, but—"

"I'm *terrified*."

He muttered a curse beneath his breath. "Listen, I'm not going to hurt you."

No, no. She shook her head, too late realizing it set her brain to rattling around in her skull. It wasn't *him* that had her mouth drying. Some people had a phobia of heights or closed spaces. Call her weak if you wanted to, but she had a thing about tarantulas crawling through her hair.

"It's not—"

"Lissie—"

They both spoke at once, stopped.

She frowned. "What did you call me?"

"Lissie," he replied. "When I was trying to get you to wake up, I asked your name. You mumbled, 'Lissie.' Isn't that right?"

A mumbled "Felicity" would come out sounding like that, she guessed. "Lissie's fine."

Though her head still ached, her thinking was sharpening with each passing second. There was a thick folder of "fan" mail in her office at GetTV that attested to some people's weird interest in TV personalities. No matter what her instincts said, if this guy didn't recognize her as Felicity Charm, maybe that was all to the good.

"Lissie's perfect." She took a deep breath, the oxygen sweeping more of the fuzziness away. "And you are . . . ?"

She wasn't sure, but he may have hesitated.

"Michael," he said. "I'm Michael."

Felicity took in another deep breath, clearing away a few more cobwebs. Feeling much closer to normal, she held out her hand. "Nice to meet you, Michael."

This time she was certain he hesitated, but then his fingers reached out and his tough, callused palm met hers.

Goosebumps bolted toward her elbow. Her head went woozy again and she clung to his fingers, not wanting to let go. *Unable* to let go, as the strangest thought yet flowered in her brain: He was her lifeline.

Felicity tried blinking it away, but it didn't budge. What was happening to her? More than anything in the world she wanted to move closer, into him. She wanted to put her head on his shoulder once more, bury her face in the skin of his neck, and smell his warm, citrus-and-leather scent again.

From scalp to toes, her skin prickled. *Again*?

"Michael?" she whispered, raising her gaze to his.

For the space of a heartbeat she thought he was as helpless against their connection as she, but then he pulled free of her and stood up. "What?" Looming over her with the moon behind him, his face was a dark, unreadable blob.

Felicity rose to her feet, too, now less concerned about dizziness than the tarantulas, the darkness, and most of all this unnerving, inexplicable link between herself and a total—not to mention dangerous-looking—stranger.

"I feel better. Fine, as a matter of fact." Physically,

anyway, and she wanted to get away from him ASAP. "I'm ready to go now."

His only response was to stare at her.

"Obviously my car isn't drivable," she went on, talking fast. "But yours appears indestructible. If you'd just take me someplace where I can make a phone call . . ."

He still wasn't saying anything.

"Because there's no cell coverage out here," she explained further, his silence making her more nervous. "And I don't think I can hope for another rescuer to come along until after daylight." Surely he didn't expect her to stay out here all night, all alone, with only the creepy crawlies for company?

He slowly shook his head. "I hate to break this to you, dollface, but neither of us—our cars anyway—are going anywhere."

"Huh? What do you mean?" She was supposed to spend the rest of the night with the creepy crawlies and with *him*? The idea was unsettling enough to send her stumbling through the sand to the shoulder of the road where their vehicles had come to rest. He was right behind her, his collision report matter-of-fact.

"Looks like your two front tires blew, that's why you lost control. Now, my Jeep *is* all right, but the problem is our bumpers are locked." He lifted his foot and tried rocking them apart, but even Felicity could see it was useless.

She could also see just exactly how much damage had been done to her beautiful, brand-new Thunderbird. And just how lucky she was to be alive. Her knees went soft as her gaze landed on the unlatched seat belt.

Oh, God. Oh, God. She'd almost been fly-splat on her very own windshield, just like her parents. They'd died on their way home to Half Palm from Las Vegas when she was four years old. "I was—I was thrown from the car?"

He shook his head. "I pulled you out. I needed to see how badly you were hurt."

He'd pulled her out.

He'd pulled her out! The stomach-clenching realization of her close call eased a little. Finally, finally, things were beginning to make sense. No wonder she'd experienced that "instant" feeling of familiarity. No wonder she'd felt a spontaneous trust for a man who wasn't remotely her type.

"Mystery solved." She had to look up a ways to find his face. "That explains why I remember you." And remembered his arms around her and her head against his chest. "It's from when you pulled me out."

One of Michael's eyebrows lifted. "Yeah? Hard to believe you'd have any memory of it. When I got you out of the car, Lissie, you hadn't just blacked out. You weren't breathing."

"Not breathing." Her stomach clenched again, and she locked her knees to keep them from wobbling. "Then how did I . . . ?"

"Mouth-to-mouth resuscitation."

"Mouth-to-mouth?" she repeated. Stupidly, but her excuse was that her brain was otherwise occupied. It was busy showing her images, like the replaying of a tape. From somewhere above, she saw herself stretched out on the sand. Michael bent over her body. The back of his shirt was ripped, too, she could see that from her position overhead, and after every breath or two he'd beg God to make her breathe. To let her live. "Resuscitation?"

"Yeah. You know." His voice was dry. "They call it the Kiss of Life."

Two

"You . . ."

Nothing else made it past the woman's lips, though she continued to stare up at Magee as if he'd just claimed kinship with Conan the Barbarian. Though that wasn't far off—not in comparison to her, anyway. Even strapped onto tiptoe by a pair of silly high-heeled shoes, the top of her feathery hair couldn't quite clear his chin.

Damn, he thought, looking down into her wide eyes with a silent shake of his head. He supposed he should have found a prettier way to tell this bit of fancy-dressed fluff what had happened.

But on the other hand, maybe it was only fair. She'd already stunned the hell out of him, after all.

And then she did it again, by pointing a fingernail at the middle of his chest. "You saved my life."

"I didn't save anyone's life!"

Magee shouldn't have shouted it. But, *Jesus*. He'd only acted on instinct. When he'd pulled her from the car and laid her flat, her mouth had been slack and her lips cold. Without thinking, he'd followed first-aid training and bent to blow two quick breaths into her.

Two hadn't done it. And not another two. After each double-blow he'd stuck to procedure, searching for signs she was breathing on her own. But her chest hadn't moved, no exhalations had brushed his cheek, and she'd stayed as silent as if she'd been buried beneath an avalanche of snow.

"I didn't save anybody," he muttered again.

"Yes, you did," she insisted. "I wasn't breathing, so then you gave me the Kiss—"

"For God's sake, I didn't kiss you, either! That's just a figure of speech." His mouth against hers had been for air exchange only. He didn't know the number of times he'd blown into her lungs or the number of times he'd pleaded for her to breathe on her own. It could have been a handful, but it had seemed days— no, months, eighteen of them—before she'd taken her first shallow inhalation.

Of course, then he *had* kissed her, he thought. Kneeling beside her, guarding each of her independent breaths, he'd held her warming hand against his mouth.

It was the most candyass thing he'd ever done in his life.

It had shocked the hell out of him then and was humiliating to think about now.

As if she could read his mind—or worse yet, remember his pathetic actions—Lissie looked down at that small, soft hand of hers, then back up at him. "This is really weird."

He grunted in reply, then closed the discussion—please—by turning his back on her to survey their tangled cars. It was time to get them on their separate ways.

"Any chance someone will come looking for you tonight?" he asked. A man could hope, even though he remembered her requesting a ride to a phone.

"N-no. It was sort of a . . . a spur-of-the moment d-decision."

Oh, great, was that a quiver in her voice? He hoped to God she wasn't going shocky on him. With her breathing restarted, he'd crossed his fingers that she'd suffer no further effects from the accident. But he'd seen plenty of tough ladies—not to mention granite-nerved guys—turn to stone, turn to tears, turn to everything in between, after a near-miss with death. And this lady appeared about as tough as the apple blossoms on the tree in his parents' Yakima back yard.

"The drive was sort of spur-of-the-moment for me, too," he murmured.

Meaning no one would be looking for him, either. He'd told everyone he was overnighting in L.A., but after his dinner meeting, after accepting the job that had been Simon's, Magee had rushed off, ready to get on with the rest of what he had to do.

"Shit." He kicked at the cars' locked bumpers, acknowledging again he'd brought this on himself. At the turnoff toward home, he'd rationalized he'd changed his life enough for one day, and opted for a head-clearing trek farther into the desert.

"Michael . . ." Lissie said in a tentative voice.

Which had led him to her.

"Michael," she repeated. This time when he didn't respond, she touched his back.

"What the—!" Somehow her fingertips had found bare flesh and he jerked, grabbing for the hand whose one light touch pulsed hard and thick through his body like bass reverb through a stereo speaker.

"Th-there's a tear in your shirt," she said, all big eyes and quivery voice again. "I . . . I saw that."

A statement of the obvious didn't necessitate a response, he figured, not when he was busy dealing with his own adrenaline hangover. After all that practice facing down danger, you'd think he'd be an expert at managing the symptoms.

Heart thumping like a drum. Heat in the blood. So much that, though the temperature must be a measly forty freakin' degrees, he hadn't felt the cold since the instant he'd first laid a finger on her. Worst of all, and new to him, was paralysis. A complete inability to look away from her face. A complete unwillingness to let go of her hand.

Remembering how he'd kissed it before, he felt like a fool.

A candyass fool.

"Michael." She swallowed, her gaze flickering down to her captured fingers and then back up to him. "I need to tell you. Something happened."

"No duh, dollface." Something had happened, all right. His first shot of fight-or-flight in over a year had torn through him, wreaking such sensory havoc that his hand was now sticking to hers with a kind of glue he'd give his right nut for on a first attempt of a new wall.

Sticking him to her.

Binding him to her.

"Shit," he muttered, panicking. He had to get loose. "I need some help here."

Well, you should have said something before, mate. No worries!

And as if that figment of Simon's voice were the signal, rain dumped down.

Magee's hand released Lissie's and they lurched apart. Looking upward got him nothing but an eyeful of torrential rainwater, but looking back at her didn't explain anything more than they were both getting drenched. They stared at each other for another startled moment.

"Let's go," he finally shouted over the sound of drops pattering against the cars and puttering onto the sand.

"Wh-what?"

She looked pitiful, her hair flattened to her head and streams running down the leather of his jacket she was wearing, the water already soaking through the layered skirt of her long white dress. Her hand lifted to wipe a strand of hair off her cheek.

The fingers were trembling.

Damn, damn, damn. He'd bet the farm she was on the verge of losing it, tipped by the cold, the wet, or just one too many surprises. He grabbed her by the elbow and hauled her toward the rear of the Jeep. "C'mon," he said.

She stumbled alongside him, her movements clumsy. "Where?"

He rolled his eyes. "Into my car." Then he was fumbling with the back door latch, his fingers sliding on the wet metal.

"Oh, of course," she replied, in an odd, teatime voice. "Thank you. Thank you so very much."

He glanced over, and her wooden expression warned him again she was probably just a few fingernails away from a post-trauma tantrum.

"It's kind of you to invite me in out of the rain." She smiled, and it was eerily sweet with the raindrops running down her face. Then she kept yakking in that well-mannered fashion, as if the moment required the making of small talk. "Did you know that what's inside a man's car reveals what's inside a man's heart? I read that somewhere."

He'd seen climbers stumble into crevasses while mumbling crazy stuff in that same half-dazed tone, so he wrenched open the door and in one quick movement picked her up and shoved her inside, then crawled in after her. Kneeing over her sopping skirt, he heard her continue the tea-party talk, punctuated by the distinct chatter of her teeth.

"Oh. Michael, inside your car is . . . nothing."

Except for the two of them, he thought, shaking his head again. He'd wanted to get loose of her, and if he could he'd put her squarely in Tahiti and himself in Timbuktu, but it appeared now as if they were stuck with each other.

* * *

Felicity blinked, trying to acclimate herself to the new surroundings. Her eyes had grown accustomed to the desert dark, but it was gloomier inside the Iron Maiden machine. There wasn't a whole lot to see, though. Metal floorboards, metal roof and sides, requisite windows. One seat. The driver's seat, of molded plastic.

At least the open floor space gave Michael plenty of room to maneuver past her toward the dashboard. She didn't have the energy to get out of his way, not when her head felt as if it had been stuffed like a pillow and her body was starting to shake. Wet leather squeaked as she wrapped one arm over the other.

Hugging herself tight didn't help.

Oh, well. She couldn't work up a worry about it, especially when she felt more numb than cold. So her arms dropped, her hands splashing into the shallow puddles her sodden clothes had created. Idly, her gaze roamed the interior of the vehicle again. Found Michael.

He was cursing beneath his breath and jabbing his keys at the glove box.

Hmmm. A concern niggled at the back of her fuzzy brain, and she remembered she'd been trying to tell him something before. She'd wanted to thank him for something. Something big. Something really big. But the rain had washed it from her mind.

Thinking back took effort, but after a moment she recalled the last thing she'd said to him. Uh-oh. Had she offended him? That was very bad of her, especially when he'd been nothing but nice in an abrupt sort of way.

"M-M-Michael," she called out, fighting her chattering teeth because it seemed imperative to sort this out. "I w-w-was w-w-wrong."

He didn't look up from his task. "Huh?"

"Ab-b-bout n-n-nothing inside your h-h-heart."

He mumbled something that sounded like, "I hope like hell you are right." Then the glove box door sprang open. "Ah-hah!"

He swung around to face her, smiling in triumph.

Oh, he had *such* a nice smile. It was white and reckless, deepening the brackets on either side of his mouth. She smiled back, she couldn't help herself. It was the strangest thing, she thought, but that he was happy made her happy.

"It's going to be okay now," he said, moving toward her. "You're going to be fine soon. Warm."

She smiled again, delighted by his interest. "F-f-fine now. Warm. P-p-perfectly warm."

He paused, his upbeat expression dying, then he scrambled forward again. "Dollface." His voice was urgent. "Get your clothes off. You need to get your clothes off right now."

She blinked some more. "W-w-whatsamatter?"

He didn't explain. Instead, he started on her himself, wrenching the leather coat away and tossing it down. But then he stopped, his hands hovering over her goosefleshed bare shoulders.

"How does this damn thing come off?" When she

didn't immediately respond, he grabbed her chin and forced her to meet his gaze. "*We need to get your clothes off.*"

His new mood baffled her, but she reacted to the command in his tone and half-lifted her left arm. He went about unzipping the dress and then working it off. Since he didn't seem to require any help, she let her mind wander.

He was mumbling again, "cold," "emotional shock," "hypothermia." Maybe she *was* cold, because her skin was so numb she didn't feel his hands on her. Amazing, because when he'd touched her before . . .

"M-Michael." It was on the tip of her tongue, that big thing she needed to tell him about. "M-Michael—"

The rest of what she'd been going to say was lost as he threw a lightweight cloth over her. Within another minute she was wrapped like a rolled taco from her head to her toes and deposited on the other—dry— side of the vehicle.

"Better?" Michael asked. He didn't wait for an answer, just held a flask to her lips. "Drink."

She didn't have any choice but that, even though the vile stuff burned her throat and a lot of whatever it was dribbled out the corners of her mouth.

"Take another."

Sputtering a refusal didn't work, and with her arms bound beneath the blanket, she could only turn her head aside. That got her nowhere, too. He forced another swallow of the stuff down her, and another, then he rocked back on his heels.

"W-what is th-that?" The numbness from before

was wearing off. There was a burning at the pit of her stomach and she was shivering so badly that her spine was banging on the metal he'd leaned her against. "P-poison?"

"No. It's . . ." He glanced down at the flask in his hand, and then his brows drew together. "I . . . It's not mine. I thought it was brandy."

He lifted it to his nose and a hint of a smile quirked his mouth. "It's tequila. Lousy tequila. The favorite of a friend. We must have mixed up our flasks."

Then he eyed her again, leaning forward.

She tried shaking her head. "F-f-fine!"

But Michael fisted his hand in the back of her hair and poured another couple of sips down her. "Sorry, dollface, but you need the heat. Champagne might be what you're used to, but this will do."

At swallow six, Felicity's shivering started to ease. But she was aware of the cold now and she could see it in every puff of breath they released. It occurred to her not only had Michael not taken his turn at the flask, but that he was still wearing wet clothes. "You," she said, working to control her chattering. "B-blanket for you, too."

He plopped down on the other side of the cargo area, resting his forearms on his knees. "There's only the one."

"I'm wound like a m-mummy," she got out. "There's enough for us both."

He hesitated another moment, then his fingers moved to the buttons of his shirt. She leaned the back of her head against the car and closed her eyes. Rain pattered down outside, a cozy sound. Despite the chill in the air, she was starting to warm nicely, she thought. As the heat in her stomach started to meander its way through her bloodstream, her still-fuzzy mind floated behind in its wake.

Her eyes stayed closed as some of her blanket wrapping was peeled back and Michael moved beneath it. When she felt metal against her lips, she took another obedient sip.

A layer of cloth away, a shoulder bumped against hers.

"Warmer?" His breath washed over her temple.

"Warm. Getting to be lovely warm." Her mind continued drifting along. "A little hungry, though."

"Unless you want to snack on packets of fast-food-joint salt or salsa, you're out of luck. That's the only stuff I found in the glove box besides the flask and the survival blanket."

"Survival blanket." Eyes still closed, she wormed a hand free to stroke the light, crinkly fabric, and words materialized in her head. "Indispensable. Versatile. Everyone should have one—more than one. Has half-a-dozen uses—as a blanket for a picnic, the stadium, on a boat. As a desert sunshade. You can even make it into a cooler for drinks."

"That's only five."

His voice snapped her out of her hazy reverie and her eyes popped open. "What?"

"You said half-a-dozen uses. That was only five."

She hadn't been aware of talking aloud, so now she could only stare at him. Like her, he was sitting up and leaning against the side of the car, but because he was so much taller than she, the blanket that reached to her neck cut him across the torso.

Revealing, even in the semidarkness, impressive masculine features: a wide plain of pectorals, heavily rounded shoulders, sinewy arms that rippled with muscles she'd been previously unacquainted with. Even his hands appeared more male than most, the palms broad, the fingers long and limber. Long enough to wrap—

Reality struck. Haziness lifted. Alarm tickled her spine.

She was stranded in the middle of the desert.

With a strange man.

A naked strange man.

Her behind wiggled. And oh, yes, she was naked, too.

Then the how and why of it came back to her, in one staggering rush.

In her mind's eye, she saw it all over again. She'd been dead. Oh, God, she *knew* she'd been dead. That's what she'd wanted to tell him before it started raining. That's what she'd tried to tell him when she'd pointed out that rip in the back of his shirt. That she'd already seen it, from outside of her body.

She'd watched the man—Michael—pull her from the car. His shirt had caught on her sideview mirror and he'd torn it free. Then he'd placed her body gently onto the sand and bent over her, breathing for her, pleading with God, pleading with her, and because he'd asked her to stay, because he'd wanted so much for her to stay, she had.

Her heart pounded against her breastbone.

"Dollface? You all right?"

"Fine," she whispered.

But much more than fine. Euphoria—she was living, breathing, thinking, feeling!—bubbled up inside and then shot through her veins. *Alive alive alive alive alive!*

Heart pounding harder, she turned to tell him, thank him . . .

And found herself speechless and staring at him again, once more fascinated by his smooth male skin and hard male muscles. My God. Just looking at them was making things inside of her stir, stretch, come awake, just as his voice had done for her when she'd been lying on the sand.

Heat flashed over her as she ran her gaze over him slowly, stroking his flesh visually like she wanted to stroke him with her hand. With her tongue.

Her tongue?

The idea of licking a stranger should be shocking. Lewd. Disgusting.

But her pulse was tripping all over itself at the thought, while desire slowly flexed its muscle in the depths of her belly. Her gaze bumped over one of his dark nipples and excitement washed across her skin like goosebumps.

She heard his breath catch.

Suddenly heat was everywhere. Pouring off of her,

radiating off of him. It was a heat that matched the heat in her belly and the heat in her blood. It was the heat of life, of the living. Of being alive.

Her gaze jumped from the thick column of his neck to that tangled hair and then to his bad-boy face. Her focus landed on his mouth, edged by dark whiskers. His nostrils flared and he sent off another blast of heat, of citrus-and-leather scent, of seductive, all-senses-alive-and-well arousal.

Her heart was a drum and desire the primal beat.

What *was* this?

She'd wanted men before—but men she knew well. She'd wanted sex before—when the time was right and the man was, too. For her, being intimate with a man had always required a crucial mental component.

But this was physical. Purely, edgily physical.

More excitement prickled her skin and she shivered.

"Michael." She lifted the hand she'd freed from the blanket.

He met it with the flask. "Take another drink," he commanded in a raspy voice.

Her gaze lifted to his. He had to know it wasn't a chill she was feeling. But despite the scorching awareness still pulsing between them, his expression was remote. Cool.

Embarrassment joined the hot tangle inside of her.

Cool. He wanted to play it cool.

And she should be thankful.

With effort, her fingers closed on the flask. She couldn't stomach another swig of the stuff, but she had to do something with herself—with her hands and with her mouth—or she just might forget who she was.

And she just might try showing him exactly how thankful she could be.

Taking a deep breath, she looked away from his nothing-remotely-like-her-type face, and said the only thing that made good sense to a woman like Felicity Charm when choosing between coming on to a perfect stranger or chugging down more bad tequila.

"Pass the salsa, please."

The night was just one stupefication after another, Magee decided, as the woman started doing salsa shooters. Salsa shooters! She might be doing them in ladylike sips, but they were salsa shooters all the same.

"When was the last time you had something to eat?" he finally ventured.

"Don't know." She was using the time-honored lick-sip-suck method: first she sprinkled salt on the side of her fist and licked it off, next she swigged the tequila, then she sucked some salsa out of a plastic packet. "I'm pretty sher—*sure*—I didn't eat dinner."

Great. Tequila on an empty stomach. "Maybe you've had enough."

She looked over at him, seeming to consider a moment. Her gaze wandered from his bare shoulders to his waist, where he'd let the blanket pool because it was getting so damn hot inside the Jeep.

"No," she said, shaking her head. "Coupla more."

He sighed. Okay, so they *were* very small hits. And

when he'd first pressed the stuff on her, half of it had spilled down her skin. Soft, satiny ski—

"You want?"

He started, then realized she was talking about the flask she was holding out to him. "No." Alcohol made him reckless, and he couldn't afford to lose even half a scruple.

Especially tonight with its surprise KOs. Discovering it was Simon's flask in his glove box instead of his own had almost wigged him out. Though it shouldn't seem so strange, Magee thought, sliding lower. When he'd cleaned out Simon's truck before putting it up for sale, he'd found not only his own second-best pair of belaying gloves but his treasured 1999 Topless Chicks Top Mountains calendar, too.

"You're smiling."

"Am I?" He looked over to find Lissie had shifted lower as well and was half-turned toward him.

"Yep. Nice smile." The hand holding the flask made a sloppy gesture toward it, sprinkling tequila over his chest. Then she smiled, and that was sloppy, too. "Uh-oh. Baptized you."

"Don't worry about it." But he edged away from her anyway, because she was definitely heading toward tipsy and she was definitely staring at his bare skin.

Then her gaze lifted from his chest to his mouth. So, hell, he indulged himself and looked at *her* mouth. That puffy, pretty mouth that he knew but that he'd never kissed. Her dark hair had dried and was sticking out in wispy tufts from behind her ears and her lashes were a thick, black fringe around matching dark eyes in the paleness of her small face. With the silver-gray blanket around her, that distracting mouth of hers was her only colorful feature.

The only thing colorful in his sight.

It was a dark pink. A bruised pink.

All night long he'd been half-hard, thinking about administrating first aid on it again—the consensual kind.

As if she could read his thoughts, the hand holding the flask jerked, spilling more tequila on his chest.

"Uh-oh," she said again, and her free hand reached out to wipe it away. But at the last second, she halted, leaving her palm a crucial inch from his skin.

The atmosphere inside the car crackled with static and the temperature jacked up another twenty degrees. He sucked in a breath. Though he'd half-expected this phenomenon to reappear, it didn't make the combustion any less powerful.

"Uh-oh," she said, wiggling the fingers of that damn hand. "Mi-chael."

"Don't," he rasped out. "You don't want to do it. You don't want to touch me."

She frowned at him. "Yes, I do."

He ground his back teeth together, cursing himself for not dealing out the facts the first time they'd almost incinerated. "Dollface, here's the beta on what's happening. We don't really want to bump bones. It's survival rush."

Her frown deepened. "Beta? Bump bones? Survival rush?"

Taking advantage of her confusion, he inched farther from her hand. "Beta—that means information. Bump bones—that's a boink, a bang, a score, a screw. Survival rush is just what it sounds like."

He'd witnessed it during climbs, even between a man and woman who held an active dislike for each other. Have them survive the same epic snowstorm or hairy roped fall and the next thing you knew, they'd be shedding their packs and their gear and going at it like rabbits. "That urge you're feeling's a reaction to stress. It'll go away."

"Oh." She looked disappointed. "I kinda like it."

Damn, he knew he should have taken the tequila from her. Without its influence, this uptight little cookie would never have made such an admission. But now the shooters had loosened her up, forcing *him* to play old maid aunt. "Too bad," he said firmly. "We're not going to act on it."

Her mouth pouted, just crying for a kiss. "Why not?" She put both hands around the flask and brought it up for another sip.

"Be—" Her movement lifted the top slope of her pale breasts out of the blanket and he had to wrench his gaze away from them. "Because, damn it, there are rules."

Like she was three-quarters drunk and he was almost—

"Naah." Her head wagged back and forth. "Guy like you, you don' follow rules," she announced.

But after what happened to Simon, Magee had vowed to change that. It was the straight and safe for him from now on. "You do."

She waved that away, wiggling closer to him as the part of the blanket covering her tits slipped southward again. "Come up with something else."

"Because we're strangers," he said between gritted teeth. "Because we'll never see each other again." A prissy woman like this one, that should change her mind.

Instead, she sent him a beatific smile. "Even better. Then if you're lousy I won' tell anybody you know."

He rolled his eyes, but was relieved when she moved back to sit straighter. And even more relieved when, with exaggerated care, she capped the flask and set it aside.

Then she fell on top of him.

Magee caught her by the wrists. Her pretty face, her pretty mouth was just inches from his and so—to hell with it—he kissed her.

Oh, God. She tasted like the best vacation he'd ever had. Four years ago, he'd headed south to cliff-climb in Mexico, but instead spent most of his time lying on the beach, soaking up tequila and spicy food and heat.

Heat. Burning heat.

He dropped her wrists and ran his palms up her spine. Then, fisting his hands in her hair, he tilted her head to change the angle of the kiss. This time, her mouth opened more and her tongue slipped out to stroke his.

On that aforesaid vacation, a rogue wave had swamped him.

He reacted the same now as he had then, jerking up,

jumping away, shaking himself like a wet dog. "Don't do that," he choked out.

She didn't say a word until he turned and grabbed for his damp jeans.

"What's wrong?"

He refused to look at her as he struggled to pull them on, she was that tempting. "I need to get out." It had stopped raining. He'd get some air, give the situation time to defuse.

"Mi-i-i-i-chael."

Her voice was a sexy purr that felt like a light scratch of fingernails against his bare skin.

"Look, you gotta understand something here," he ground out in warning. "I'm no saint, dollface. I'm just trying to act like one."

"Silly Michael. Be brave. I won' hurt you."

Oh, he had plenty of courage. And it was true that he'd never been known for turning down sex. But things were different now. He had obligations to fulfill. Promises to make.

So he was doing the smart thing. The climbing tribe had nicknamed him "Lucky Bastard," but his legendary good fortune had never been due strictly to chance. It was in part because he used his brain when deciding between continuing on or bailing out.

And it was bail time, baby.

Without even waiting to shove his feet in his boots, he thrust open the back door and leaped from the Jeep.

The cold swamped him, but it wasn't unpleasant. The clouds—not that he'd ever seen any before the rain—had disappeared and the moon was out once again.

Then Magee saw that something else was out, too, creeping up from beneath the sand.

Somethings.

He froze, as all around him dozens upon dozens of tarantula spiders—as big as his palm!—emerged from the desert floor and went on the prowl. His skin crawled right along with them.

Okay. Well. Damn, damn, damn. This changed the danger/courage equation entirely.

With a sound oddly like Simon's laughter ringing in his ears, Magee opened the Jeep's back door and dove back inside.

Three

Before disappointment had a chance to sink in, Michael was back inside the car. Felicity smiled. *He'd changed his mind!*

Without a word, he leaned across her to swipe up the flask of tequila. A healthy slug went down his throat. And then another.

They were going to have sex after all!

She hoped so anyway, because the salsa shooters hadn't taken the tiniest edge off her need. And oh, did she *need*. The feeling was exhilarating, exciting, excruciating.

She didn't give a hoot if it was survival rush or a reaction to stress or anything else. And acting on it only made complete sense, she told herself. It was absolutely necessary. She'd had that strange, scary sensation of being outside her body, and now she needed something—apparently sweaty sex—to put herself firmly back inside it.

No, no. Sweaty sex would put *him* firmly inside her.

She giggled at the idea, then sobered, a second

thought flitting through her tipsy brain. Inside her? She was going to let a man she didn't know inside of her? That wasn't what smart, hardworking Felicity Charm would *ever* do.

"Look, Lissie . . ." Michael began, then stopped to take another draw on the flask.

Lissie? Oh, *yes. Lissie.*

Felicity Charm, America's Sweetheart of Sales, wasn't going to be doing the wild thing with the wild man who wasn't her type. It was *Lissie.* Lissie, who wasn't the It Girl of anything, which meant she was free to do things that Felicity couldn't.

"Look, Lissie, I'm not back . . ."

His words drifted off again as she reached up and combed her fingers through his hair. Lissie got to do stuff like that, the lucky girl. "Kiss me," she demanded.

And because Lissie wasn't one for waiting, she yanked on his hair to bring his mouth down to hers. The kiss was hard and hot. His lips moved under hers—oh, nice—but then she realized he was trying to tell her something. She eased her hold on him, giving him half an inch.

"I still think this isn't a good idea," he said.

But since one of his arms was clamped around her back, she guessed he didn't think it was such a terrible idea, either. His reluctance, however, was becoming annoying. He was her bad boy! The dark, untamed stranger destined to fulfill this need he'd awoken inside of her.

Determined to get what she wanted, she reached

down and palmed the fly of his jeans, making him groan. "Then you're thinking with the wrong head," she whispered. Half-delighted and half-appalled by what she'd said and done, she stroked him once more.

In response, his mouth descended all on its own and widened over hers, widening hers, so his tongue could thrust inside. The delicious intrusion made her tremble. Then his lips were gone, trailing over her cheek and toward her ear. "Really. I didn't come in for this, for you."

He bit down on her lobe and she squeaked, her fingers contracting on his hard, happy erection. He groaned again.

"I don't care," she answered, not as long as he was going to do something about all these hot, primal impulses clamoring inside of her.

"We have nothing in common," he murmured, moving back to her mouth.

"Who cares about that, either?" They needed nothing in common besides—what did he call it?— wanting to bump bones right here, right now.

On their next kiss, he dropped the flask. It clattered against the metal floor as he tugged her lower. Then she was flat on her back and he was on his elbows, leaning over her.

Her palms rested on his wide, naked shoulders. His head lowered, his rain-scented hair the dark curtain that made what they were doing more private, more intimate, more breath-stealing sexy. His lips brushed hers and she moaned, the brief connection flinging heat in every direction over every inch of her flesh. Her fingers clenched onto heavy muscle. She needed his weight, his skin, his taste against every pore.

"Take me now," she heard herself pleading.

But Lissie wouldn't beg, she realized, Lissie would do the taking herself. The concern cartwheeled away as his tongue twined with hers again. He could take her this time, she consoled herself, then Lissie would take him the next.

He was kissing down her neck, the stubble of his beard scraping against her skin, teasing more nerve endings to the surface. Then, half-sitting at her side, he hooked his fingers in the blanket between her breasts and tugged, trying to draw it lower.

She held her breath. Yes. *Touch me there. Yes*.

But she was swaddled so tightly, the fabric wouldn't budge. He tried again, again making no progress. Her focus narrowed to his two fingers, the backs of them hard and hot against her breastbone as his hand worked at moving the stubborn blanket away. Worried he'd give up, she shimmied her hips, trying to loosen the maddening material, but that didn't help, either.

His fingers slid out and away and she almost cried, but then he brushed his palm over one blanket-covered nipple.

Yessss. Lissie was nobody's sweetheart, nobody's girl. She was a woman, a needy woman, and she arched her back to get as much of his attention as she could. He laughed, a dark, dangerous sound, and the wickedness of it thrilled her, making her needier, hotter, wetter.

More demanding.

Knowing exactly what she wanted next, she sat up. Then, curling her own fingers into the layers of blanket, she yanked them past her breasts.

He stilled. Her naked skin shone pale in the darkness. She wasn't very big—no! Lissie knew appearances didn't matter, only desire. Desire and touch. So, her gaze glued to his face, she palmed her breasts herself. Once, twice. Her hard nipples pulled tighter, stiffened.

The lean angles of his bad-boy face sharpened. "Do that again," he ordered roughly.

In their cocoon of fogged windows, his breathing sounded loud and harsh. "Again," he commanded, his voice hoarse.

Watching him, Lissie slowly moved, reaching up and behind to find the cold glass. She dragged the flat of one hand down the wet surface. His breath hitched as she slowly drew that same hand across the heated skin of one of her breasts, letting it catch on the nipple and then letting the nipple pop free.

"Jesus," he muttered. "I was nuts *not* to come back for this."

She'd never felt so liberated from her inhibitions—and her image. Her hand made a languid pass over her other breast. "So," she said softly, prolonging the anticipation, "why *did* you come back?"

Her hand stretched back up toward the glass. He

tracked the movement with his eyes, and she thought he'd forgotten her question. Her palm flattened, then inched down the slick glass.

"You'll laugh," he finally said.

This time she brought her cool, wet hand toward his chest. His skin twitched. "I won't laugh," she replied, her palm hovering near one of his dusky nipples.

He was breathing harder.

"I'd never laugh," she added, still delaying the touch. Making him wait. Anticipate. "Tell me."

The power was in her hands. It *was* her hands. She allowed her damp thumb to edge closer to his nipple, pause again. He groaned.

"Tell me," she insisted, just for the wicked, naughty fun of having him at her mercy.

"Because the tarantulas scared the shit out of me."

Felicity froze. Tarantulas? *"Tarantulas?"* Her hand dropped and her legs jackknifed toward her chest, the blanket restricting her movement to a spastic kick.

He stared. "What's wrong with you?" His eyebrows rose as she desperately yanked at the part of the blanket caught beneath him.

"We have more in common than you thought." With the end free, she threw it over her shoulder, toga-style, then arranged the rest of it to re-cover her breasts. Pressing her spine against the side of the car, she tried making herself smaller as she peered about. "Did one get in? Could one be on you?"

"Lissie—"

Something touched her foot and she shrieked. "Get it off! Get it off! Kill it!"

"Take it easy. That was my hand," he said. "Jesus, you really *are* scared."

She wanted to slap him. "Of *course* I'm scared."

"Don't you think—"

"I don't want to think. If I think I'll hear them. I'll hear their long fangs clackety-clacking and their fat hairy legs rub-a-dub-dubbing my way." She shivered.

"Now *you're* scaring me."

"Shut up, shut up." There was no way to explain her irrational fear. There was no way to explain her equally immense regret, either. Thanks to him, she'd lost her chance to experience purely physical passion. "I could kill you for this!"

"You've had your shot at that once tonight already," he said dryly. "But now I take it the mood is dead, too?"

She shot him a dirty look, then scrubbed her face with her hands. As illogical, but certainly as *real* as her spider fear was that notion that she'd needed sex. Right now. Tonight. Sex to cement herself back inside her body.

Remembering that sensation of floating above the scene of the accident, she shivered again. Damn him for leaving her hanging like this!

"Lissie, I . . ." He studied her in silence for another moment, then scooted nearer. "I'm going to get close enough to touch you."

"*What?*"

"I'm trying to save you from another bump on the head. When I brushed your foot a second ago you nearly hit the roof."

"Hah-hah," she said, eyeing him as he settled beside her again. His bare shoulder jostled hers and her stomach jumped. "Are you certain you didn't bring one inside with you?"

"Chill, dollface." He turned toward her, laying a soothing stroke to her jaw with the back his hand. "Why don't we talk about something else?"

She appreciated the calming caress and then the next one after that, but relax? No. "Have you ever seen tarantulas migrate?"

He shook his head. "Lissie—"

"They come out of the ground and start walking. They stop at nothing. They'll crawl over things in their path rather than going around them."

"Gotta admire their determination," he murmured, stroking the other side of her jaw. "Where are they heading?"

His knuckles played across her bottom lip, but she pretended not to notice. "Not where, but *who*. They're looking for babes."

His hand halted. "*Babies?*"

"Chicks."

"Chicke—"

"I mean women." She batted his distracting hand away. "No, I *mean* lady spiders."

"Now I get it." Michael leaned over and kissed her softly on the mouth. Then he kissed her again. This time, despite herself, her lips clung to his, but he lifted his mouth and went back to stroking her face. "They want to mate."

"They want to mate," she agreed.

His lips touched down again, finding the corner of hers, and one of those wonderful hot shivers rolled over her. Oh, maybe she still wanted to mate, too.

"Hmmm. I think I'm starting to understand those guys," he said, working his way toward her ear. "They're not so different from you and me, right?"

Not so different from you and me. Maybe she *could* forget about them, she thought, as his lips settled against hers again. Her knees were still plastered to her chest, but her tense muscles were warming, loosening, wanting him once more. When his rough-surfaced palm slid between the blanket and her breast, she gasped. When he took the kiss deeper, angling his head to thrust against her tongue with his, she slipped her hand beneath the waistband of his jeans.

He groaned into her mouth, the sound making her light-headed with lust. His fingers kneaded her breast and she went to work on the buttons of his fly so she could knead him, too.

Incredible, she thought. It was incredible that she could get this far with a total stranger despite tequila and tarantulas and the image she'd been working on for a lifetime. But then it hit her. Of course. It was *because* he was a total stranger.

A woman who'd almost died deserved a dark stranger and a solitary night of unbridled sex. Felicity unfastened the last button and pulled apart the edges of his jeans.

Just that made him groan again, and she almost lost it. Oh, yes, with him she could let go and discover pure, physical passion. It was a woman's secret dream, the fantasy that had been described years ago in the book *Fear of Flying,* a book she and some boarding schoolmates had found tucked behind a drawer in an old unused dresser. Felicity remembered that the author called it the zipless fuck.

She reached in and palmed his hot, smooth skin. Inside her own body there was softening, heating, all the preparing necessary to take in the hardness she cradled in her hand. More shivers rolled over her sensitized skin. She'd never been so turned on by touching a man! The moment was priceless.

"Jong," she murmured against his mouth. "It's so Jong." Erica Jong's zipless fuck.

"Thank you," he whispered back, pushing up against her hand.

She lifted her head to explain. "No, I mean—" Then she saw a strange expression cross his face, and she stilled. "What? What is it?"

"Tell me more about these eight-legged friends of yours." He took his hand off her breast and slid away from her.

"What? More about tarantulas?" She glared at him, her body wet and ready, her pulse pounding for that dark-stranger-solitary-night-of-passion. "The females kill their mates after sex. Sometimes *before* sex." Her hand grabbed his, ready to place it right back where she wanted it.

"They don't knock?"

Her eyes widened. "No." Then she heard it, the knock on the fogged-over back window. "*No.*"

"Well, then, dollface, I guess we've been caught red-handed, or, should I say, with our pants down."

As the sky turned pink with dawn, Magee stood alone in the desert. The tarantulas had returned to their underground homes after the rainwater had drained, and the tow truck operator was just now driving away, hauling the convertible Thunderbird behind him. Through the truck's rear window Magee had his last glimpse of Lissie—the back of her head, anyway—shrouded sari-style by the survival blanket.

She'd left him behind without a backward glance, let alone a goodbye kiss. It was as if they were complete strangers.

Which, of course, they were.

Thank God.

He'd done his part to keep it that way, refusing to exchange insurance information. Repairing the Jeep's bashed headlights was on him, an object lesson in what could happen when he deviated from the straight, narrow, safe course he'd assigned himself.

Last night he should have been making a marriage proposal instead of making out with a feathery-haired woman whom fate had pushed into his path. Shaking his head, he climbed into the driver's seat of his Jeep. She had her regrets, too, he knew, because with the tow truck driver on scene she'd kept her head down and her voice hushed.

Only twice had he seen any animation in her. First, when she'd babbled some cock-and-bull story explaining her nakedness—"a previously undetected dermatological, allergic reaction to white chiffon evening gowns"—that had him choking back laughter and the tow truck operator scratching his head. Then, after the driver explained he'd come out their way upon receiving a tip from Billy's Tire Repair about a stranded car, she'd released one of those tarantula screeches of hers and stomped off, muttering darkly.

He should pity Lissie's next victim, Magee thought as he started the Jeep's engine. But as he turned toward Half Palm, he could only feel relief that she was moving on to wreak havoc in some other man's life.

Eyes closed, Felicity rubbed her cheek against something furry. "Michael," she whispered. It must be his warm chest pillowing her head. "Michael." She smiled drowsily.

He started to purr.

Felicity's head shot up and her eyes popped open. "Ouchouchouch," she moaned, squinting against the bright sunlight that was sending a shaft of pain through her head. The purr-er wasn't Michael. She wasn't in the back of his car. She was at Aunt Vi's, in the bedroom she used to share with her cousin Ashley. And sharing the bed with Felicity were four tattered-looking cats. They all blinked back at her.

She flopped back onto the pillow, careful to miss the curled bodies of a matching pair of ugly tabbies. Tugging the worn quilt up around her ears, she decided to escape back into sleep.

Tomorrow, next week, next year—yes, next year—

would be soon enough to tackle the problems await-
ing her.

A light knock sounded on the bedroom door just as
small paws minced up her chest.

Felicity opened one eye. Met the moss-green ones
of a short-haired black cat with ears bigger than its
head. It found the level ground between her breasts
and sat, then lifted a foot and began cleaning bubble-
gum-pink pads.

The knock sounded again, followed by Aunt Vi's
voice. "Felicity? Are you awake?"

The cat stopped licking and looked at her. Felicity
gave a small shake of her head, then placed her forefinger over her lips. Then another cat, carrying something in its mouth, romped up, displacing its
black-haired buddy.

"Felicity?" At Aunt Vi's renewed knock, the
romper dropped the something in its mouth, right below Felicity's chin.

Wet with cat spit, the thing was huge, black, and
hairy. Certain it moved, she let out a shriek and leaped
from the bed, scattering the cats that proceeded to escape through the opening bedroom door. Aunt Vi
peeked in.

"You *are* awake! Did you have a good rest?" Aunt
Vi was smiling. She made no comment about the fact
that Felicity was on top of the unslept-in twin bed and
hopping from one foot to the other.

"A great rest," Felicity replied. "Until that—that—"
She pointed a finger at the wet, black, spidery thing
lying on her rumpled coverlet.

"That's exactly what I called you about." Aunt Vi crossed to the bed and grabbed up the disgusting thing. Then she held it under Felicity's nose, even as she cringed away. "*This* is why we need your help."

Felicity twisted her hands in the old flannel nightgown she was wearing and looked at the juice-can curlers rolled into Aunt Vi's grayish brown hair instead of what she was holding. "Auntie, you know I can't help with tarantulas."

"Tarantulas! No, no, this is why I'm worried about Benjamin. He must be in trouble. Why else would he think he might need a disguise?"

Swallowing, Felicity peered at what was in her aunt's palm. Okay, it definitely wasn't alive. "But what the heck is it?" she asked.

"A mustache. He borrowed it from Uncle Leo a couple of weeks ago. Benjamin had been missing for several days before Leo told me about it—and that's when I called you. What do you think we should do?"

With the tarantula threat on hold, Felicity dropped onto the mattress and put her head in her hands. What should "we" do? Her purpose for coming to Half Palm was to extricate herself from the Charms and their attendant problems.

But she needed to get her bearings first. "Aunt Vi, I . . . I need a quick shower, and then we'll, uh, talk, okay?"

Aunt Vi patted her shoulder, as the four original cats and two others leaped onto the mattress to arrange themselves around Felicity. "I'll have coffee

ready. Ashley and her boyfriend are coming for lunch
in half an hour."

Looking up, Felicity stroked the tabby that had settled onto her lap. "Ashley's seeing someone?"

"It's been eighteen months since Simon was killed."

"That long?" Felicity suppressed a twinge of guilt
that she hadn't made it to Ashley's husband's memorial service, or even talked to her cousin except for a
single sympathy phone call.

It wasn't as if they had anything in common, after
all.

"She's living with the man," Aunt Vi said. "I think
you'll like him."

Twenty minutes later, Felicity entered Aunt Vi's
Depression-era kitchen. Looking around at the worn
tile, the chipped sink, the cheap cabinets, she wasn't
surprised to find nothing had changed.

But *she* had! That's what the visit to Half Palm was
for, to show the Charms just how unlike them she'd
become. Now she only had to figure out some quick,
painless way to make it clear she was breaking her ties
with them.

Aunt Vi turned away from the counter to hand Felicity a thick mug filled with coffee. "Oh, good. You
found some of your old things."

Felicity tugged on the hem of the tight T-shirt she
wore, then sank onto the plastic cushion of one of the
metal-legged chairs drawn up to the formica table. To
ease the equally snug fit of her pair of worn jeans, she
wiggled.

"They were all there. Right where I left them when I went off to USC." The whole house was exactly as she'd left it, from the boarded-up second story windows to the neglected pots of cactus lining the cracked-cement front walkway.

In the case of her clothes, she supposed she should be glad. While she'd planned to arrive in Half Palm dressed in her awards-ceremony finery and driving her beautiful new convertible—undeniable proof she didn't belong in this place with them—instead she'd been towed into town wearing nothing more than a survival blanket.

Thank God it had barely been daylight.

Even though brewed in a chrome percolator that must be as old as she was, the coffee tasted good. Felicity gulped it down with her eyes closed, aware that Aunt Vi was hovering in a way that spelled out more trouble.

With half the cup downed, she made herself look up.

Aunt Vi smiled. "Good news!" From behind her back, she whipped out something that she then set in front of Felicity.

Her mug at her lips, she froze. Her Joanie.

Aunt Vi came around behind Felicity as if to admire the statuette from her same angle. "Is this what you told me about when you arrived this morning? Is this your award?"

Felicity found she couldn't speak. It couldn't be! Her Joanie, her perfect, gleaming prize, was now nicked, dented, and scratched.

"Your Uncle Billy brought it over," Aunt Vi continued. "He thought you might want it with you since your car won't be ready for . . . uh, for a bit."

Felicity swung around to look at her aunt. It was better than looking at the scraped and bent disaster that had once been her golden Joanie. "What do you mean, my car won't be ready for a bit? I told Uncle Billy to get it to the point where I can drive it back to L.A. I'll have the body work done there."

Aunt Vi shrugged, moving across the kitchen with Felicity's cup to pour her more coffee. "I don't know. Something about a drive shaft? He said it isn't safe to tow it any farther."

Felicity could feel her blood pressure rising. It was a burning sensation that rose from somewhere around her stomach to wrap strangling hands around her neck. "Aunt Vi, do you know why my car is at Uncle Billy's in the first place? Did you know he's up to his old tricks?"

Aunt Vi fluttered her hands. The Charm women all fluttered when directly asked about nefarious practices. Add to that the fact that Aunt Vi was born a ditherer, then straight talk and simple action were outside her MO. "I don't know anything."

Felicity sighed, because *that* was the first thing Charms were taught. If anyone asked, deny, deny, deny. "He's salting the outlying roads with nails, Aunt Vi. Remember that little scam of his? The one he used some years ago to pick up business at the tire repair shop? I thought he'd sworn to the sheriff he wouldn't do it again."

"We have a new sheriff now. Sheriff Mendoza retired." Aunt Vi set the refilled mug beside the mangled Joanie. "He's living near his daughters in Tempe. I miss that man." She beamed a fond smile.

Felicity rolled her eyes. The only thing a Charm would miss about an authority figure was the opportunity to avoid one.

"Aunt Vi, I could have been hurt," she said, shoving that out-of-body memory from her head. "And not just me, there was also M—"

But there was no reason to say the name aloud, not when she was halfway to convincing herself the whole Michael part of the night before had been some weird after-accident dream as well. Felicity would *never* have begged a stranger for sex!

It simply *had not* happened. Her lingering headache was easily explained by her head hitting the car window. The minor muscle pain an aftereffect of the collision, too. Neither had anything to do with shots of tequila or lovemaking on metal floorboards. Bottom line, since she'd never see the man again, as far as she was concerned, Michael did not exist.

The kitchen's back door squealed as it swung open. Felicity looked up and found herself leaping to her feet to rush the newcomer. Without thinking, she reached out with both arms. Squeezed.

Then, embarrassed by her enthusiasm, she released her cousin Ashley, stepping back from the taller woman who'd been like a sister to Felicity until she'd left Half Palm. "I . . . I'm sorry, Ash. I don't know what got into me." Several cats had come through the back door, too, so Felicity slid past the awkward moment by picking one up. "How, uh, are you?"

"It's good to see you." Ashley smiled, then tilted her head. "I like Felicity's short hair, don't you, Mom?"

Like everything else in Half Palm, Ashley hadn't changed a whit. She was still tall and slender, with a long fall of blond hair in a precise center part. Growing up, Felicity had wanted Ashley's height and Ashley's hair and . . . well, just about everything that Ashley had.

And Ashley had something very, very special that Felicity had only seen pictures of. "Where is she, Ash? Where's your baby?"

"Not a baby anymore." Ashley's smile was sadder now. "Anna P's turning four."

"So that's what you call her." Felicity had sent an engraved Tiffany cereal bowl and cup at the baby's birth, engraved "Annapurna." Her daddy had named her for the first mountain he'd climbed after meeting Ashley. "Where's your Anna P.?"

"Magee's bringing her," Ashley answered. "My housemate. We had to come in separate cars because I'm going to work straight from here. They'll be here any minute."

"Well," Aunt Vi said. "We'd better get lunch out, then."

Felicity followed her aunt's direction, moving into the living area to unfold the metal TV trays and then set them with mismatched silverware and plastic-ware plates. At one point she found herself in the kitchen alone with Ashley, and though it wasn't part of her cut-herself-free-of-the-family agenda, Felicity couldn't help but ask.

" 'Housemate,' Ash? Aunt Vi calls this Magee your boyfriend."

Her cousin didn't meet her eyes. She lifted a hand, let it drop. Like her mother, Ashley was a natural ditherer, but this felt more like reticence, not helplessness. "He was Simon's best friend," she finally said quietly. "And he's been taking good care of Anna P. and me. We've needed that."

Thinking of Simon, Felicity quieted, too. She'd met him once. Right before their daughter was born, he and Ashley had visited L.A. and Felicity had taken them to dinner at Fidel's in Manhattan Beach. With his Australian accent, his golden hair, his brawny arms, Simon had been larger-than-life. Felicity had expected the evening to be awkward and small talk hard to come by, but they'd ended up closing down the restaurant thanks to his outrageous, funny stories of climbs and other climbers.

The memory made her smile. "I liked Simon," she said softly.

"You'll like Magee, too," Ashley replied.

"Of course she'll like Magee," a male voice said from behind Felicity, accompanied by a round of little girl giggles.

That voice! Felicity froze. *It couldn't be. . . .*

"Tell her, Anna P.," he went on. "Tell her everybody likes Michael Magee."

Four

Crossing his arms over his chest, Magee leaned against the kitchen wall and looked toward the woman washing the lunch dishes. "Need a hand?"

She jumped, splashing water and soap suds on the apron she wore over skinny Levi's and a striped T-shirt. Turning, she hissed at him, "How *could* this have happened?"

He lifted an eyebrow. "You eat, the dishes get dir—"

"You are so not funny." She darted a nervous glance past him to the living room beyond.

"Your aunt and Ashley are outside with Anna P.," he said. "We're all alone."

Mimicking his pose, she crossed her arms over her chest and frowned at him, even as a flush crawled up her neck. Looking at all that embarrassed color only improved his mood. An hour before, he'd nearly dropped Anna P. when he'd walked into the kitchen and got his first glimpse of Ashley's cousin, but the instant horror written all over "Lissie's" face had eased his.

Her obvious discomfort told him his task was going to be easy. In order to do what he planned—what he owed Simon—and take care of Ashley and Anna P. for the rest of his life, he had to ensure that the events of the night before would stay out in the dark desert and never come back to haunt him.

But the woman across the room got in the first word. "I think I should tell you . . ." she started, and the blush on her face deepened, turning her fair skin a clear pink. Even her full lips took on more color. "I want you to know . . ."

It was clear she wanted to leave last night behind, too, so there was no point in prolonging her misery or postponing his move. He stepped into the awkward silence she couldn't seem to fill. "I'm not sure I caught your name when we were introduced before lunch. Felicity, is it? And I'm Michael Magee, though most people just call me Magee."

She blinked. The eyes that had been dark pools the night before, he realized, were really a deep, bottomless blue. Thanks to a nothing nose, small chin, and short, feathery haircut, the big eyes and pouty mouth dominated her face.

"Magee?" she said, as if trying the word out.

He nodded. "Magee."

Her gaze stayed trained on his. "And I'm—"

"Felicity," he supplied. "It's good to meet you."

Then she nodded, too, and just like that, he thought with relief, they'd agreed to pretend the night before had never happened. It was the easiest way to play it.

"Well, then, it's good to meet you, too." She strode forward and held out her hand.

Without thinking, he shook it. Damn him.

Because for moments more than was necessary, her fingers clung to his. He gripped back, only able to hold on as an unexpected, electric jolt of lust buzzed through his body. Their eyes met, and Magee took a screamer of a fall into that bottomless blue.

"Magee? Felicity?" Ashley's voice floated toward the kitchen.

He jerked his hand back, his elbow slamming into the kitchen wall. "Shit!" The shooting pain at least gave him something else to think about as Ashley entered the kitchen, a drowsy Anna P. half-asleep in her arms.

For her part, Felicity had retreated to the sink and shoved her hand into the sudsy water as if trying to wash away his touch. "Did you need something, Ash?"

"I was hoping you two were getting to know each other better," she said, smoothing her hand down the little girl's back.

"We were just getting to that getting-to-know-each-other part, weren't we, Magee?" Her expression unreadable, Felicity turned toward him. "I understand you were a friend of Simon's. Are you a climber, too?"

"I was." At the thought, an ache in his ankles joined the throb at his elbow, but he managed to match her polite tone. "Simon and I were climbing partners the last several years."

"Ah." Knowledge sparked in her eyes and her voice slowed with speculation. "I had a long dinner with Simon once. I think he told me about you."

Magee stifled a groan. Simon had been famous for telling the best stories about other people at their worst. "But now you," he interjected hastily. "What is it you do? Something in television, right?"

"GetTV. I host a couple of their bestselling shows. You've probably heard of my *All That's Cool Afternoons*?" When he didn't respond, her eyes widened. "*Girl Stuff Saturday Mornings*?"

He shrugged. "I don't know GetTV."

He might as well have slapped her. "Everyone knows GetTV! Salon.com calls it a cross between eBay and MTV's *Cribs*. *Time* magazine pronounced it the hottest thing in reality TV."

"Sorry, I don't know it. What is it again?"

"An electronic retailer." When he continued to just look at her, she made an impatient gesture. "You know, so people can shop while watching television. You do know what shopping is?"

Her snotty tone bugged him. What was her problem? Was she offended by some story Simon had told on him, or just pissed at that heat sizzling between them? That wasn't his fault—that was an equation as simple as $XX + XY$. "Listen . . ."

"You know men, Felicity," Ashley said, jumping in. "They're not the most enthusiastic shoppers."

"Oh, really?" Her cousin's lip curled. "Because in my experience some of them have been *overly* enthusiastic. No matter what the product is, they just have to have it."

Oh, yeah, Felicity was trying to blame him, all right.

"Ashley, I don't think your cousin understands men at all," Magee said through his teeth. "It's true that under certain circumstances a man might not refuse a free sample—who would, especially when the salesgirl insists by pressing it into his hand!—but that doesn't mean he wants a second taste, let alone the whole enchilada. It isn't that good."

"Salesgirl insists! Are you claiming you were *forced* to . . . to . . ."

"Is GetTV selling a line of Mexican food now?" Ashley asked, her eyebrows drawing together.

Felicity answered her cousin, but her gaze was narrowed at him. "As a matter of fact, we've had great success with our food products. We've never had to beg anyone to take a sample because everything at GetTV is top-quality."

"Is that so?" Something new on a nearby countertop snagged his attention and he reached over to snatch up a mangled piece of statuary. "Well, if you bought this from GetTV, dollface, you got taken."

In a flash, she rushed over to grab it from him. "That's a Joanie. *My* Joanie. I won it last night for being voted Host of the Year."

"Sorry, but it looks like the booby prize to me. Couldn't they have polished it up for you?"

She glared at him. "It *was* polished. It was *perfect.*

But then it was tossed around in the trunk during the accident."

"Accident?"

At Ashley's voice, both Magee and Felicity whipped their heads toward her. Magee had almost forgotten the other woman was in the room.

"Mom didn't tell me you were in an accident," Ashley said.

"Oh. Uh. Uh, it's really not worth mentioning," Felicity stuttered out. "No harm done, except I'm stuck here until Uncle Billy makes some repairs. Which, at his usual snail's pace, means I won't be heading back to L.A. until tomorrow morning, I suppose."

She was just passing through! Magee breathed out a silent sigh of relief. Once he made it through the next few minutes, then he'd never have to see the pain-in-the-tail chick again. Ashley would agree to a quickie Vegas wedding, he was sure, so he wouldn't even have to endure a reception line that included her cousin's congratulatory kiss.

"Tomorrow?" Ashley shifted Anna P., her eyes widening. "But Felicity, what . . . what about Ben?"

Ben? "What about your brother, Ash?"

Her cousin spoke right over him, gripping that ridiculous statue in both hands as if it was a talisman. "Come on. So he hasn't called or come home for a week. Maybe if it was another twenty-one-year-old we should worry. But it's Ben, Ash. *Ben.*"

Magee relaxed, because he wasn't too worried about week-gone Ben, either. The kid had a good heart but a soft head, and at twenty-one he had likely gone off with a girlfriend or gone on a camping trip and merely forgotten to let anyone know.

But if Ash was anxious . . . "Is there something I can do?"

"No, Magee," she said, darting him a guilty look.

Felicity shot him a suspicious one. "We have a passel of relatives around here with nothing better to do than be on the lookout for Ben. Why involve me, Ashley?"

When her cousin gazed back without a word, Felicity closed her eyes and sighed. "Okay, fine. Don't answer that."

Apparently Magee had missed something in that last exchange. "I don't get it. Why should it be you?"

"Because being irresponsible is what the Charms do," Felicity answered. "Meaning they're high on plans and low on results."

Ashley shifted Anna P. so that the angelic face of the snoozing little girl was facing her cousin. "But you're the different one, Felicity," she said softly. "Isn't that what you've always wanted?"

Felicity's gaze was on her cousin's daughter, and she didn't look like the same woman who'd been spitting nails at Magee a few minutes before.

"I'm the one who doesn't belong," she said softly. Then she shook herself and focused on Ashley again. "Okay, okay. I'll do what I can, but only until Uncle Billy makes my car drivable."

Magee's instincts, the ones that had earned him the

Lucky Bastard nickname, were jabbed awake when Ashley turned to him. "And you can do something, Magee. You'll help my cousin, won't you?"

"*No!*" He glanced over at Felicity, who'd yelled the same word at the same time. Anna P. squirmed, crying out in her sleep, and Magee quieted his voice.

"Listen, Ashley, I would, you know I would, but Felicity and I don't really know each other—"

"Just for today," Ashley said. "Simon would want you to."

That ended the discussion. At least for Magee.

But it didn't stop him from muttering at Felicity once Ashley left the kitchen to put Anna P. down for her nap. "You can still say something. Tell her the same thing I did. Tell her that we don't really know each other."

If looks could kill, she'd just shoved him off the summit of Yosemite's El Capitan. "But I do know you, *Michael Magee*. I remember that Simon told me plenty about his climbing partner . . . including the nickname you were given for your many amorous adventures."

Oh, hell.

She crossed her arms, tapped one toe. "Let's see. It went like this, I think. The more difficult the location, the more chance you might be discovered, the better you like doing it, isn't that right . . ."

He sighed, waiting for it.

". . . *Thrillbanger?*"

Felicity grabbed a baseball cap from her old closet, then jammed it over her hair as she followed Magee down the crumbling cement walkway. Over her shoulder, she waved at Aunt Vi, who was standing in the doorway and smiling at them through a curling rip in the screen.

At the end of the walk, he held open the door of his beater-mobile for her, and Felicity stopped short, surprised by the passenger seat that hadn't been there the night before.

"For Anna P.'s car seat," he explained, apparently reading her thoughts.

She spied the padded contraption now stowed in the cargo area, where last night— Hastily diverting her thoughts, she slid onto the seat and let Magee shut the door behind her.

Okay, he could display good manners. And perhaps he'd been kind to Ashley and Anna P. But didn't Felicity know for a fact that he possessed some dangerous Pied Piper qualities? Look at what happened last night! She'd acted completely out of character, and the culprit wasn't his so-called "survival rush" or even that out-of-body weirdness that she wasn't going to think about.

No, now that she knew Magee was the infamous Thrillbanger, she could squarely place the blame for that near-sexscapade on him.

She scrutinized the man as he walked around the car to the other side. Same wide-shouldered, lean build. Same who-needs-a-stylist inky-colored hair. He was dressed even more casually today, in another pair of jeans, beat-up hiking boots, and a faded T-shirt that said—oh, sheesh!

I'm
Unreliable
Irresponsible
Immature
Undisciplined
Inefficient
Disorganized
Inconsistent
and
Unmotivated
but
I'm Fun!

She was willing to bet that meant he didn't have a job, let alone a whiff of ambition. While that might make him fit right in with the Charms, she'd make darn sure he wasn't planning on leading the family down some thorn-filled primrose path. Though she doubted she had a prayer of finding Ben by morning, her good deed, she decided, would be to instead discover enough about Magee to warn Ashley and the rest that they should steer clear of him.

Magee ducked into his seat and glanced over to catch her looking at him. She quickly transferred her gaze, pretending an avid interest in Aunt Vi's house.

His head followed hers. "How long since you've been back to the ancestral home?" he asked.

Ancestral home? Felicity looked up at the ramshackle farmhouse. It was shaded by two sparse California pepper trees, their branches of thin leaves and clusters of pinkish berries brushing against the second-floor windows that had been boarded up as long as she could remember.

The first Charms had come to the area in the late 1800s, taken in by the advertising of a Palm Springs hustler who'd stuck oranges and grapefruits on the spines of the Joshua trees, then photographed them. Lured by the get-rich-quick promises, her great-great-grandfather had rushed from the Midwest to buy some acres of his very own sand, without considering whether arid dunes could truly support flourishing citrus groves.

"I'm not 'back,' " Felicity corrected, shaking her head. "I'm visiting."

Though she hadn't intended visiting, either. She'd intended on breezing through and permanently locking the door to her past even as she continued speeding out of town.

"Yeah? How long ago was your last visit, then?"

"I haven't actually lived in the house—in Half Palm, for that matter—since I started boarding school in Palm Springs. I was eleven years old."

"That explains your wardrobe."

"What? No." She tugged on the hem of the too-short T-shirt. "I was even smaller at eleven than when I wore this." Which had made her the designated fall guy in any con gone awry. To most, she'd looked too young and too innocent to bear the blame.

The sound of his car starting reminded her she was

supposed to be grilling *him*. "So . . . what about you?"

He glanced in the sideview mirror as he maneu-vered onto the road, then down at his own T-shirt. "I think I found this last week in the freebie box at the Wild Side."

"I wasn't asking about— The wild side?" See, this was exactly what she was talking about. Wild side, freebie boxes. The man was a derelict, and it was her duty as the only discriminating member of her family, not to mention the member who wanted to run away from Half Palm with a free conscience, to discover just how much trouble he could cause the Charms.

"The Wild Side is where I'm taking you, dollface." She made a strangled noise and he grinned.

"Not to worry," he said. "It's a climbing store. We can ask about Ben there."

That grin of his was displaying a bunch of white teeth and deepening the brackets around his mouth and the sun lines at the corners of his eyes. She crowded the car door, keeping clear of the thrill-banger rays it was beaming out.

"Where's this climbing store?" she grumbled. Not far, she guessed, given that the national park known as Southern California's uber-destination for rock climbing wasn't far from Half Palm.

With her nose glued to the window, she catalogued the scenery outside. Barren lunar landscape: check. The occasional home, cobbled together with scrap wood and aluminum: check. A far cry from the lux-ury, prestige, and well-watered beauty of other desert communities: check, check, and check.

But as they neared the entrance to the national park, she spied signs of actual, civilized civilization. "Bed and breakfasts?" she wondered aloud. "A *day spa*?"

"Climbing's attracting a well-heeled clientele these days. Very in with the high-tech set." Magee glanced over, grinning at her again. "Or should I say 'cool'?"

She pretended to ignore that stupid, lethal smile. "High-tech set?"

"You know, the digitheads and the geeks. It's the angles they're attracted to. The angles and the independence."

The angles and the independence? She thought rock climbing was about throwing up a rope and then winching yourself to the top of something. "What attracts you?" she asked, curious.

There was a long pause, then he reached over and caressed her knee. "C'mon, dollface," he said, his voice amused. "I don't have to tell you, do I?"

She pushed his hand away. "You know what I'm talking about. Which is it you like about climbing, the angles or the independence?"

His face hardened as he pulled into a tidy little strip mall. "Neither. I don't climb anymore."

He didn't say another word as they climbed out of the car and she trailed him toward a store that proclaimed itself in neon tubing as the Wild Side. She might have let the silence stand, but a worry nagged at her, despite the old clothes and the ball cap she was wearing. Before his hand clasped the metal handle of the plate-glass door, she grabbed his wrist.

He twitched. She kept her eyes on his sinewy fore-arm instead of looking at him. "Look, will you do me a favor?"

"Does it involve my clothes on or off this time?"

She wished she could ignore that, but thinking of him naked made *her* twitch. So she let out a long sigh and then looked up.

His face revealed nothing.

So, fine, she wouldn't let *him* know that he was working his thrillbanger trickery again and that there was a needy little urge bubbling through her bloodstream. Letting out another breath, she let go of him.

"Would you please, uh, not mention me by name in there?" She nodded toward the shop.

He just looked at her.

"Because, well, believe it or not, I get stopped on the street. People recognize me. Probably not dressed like this." She pulled the hat lower over her eyes. "Especially if you don't use my name. But you see, Felicity Charm, she . . . she . . ."

Felicity Charm couldn't afford to let anyone find out about her real relatives. The public loved and approved of the fictionalized Charm family, which was part of their love and approval of *her*.

His eyebrows lifted. "Felicity wouldn't be seen with a man like me?"

She made an offhand gesture that encompassed everything from his untamed hair to that telling T-shirt. "Well, of course she wouldn't, but—"

Hearing what she'd said, she tripped over her own

tongue. "*No,* that didn't come out right. It wasn't about you. I meant, I mean . . ."

"I get you." Magee pulled open the door then reached around to shove her through with his palm on her behind. "No real names, right, sweet cheeks?"

Two minutes later, she realized she might as well have saved her breath. Because not one of the dozen or more young men and women in the store spared her a glance. The best she got was an elbow, as the climbers browsing in the store gathered near Magee.

She found herself on the outer circle and unable to decipher a word of their conversation. Bemused, she took the opportunity to check out the store. The truth was, she knew little about brick-and-mortar retailing, other than that the merchandise was left to speak for itself. On GetTV, that's what she did—speak for the merchandise—giving it an image that customers wanted to identify with . . . and own.

But there was image at work here, too, she decided, spinning in a slow circle. The bins of metal clips and straps and lethal-looking tools, the stacks of dried food and racks of backpacks, the shelves of color-coordinated clothing, didn't dominate the store as much as the bigger-than-life color photographs hanging high on the walls—photographs of climbers caught in improbable conditions and positions.

One of the photos commanded her attention and wouldn't let go. A golden-skinned, buffed, and bare-backed man was stretched over a rock wall, hanging by nothing but crimped fingers at the end of one bulging arm. His other hand reached impossibly higher.

It was an image that captured pure, physical strength. It was raw male power.

It was Magee.

And it was the female in her that responded to it with such a hot, weakening rush. Her gaze jumped across the room to make sure he hadn't noticed, but wouldn't you know, his eyes met hers over the knot of people around him. A shiver burned down her back as that connection she'd felt with him the night before rebuilt, stretched taut. In a rush, her nipples tightened, too, and her inner thigh muscles clenched.

No, no. She already knew this about him. *Those thrillbanger tricks.* Her feet shuffled back and then her body bumped a countertop, scattering a stack of magazines and papers and cutting the link between them.

Felicity dropped down to gather up the mess.

"Can I help you?" a female voice asked. A pair of hiking boots entered her field of vision.

She shook her head, stacking up flyers for climbing classes, adventure vacations, and the National Outdoor Products Trade Show taking place at the Palm Springs Convention Center the following week. Then she piled up a selection of magazines: *Climbing, Climber, Outdoorsman, Rock & Ice.*

When she replaced them on the counter, her fingertips slid across a glossy cover. On a whim she flipped through the pages, noting the colorful clothes, shoes, and gear. "Very in with the high-tech set," she murmured to herself, and then picked up another magazine.

This time the merchandise caught her eye, and so did Magee. Not only was he featured in ads for a company named Mountain Logic, but she found him mentioned in an interview with an up-and-coming climber. According to what she was reading, Magee wasn't just your average guy who liked heights—in his world he was a legend.

An out-and-out rock god. A rock star.

Felicity cast him a sidelong look, but found it intercepted by a young woman instead.

"Did you need something?" she said.

It was the voice from a moment ago, and it belonged to a sales clerk dressed like Magee in jeans, T-shirt, and boots. Her strawberry blond hair was fashioned into more than a dozen braids, each fastened with a different colored rubber band. There wasn't a smidgen of mascara on her pale lashes, and though she wore lip gloss, her nose was peeling.

"Did you need something?" the girl asked again.

Felicity tugged on the brim of her hat. "Oh, no, thank you. I'm fine." She nodded toward Magee. "I'm with him."

The girl's eyes rounded. "You're with the Lucky Bastard?" Her freckles disappeared into a flush on her cheeks. "Magee?"

Felicity cleared her throat. "Well, uh, yes."

"Then you *are* fine," the salesgirl muttered. She

frowned, and her gaze ran over Felicity, as if seeking out flaws. "He tells me I'm too young for him."

"Hmm, well . . ." She supposed it was comforting to discover he wasn't into jailbait, because the girl looked approximately fifteen years old. "But you see, we're not exactly—"

"There you are, angel thighs!" Magee's hard arm wrapped around Felicity's waist and squeezed. "Now, don't you be corrupting my little friend Gwen."

"Corrupting? I wasn't—"

"You weren't telling her how we spent last night, were you?" He spun Felicity so that they were face-to-face. Then he leaned over her so that the brim of her hat and the fall of his too-long hair curtained their faces. "Follow my lead," he whispered.

Oh, no. Hadn't she already cautioned herself about his Pied Piper talents? "Wait . . ."

But he was already mashing his lips against hers. She stiffened at the outrage of it all—Lucky Bastard? Presumptuous Bastard!—but then he gentled the kiss and she found herself moving closer, as if he were reeling her in with that invisible cord he kept spinning between them. She went on tiptoe, her tightening nipples brushing against his chest.

He lifted his head, giving her a wry smile before he turned her in front of his body to face the salesgirl. "Did you two get introduced?" he asked, his big hands kneading Felicity's shoulders.

"No," the girl said, crossing her arms. "Who is she?"

"This is Lissie," Magee said, still massaging.

"The one who's been keeping me so busy lately. And Lissie, my sugar lady, this is my little friend Gwen."

Little Friend Gwen looked as if she wanted to grind the sugar lady into little tiny granules. "Just exactly how many can she hang?" the girl asked Magee.

"Hang?" Felicity turned to glance up at Magee. She had no idea what that meant, but she knew who deserved a noose around his neck. "Yes, exactly how many, studly hips, *can* I hang?"

"I'll bet she can't do five pull-ups," the girl scoffed, a challenge in her eyes. Without waiting for an answer, she headed toward an office doorway where there was a chin-up bar installed.

Felicity whirled on Magee in panic. "I'll bet I can't do *one*."

"Don't worry about it," he murmured, then raised his voice. "Gwen, we don't spend our time together working on our climbing techniques. We do more . . . adult things, do you understand?"

The girl turned, her face bright red. "Oh. Oh, I guess."

Felicity felt Gwen's misery and tried to smooth the moment over. "Yeah, you know," she said. "We go to the theater, opera, out for drinks. . . ."

The girl narrowed her eyes. "So the two of you will be at the Bivy tonight?"

Magee's grip tightened on Felicity's shoulders. "Sure, it's my shift."

"So she'll be there with you?" Gwen asked, gesturing with a belligerent chin. "Since the two of you are so tight and all."

"Of course," Magee replied, his voice light. "She'll be there."

Once they were out of the store, it took him two minutes' worth of curt sentences to explain the situation with Gwen. The girl—the little sister of a long-time friend of his—had been making plays for him for years and seemed immune to the usual discouragement. It had only gotten worse since she turned twenty-one. In hopes that the girl would finally look for someone her own age, he'd tried to pass off Felicity as the new woman in his life.

"But the mention of opera made her suspicious, damn it." He shot Felicity a disgusted look. "As if I'd go to the *opera*."

She was out of sympathy and patience. "How was I to know? I like the opera. I like men who go to the opera. Let me tell you, one 'sweet thighs' does not a whole explanation make."

"I didn't plan it," he muttered. "It just occurred to me as you were standing there that I could throw Gwen off the scent."

"What's the Bivy, anyway?"

"A bar."

"Ah." So it appeared he did have employment of sorts. At a *bar*. "Wait—that's where Ashley works, too, right?"

He grunted, then started the car and pulled out of the parking place with a jerk. "She has some waitressing shifts and does the accounting."

Thinking of her cousin brought to mind another murky point. Just how involved *was* he with the Charms? Aunt Vi said boyfriend, while Ashley claimed him as mere housemate.

She half-turned, pinning Magee with her gaze. "So why are you dragging me into this? Why don't you use Ashley as your scent-thrower-offer? For goodness' sake, you *live* with her."

He mumbled something.

"What?" Felicity asked. "I didn't hear you."

"I said I already tried that and Gwen didn't buy it for a minute. She claims I could never be in love with Ashley."

Five

That evening, Felicity drove Aunt Vi's Dodge Dart to the Bivy. Not for Magee—she was going to stay away from him. His girl problem wasn't hers. But there'd been no word of Ben at the Wild Side or anywhere else they'd stopped that afternoon, so she'd placated a fluttering Aunt Vi by promising to ask around the bar, purportedly a favorite hangout of her missing cousin's.

Then there was her hope that the people, the noise, and a task to accomplish would put an end to the disquieting memories of the night before that kept popping up to plague her. She wanted to forget everything about it.

Following Aunt Vi's directions, Felicity found the Bivy easily enough, but not a place to park. Though the plain stucco building was surrounded by a generous lot, the only space available was in a dark corner between a shed and a dilapidated truck topped by a camper shell covered in bumper stickers.

She paused to read a few.

MEAT IS DEAD
Boy Bands: Spawn of Satan
Frodo Has Left The Shire
CARPE GENITALIA

Oh-kay, that told her something about the clientele of the place. Glancing down at her dressy, scoop-necked minidress—a DKNY lycra-cotton in French blue—she second-guessed her earlier mad dash to Palm Desert, one of the more prominent desert communities.

But it had been an interesting trip down Memory Lane regardless, she consoled herself. Instead of hitting Saks Fifth Avenue or one of the trendy boutiques, she'd found herself combing the racks of the many consignment shops, replaying how she'd supplemented her wardrobe during her years at boarding school. When she'd found the DKNY dress—original price tag still in place—she'd experienced that old familiar mix of acquisition joy and secretive shame, too. It was a good reminder of how far she'd come since then . . . and why.

So, taking a deep breath, she slung the new—to her, anyway—Kate Spade purse over her shoulder and, in matching pumps, strode to the bar's door.

It opened just as she reached for the odd, axelike device that served as a handle. Barraged by the notes of an old Stones' song, "Brown Sugar," she froze, leaving her easy pickings for one of the two scruffy young men on their way out.

"Look!" he said, lifting her up by the waist to bring her face level with his. His sun-streaked dreadlocks stood out from his head like a scrub brush. "Look who it is!"

Felicity's stomach dipped, even though her earlier experiences in the day had made it obvious that her face was as unfamiliar to the climber crowd as its members were to decent haircuts and quality styling products.

He grinned. "It's the bluebird of happiness!"

As pickup lines went, it was original, Felicity admitted, but she felt compelled to object to the manhandling part, especially when the first guy handed her off to the second. "Hey," she said, trying to appear authoritative while staring down at this one's crocheted beanie. "I, um, like standing on my own two feet."

He blinked up at her. "I'll take you where you want to go."

"She wants to come to me," a new voice called out over the music.

Crocheted Beanie instantly dropped her. The soles of her shoes hit the inches of sawdust covering the floor, sending up a small cloud. His buddy groaned. "Jeez, Banger, can't we have just *one* of them first?"

As the two young men continued on their way out the door, Felicity gathered her dignity and then raised her chin to meet the unreadable gaze of her would-be protector.

Magee lifted a brow. "Something the matter? You look ticked off."

"I can't think why you'd say that, *Banger*," she retorted, sweeping past him. "Your friend told me I'm the bluebird of happiness."

"Wait." He caught her elbow and hauled her back, jamming her shoulder blade against his chest. "Stick by me tonight."

As if. Turning her head to say it aloud, she sucked in a breath—and then wished she hadn't. This close, the scent of him invaded her lungs and invaded her head with flashbacks of the night before. This was exactly what she didn't want! But it was there anyway, the rain, the heat, the silky slide of his hair through her fingers. The weight of his body on hers and how she'd wanted to cradle him between her thighs so he could fill the emptiness inside her.

Aah! She wanted to stamp her feet and scream in frustration. The man was at it again. Trickery. Thrillbanger trickery. She tried stepping away, but his grasp only let her get so far.

"Let me go, Magee," she said. "Your romantic trouble is your own."

"*You're* trouble, walking in here looking like that."

She glanced toward the crowded barroom floor, noting that the women were wearing jeans, jeans, or jeans. A colored bandanna twisted and tied around the neck appeared to be the accessory of choice. "I'll take that as a compliment."

"Some will take it as an invitation. The men in here aren't the well-behaved clubby types I'm sure you're accustomed to."

"We women have learned to say no, Magee. It's our evolutionary edge." She glared at him.

His hand slid up her arm and hauled her closer. "Damn it. You're still blaming this on me, aren't you? That's why you're giving me the Ice Queen eyes."

She held herself very still. He couldn't know, could he, that every tender place on her body was throbbing—her wrists, her throat, her armpits, even! And she refused to give him the satisfaction of knowing how well his deviltry worked. "I don't know what you're talking about."

"This." Two of the fingers holding her upper arm uncurled. "I'm talking about this." They stroked along the outer curve of her breast.

Her breath caught. Her nipples tightened into hard points.

His gaze seemed to burn them. "Now go ahead, dollface," he said softly, his fingers moving in yet another secret caress. "Say no."

It took everything she had to wrench away from him. "*No*. No, I will not fall for your chicanery again."

He blinked. "My 'chicanery'?"

"It means wiles, tricks, shenanigans," she explained. "This game that you play."

He had the nerve to look insulted. "You really don't think much of me, do you?"

"I think you're good at this . . . this . . ." She waved her hand. "Thrill business. And that you enjoy how you can make me . . . respond."

"I guess that's something—being good at the thrill

business." He crossed his arms over his chest. "But if you're so smart—and you must be, knowing big words like *chicanery* and all—how come *your* response is *my* fault?"

"Because." She turned to stalk away from him, but he clapped a hand on her shoulder.

"I'm not *that* dumb, dollface. Because why?"

"Because it's obvious you're doing something to mess me up." She spun back to confront him, angry at how susceptible he made her. "My head rules my hormones. My brain commands my body. The fact is, I have a strict, short list of qualities that interest me in a man, and nothing about *you,* Magee, is on it."

Without giving him a chance to reply, she whirled away and marched toward the bar. Ashley stood at one end, in conversation with the bartender.

The man looked over as she slid onto a stool beside her cousin. "Hello, there," he said, giving her a friendly smile. "You a friend of Magee's?"

The curiosity in the bartender's eyes made it clear he'd witnessed at least some of the little scene by the door. Her cheeks heated. "Actually, I'm a friend of Ashley's."

"She's my cousin," Ashley corrected. "Felicity, meet Peter."

Though there wasn't even a hint of rebuke in the other woman's voice, Felicity felt her flush burn hotter. "Nice to meet you, Peter." Like Magee, he had that outdoorsy look, too, though with lighter brown hair streaked with gold, tanned skin, and those wide climber shoulders and ropy arms.

"What can I get you?"

Not until she'd ordered a glass of wine did she real-ize that Peter was in a wheelchair. In a practiced move, he pivoted for the bottle, pivoted back to pour her glass. There had to be a raised floor on the other side of the bar, because he moved at eye-level, easily handling her order and then rolling on to help a cus-tomer sitting farther down the row of stools.

Someone in the crowd of tables shouted Ashley's name, and she made a face. "Sorry, Felicity. It's going to be busy night. We probably won't have a lot of time to talk."

"Don't mind me." Now that she'd made it through the Magee gauntlet, nothing could mar the evening. "I'm fine on my own. Really."

"Ashley!" came from the tables again, and with that her cousin was gone.

Leaving Felicity by herself for, oh, something like two seconds. Before she had a chance to even sip and swallow, the empty seat beside her was filled by a very polite young man. His just-as-polite friend hung at her shoulder. Faces as scrubbed and fresh as mis-sionaries, they watched a snowboarding competition on the TV over the bar, explaining to her some of the finer points in a friendly, harmless manner.

A few minutes later, she found herself request-ing the Bivy's world-famous cheese fries. In the time it took her order to arrive—and her stomach was growling at the prospect, thanks to their effusive recommendation—they entertained her with their life stories. Both of them were college students on sabbatical, they told her, taking some time to travel around the U.S. in order to narrow their career focus.

Translation, Felicity thought, grinning to herself: They'd flunked out of school and were bumming around the country until their money ran out or their parents found out, whichever came first. Amused by their air of exuberant innocence, she bought them a couple of beers that arrived just as her cheese fries were placed in front of her.

"Let me get you some napkins," one of the missionary-faced boys said helpfully, then thrust a handful toward her, knocking her little Kate Spade purse to the floor. "Oh, sorry!"

"It's okay." Felicity slid off the stool to retrieve the purse, and when she came back up, both boys were gone.

Along with their beers, her wine, and the order of cheese fries. She scanned the room for them, even though the obvious was obvious. She'd been scammed.

"The Olson twins get you?" Peter rolled up and quickly poured her another glass of wine.

"They looked so sweet . . ." And a Charm should have known better! The knocked-over purse had been classic misdirection and she'd fallen for it hook, line, and sinker. "I feel like an idiot."

"Don't worry about it. I usually chase them away from newcomers, but Magee had sent them over."

"What?"

Peter shrugged. "I guess he wanted you kept busy. He said they were the lesser of the evils in the room."

"*What?*" He thought she needed a babysitter, and

he'd sent those two . . . two . . . petty criminals to do the job? She gulped down the wine, trying to cool off her temper.

"You and Magee . . ." Peter rolled closer. "You seem pretty . . . chummy."

She shook her head. "I just met him."

"Last night. He told me about it."

"He did?" If she hadn't wanted to avoid further contact with him, she would have gone after Magee and removed every hair from his head, follicle by follicle. "Exactly *what* did he tell you?"

"That you were in a car accident. Finding you like that shook him up, you know."

The fire went out of her. "I know," she heard herself answer. And then, though she'd been assuring herself all day that it hadn't happened, that it *couldn't* have happened, that tape in her mind restarted. From high above, she saw herself, she saw him. "His voice brought me back," she murmured. His voice and his despair.

"Brought you back?"

Felicity was still caught up in the memory. "I had a choice, and because of him, I decided to—" Then, horrified at what she'd revealed aloud, she quickly glanced at Peter.

He stared back at her, his eyes steady. "I lost the use of my legs in a crevasse fall almost three years ago. My partner had to go for help to get me out. I spent the night alone. I knew it was bad. I couldn't feel my legs and the temperature dropped until I was so cold I couldn't feel anything."

"I'm . . . sorry."

"Then I had an NDE—a near-death experience." He topped off the wine glass in her nerveless fingers. "It was just like people say. I was above my body, looking down on it, when help arrived. They were working to get me out, and I was surprised by all their desperate efforts. I wanted to tell them I was okay, not to worry about that broken shell in the crevasse."

Felicity's hands shook as she took a gulp from her glass. "And then what happened?"

"I was turning toward this light, a beautiful light more warm and accepting than anything I'd ever seen or imagined, when I heard my climbing partner screaming my name. I knew if I kept going toward the light, he'd always believe he failed me. And I still wanted to go. So damn much. But I saw how careless, how selfish that would be. How careless and selfish I'd been for most of my life. And though it hurt like hell to go back into that broken body, I was certain I had more to do here. Amends to make."

A beat or two of silence passed. "Did something like that happen to you?" he asked softly. "Did you see the light?"

"Of course not!" The idea terrified her. Not just because it was weird, but because . . . "I have to go." She slid off the stool and stumbled away, wondering if what had—and hadn't!—happened the night before would ever leave her in peace.

* * *

"What did you say to my cousin?"

Peter didn't look up from the beer mug he was filling. "What's that, Ash?"

"My cousin. She jumped up from her seat like it scalded her. Did you—did you make a pass at her or something?"

Surprised by the note of truculence in her voice, he lifted his gaze to hers and raised his eyebrows. "Would that be so shocking?"

"No!" She swallowed. "No. Of course it wouldn't. I'm sure you, uh . . ." Her beautiful face flushed red and she fumbled with her pad. "I need three drafts and a bottle of Miller Lite."

Peter went about filling the order, moving with extra care because he had a sudden sense of sands shifting beneath him. *What's going on here?* He glanced up, and kept his voice casual. "What does Magee think of Felicity?"

Ashley looked over, a frown between her clear blue eyes. "Think of her? I don't know. They only met this afternoon."

"Ah." Interesting that his pal Magee hadn't said a word about the night before to the woman he lived with.

"Why?" Ashley asked. She slid her tray onto the bar so that she could lean closer. He could smell that wildflower perfume she wore—the scent of the desert in spring. "Do *you* think something about her, Peter?"

Dragging his attention from Ashley, he looked over her shoulder to see that Felicity had been drawn into

a game of darts. Maybe his talk of NDEs had un-
nerved her into tossing back too much wine, he
thought, because she was laughing as one of the regu-
lars tried to correct her technique by octopus-arming
her from behind.

"I think she's . . . intriguing," he replied. Even
more intriguing was the dark expression on Magee's
face as he watched the scene at the dartboard from the
other side of the room.

"Well, you're not her type," Ashley said, setting the
last beer on her tray with an emphatic clack.

That Ashley was warning him away from her
cousin was the most intriguing of all. He felt the
ground beneath his chair shift again.

He slanted her a glance, then tossed out a test question. "Because of my legs?"

"Your legs? What does that matter?"

"It matters a lot." Peter grabbed a rag and started
wiping. "To some women, anyway."

The tray hit the bar. "You give me her name. Their
names." Ashley's voice was as fierce as he'd ever
heard it. "If anyone's insulted you, I'll—"

"What, Ash?" The foundation beneath him was
moving again, and he gripped the counter below the
bar to keep himself steady. "What will you do?"

"I . . ." Her shoulders slumped. "Oh, you know me.
Nothing, I guess."

He sighed out a long breath and forced his fingers
to relax. "That's all right, Ash."

For a second, just a second, he'd thought . . . But he
must be wrong. If Ashley was going to turn to anyone,

it would be Magee. When he'd moved her and Anna P. in with him, Peter had sat by like a stone because he'd thought Simon's widow and daughter and Simon's best friend needed to help each other heal. But later he'd wondered if he'd bungled once again.

As the evening wore on, he kept one eye on Ashley and one on her cousin. Felicity had found herself a group of dance partners and Magee didn't look any happier about that than he did about the dart lessons. Ashley moved in and out of the tables with her usual grace, but the new, speculative glances she darted his way puzzled him.

Then he figured it out. *Well, hell!* As humiliating as it was to acknowledge, Ashley must not have regarded him as a sexual being since his accident. Okay, so he had to admit that until tonight he'd never said anything to her about women, romance, or sex, but she'd been married to someone else, and then was a new widow!

It hadn't seemed . . . appropriate.

But maybe those shifting sands signaled a change after all. Maybe it wasn't too late to reassert himself in Ashley's eyes. So, the next time she came by with a load of dirty glasses, he put his hand on her arm.

She froze.

"Thought I'd ask your opinion, Ash, since we were speaking of me and women. What do you think about Elaine?" He tilted his chin in the direction of a thirty-ish woman at the end of the bar.

Ashley blinked. "Well, I . . . I don't know. Doesn't she work at the library?"

"Uh-uh. As a matter of fact, before our first date, she did some research."

"Research?"

"Yeah. When I called to ask her out, she asked *me* at what level my spinal cord was damaged. Then she told me she'd get back to me on the date."

Ashley glanced down the bar at Elaine again. "That's . . . odd."

He shrugged. "Not so. She called me back the next night and said it was a go. Her research had paid off and I passed."

Ashley made a face. "Something tells me I'm not going to like her at *all* after this."

Peter stifled his smile. "She had a right to know what she was getting into. Who would want to be saddled with a dud of a date? Once she found out I could control all my . . . faculties, let's say, then she agreed to, uh, exploring our mutual interests."

Ashley was staring at him. "That's cold-blooded and just, well, icky."

He lifted a brow. "Is it? Is it so cold-blooded to want to be with someone who can meet your needs?"

She rushed away. From the disgusting idea of him and his useless legs having sex? But perhaps it was another answer altogether, because a few minutes later Elaine yelped and jumped to her feet. The back of her denim shirt was drenched.

Behind her, Ashley stood with an empty beer mug in her hand. Murmurs raced down the bar. Consensus was that while her apologies sounded insincere, the spill *must* have been unintentional.

No one could think of anything that would motivate gentle Ashley to attack a woman she barely knew.

Peter hid his grin. Progress! Now he was sure of it. But if there was one thing the long rehab process had taught him, it was patience. To proceed with little steps. Still, his mood was flying high when Magee stomped behind the bar to pour himself a cup of coffee.

"Females!" He slammed the pot back on the burner. "What the *hell* are they good for?"

"I thought you'd figured that out a long time ago, Banger," Peter replied.

Magee rounded on him. "*Don't* call me that. Jesus, a guy sows some wild oats—"

"Some?"

"C'mon. I was in my twenties," he protested. "It was part of the lifestyle. It's not as if you were any better."

"Compared to you? I was Saint Peter."

"You are Saint Bullshit, my friend. We were all part of the 3-D Club, remember? What did Simon call it? Danger, Debauchery, and—"

"Demons," Peter finished for him, then tilted his head. "Have you ever figured out what yours are?"

Magee swung away to refill his coffee cup. "You know I don't navel-gaze."

"Might do you some good."

"Fine." The contents of the second cup of coffee were tossed into the sink and Magee turned to survey the room moodily. "You want to get serious? Then you should be seriously thinking of buying me out of this place."

"What? What's this about?" Peter's blood went

cold, then froze as Magee's wandering gaze found Ashley and stayed on her.

"It's time to do what's right, Peter. It's time I got a move on and wrapped things up." Then Magee's head jerked left. "Oh, damn. *Now* what's she doing?"

Peter watched his friend stride off after a flouncing blue skirt. Despite that, he didn't feel like smiling any longer, not even with Ashley heading toward him. He might have the patience, but there might not be the time. Not when he feared that one of the "things" Magee was threatening to wrap up was Peter's first and only love.

How was he ever going to let her go? Magee thought in exasperation, following Felicity and her escort into the parking lot. He'd have to go through the rest of his life thinking he'd saved her cute little ass, only to lose her to some stupid decision like driving herself home or letting the animal she was with do it for her.

An animal who apparently didn't remember that Magee had already confiscated his keys. "Joe," he called out, approaching the couple from behind. They were standing together in the deep shadows, away from the lights illuminating the parking lot. "Gordon's giving you a ride home tonight, remember? He's your designated driver, dude."

Joe slowly spun, almost losing his balance in the process. He clutched at Felicity to keep himself upright. "I 'member."

Despite the shadows, the look Felicity sent Magee

was sharp as a tack. Maybe she hadn't drunk as much as he thought. "You can go back inside, Dad," she said, her voice like a shard of ice. "Joe asked me to come out here and wait for the cab with him."

Oh, this was good. "Joe said he called a cab?"

"Yes."

Joe himself shook his head. "No cabs in Half Palm," he said mournfully. "I made that up."

Her head whipped toward him. "What?"

Joe pawed at her hair with a clumsy hand. "Pretty Lissie. Such a pretty, pretty Lissie."

She took a step away from him. "You said you had an idea of where Ben might be! That you'd seen him at the casino in Palm Springs and that if I came out here you'd tell me where you think he might be now!"

Joe shook his head, even more disconsolate. "I made that part up, too. Okay, pretty Lissie?" He reached a hand toward her hair again.

She smacked it away. "No, it's not okay."

The smack put Joe off balance for the second time and he lurched around in a large circle. It was at times like this that Magee remembered how often debauchery included making a fool of oneself. As Joe stumbled closer, Magee grabbed hold of his shoulders and steered him in the direction of the bar entrance. "Dude, straight ahead. Go inside and find Gordon."

Joe tripped forward and finally made it through the bar door.

Magee looked back at Felicity. She raised an eyebrow. "You better go back inside, too. I saw you cleaning tables and such. I'm sure your boss doesn't want you loafing around out here."

She thought he was the bar's busboy.

He bared his teeth in a smile. "Oh, I don't mind sacrificing minimum wage plus my share of the tip jar for you, dollface."

"I didn't ask for and I don't need a keeper. Especially one like you."

Oh, yeah, that's right. Nothing about him was on that short list of hers. "Believe me, dollface, I didn't follow you for your benefit. Until you're at least fifty miles out of range, I think it's in my own best interest to know exactly where you are at all times."

"Oh, I can't wait to hear your explanation for that."

"I told you last night. The way I see it, you're my spitwad of bad karma—payback for my wicked deeds—and I don't plan on being blindsided again."

It made sense to him. More than half the climbers he knew were Buddhists or at least claimed to be, and he'd been soaked in enough of their yammer to have absorbed the law of karma. Last night he'd postponed fulfilling his obligation and making that proposal of marriage, consequently he'd been struck by the dollface's car—and then by this raging case of protective . . . horniness for the dollface herself.

"You're bad karma," he said again.

"Wait just a minute," Felicity said as she marched closer. "You're saying *I'm* a problem for *you*?"

His gaze ran from her face, which was all dark-lashed eyes and pink, puffy mouth, down her slender curves in the tight-fitting dress, to those sex-and-the-single-girl shoes. Jesus Christ, he thought, she was a problem for him, all right. He was a man who liked women in rough-terrain boots, but the whole tippy-toe thing acted like a direct power source to his penis. "Hell, yes."

"No." She shook her head. "The problem is your thrillbanger tri—"

"Give us both a break, dollface." He wasn't going to let her ignore the truth any longer. "This isn't something I'm doing to you. It's—look, it's working both ways. Your yin is batting its bedroom eyes at my yang. My kayak is all packed and ready to explore your tunnel of love."

Her jaw dropped. "Well, I never—"

"Then maybe it's high time you did," he said, gripping her shoulders and pulling her close. "Feel it, baby." She grabbed his shirt, and the side of her fist pressed against his thumping heart, working triple-time to keep his erection stiff. "This is physical, nasty, steamy, forget-your-friggin'-list lust."

And forgetting everything but that, he lowered his mouth.

Six

With Anna P. riding piggyback, Magee jogged up the front walk of the Charm house. No more private chats with Felicity, he warned himself. No private moments of *any* kind. No truth-baring and no skin-baring, either. Last night, trying to make a point about the chemistry between them had only proved what an idiot he was. The kiss had turned wild in a heartbeat. Her dress had been half-unzipped when they'd been caught in the headlight beams of Gwen's car.

He'd been so hard and hurting that when Felicity had stuttered out some excuse to the younger woman about Magee helping her with a moth that had flown up her dress, he hadn't had the breath to call bullshit on her. He figured Gwen had caught on, though, which was the good news.

But now it was time for bad news. Get in, give it to Felicity, get out. Though it was nearing midday, he guessed he'd find her inside.

In fact, it was she who opened the door. Staring down at her bare toes, her face went red, but then she widened the screen so he could gallop the little girl into the living room. He slid her onto the couch to a litany of "good horsie" praise. In return, he mussed the bangs she'd insisted he straighten with a wet comb five minutes before they'd left.

"Magee!"

Her kid-pout made him laugh. "No, baby, it still looks fine. But a person shouldn't be so hung up on appearances."

"Not a baby." She hopped off the couch, heading for the VCR and the box of the videotapes beneath the TV set.

Magee glanced over at Felicity, who'd trailed them into the room. "Vi watches her on Sunday afternoons."

Felicity's gaze was on the little girl now poking through the tapes. "I know. She's expecting her."

In her high school jeans and T-shirt again, Felicity looked younger than Gwen and a thousand times more harmless than Anna P. Magee shook his head. Who the hell was she, really? Lissie, with all her passion? Felicity, with her hormone-ruling head and short list of acceptable-man qualities? Or this barefoot young woman in a run-down living room who couldn't keep her eyes off her cousin's daughter?

Blowing out a breath, he shoved his hands in his pockets and decided to get business done. "Felicity—" She looked up, and the rest of his words froze.

Damn, damn, damn, whoever she was today, yesterday, any day didn't seem to matter. One look into those blue eyes and he was once again drowning in that uncontrollable urge to drag her off, strip her down, and do it dirty. Unlike Peter, he wouldn't try to claim sainthood for even a second, but he'd never had a case of the jones that burned like this one.

He glared at her, but her gaze cut back to Anna P. "Does . . . does she remember her father?" she asked softly.

Well, hell, the only thing he wanted to think about less than sex was Simon. But ignoring it was out of the question because a telltale upward peek from the little girl made clear that Anna P. had heard Felicity, too.

"Sure, she remembers him." He forced himself to sound casual, to act casual as he moved to a table under the window and scooped up a frame. He showed it to the little girl, even though he himself couldn't look down at the grinning face in the photograph. "Tell Felicity who's in the picture, sweetheart."

Anna P. glanced at it, then went back to perusing the tapes. "That's my daddy, mate," she said, her accent going pure Aussie. "My daddy that used to sing my special song, 'Anna P., Anna P., the only little girl for me.' "

Felicity laughed. "That sounds just like him."

Magee forced himself to relax and ruffled Anna P.'s bangs again. "We have video," he explained.

"Daddy died," Anna P. added matter-of-factly. "Under lots of snow."

Magee's grip on the frame tightened as he walked it back to its place. The tragic words in that little voice tore at him.

"Well, you know what?" Felicity replied. "My

daddy died, too. Along with my mommy when I wasn't much older than you are now."

Staring out the front window, Magee pretended he hadn't heard that, because he had a thing about dead fathers. He rubbed his hands over his face, feeling every sleepless hour of the past two nights. The first had been filled with rain and tequila and tarantulas and then last night he'd come awake in a sudden panic, a nightmare of being smothered in a landslide of pencils, printouts, and PCs still lying like a heavy weight on his chest.

He'd breathed deeply, that weight morphing into a memory of Felicity lying across him in the back of the Jeep. The hours until the alarm had been filled with cursing himself, her, and the hard-on stretching toward his navel.

The robotic hum of the VCR as Anna P. ejected the tape already in the machine must have masked Felicity's movement, because the next thing he knew she was standing beside him.

"What was he thinking?" she whispered, picking up the photo. "How could he have risked his life after she was born?"

"It was his last climb," he said. "He'd made plans to change his life, but then . . . but then bad luck caught up with him." Or Magee hadn't.

He swung around to check on Anna P. Her small fingers flattened as she pushed a new tape in the machine. She was settling in and he could be on his way.

Halfway across the room, he remembered the message he had for Felicity. "Hey . . ." The word trailed off as he saw an image of her materialize on the television screen.

Anna P. caught his eye and smiled, her voice full of Aussie mischief. "Where you going, mate? Sit down with me and watch."

She had him wrapped around her little finger, Magee had to admit that as he sank onto the sofa cushions. But he wasn't the only one. When Anna P. ordered Felicity to sit down, too, she also obeyed.

Her face was flushed again, though, as she threw him a glance. "GetTV," she said, gesturing toward the screen. "I send Aunt Vi production tapes every once in a while since she can't get cable in Half Palm."

He looked back at the screen. It was Felicity, all right, a city Felicity, wearing a white shirt, a tight, bilious-green knee-length skirt, and a pair of chunky-heeled sandals. Despite the constricting outfit, she was curled up on an armchair and proceeded to smile at and chat with the camera as if they were best friends.

"Don't you hate worrying about losing your cell phone? Have you ever mixed yours up with someone else's?" She launched into a story about mistakenly trading cell phones with another woman on a Friday night and being plagued all weekend with calls from a personal trainer, a dog trainer, and a gravel-voiced man calling himself Sir John who'd promised to train her.

"But look! The must-have solution!" From a table beside her, she whipped out a piece of jewelry that she flashed for the camera with perfectly manicured fingers. "Cell phone charms! You can personalize your phone to signal your mood, your current dating status, or even your beverage of choice." The camera zoomed in on the charm, a tiny margarita glass.

As she waxed on about how to order—"try our keep-it-simple payment plan!"—Magee still couldn't believe such items existed or that any sane person would bother with them.

Still . . . "Hey, does that set come with a shot glass?" he couldn't resist asking.

She tried sneering, but there was something about her girl-next-door features that couldn't make it stick. Instead, it slid into an embarrassed frown. Laughing to himself, he settled back on the couch, content to have her televised image yak him right out of his unwelcome yen for her.

And if the cell phone charms hadn't proved they were from two different galaxies, the battery-operated ice cubes she featured next were evidence aplenty. Holding up a boxful of them in "Age of Aquarius" colors, she went about convincing the viewers they were a "must-have," too, for the next "must-do" party. His jaw gaped when she mentioned that the last time they'd been featured on her *All That's Cool Afternoon,* they'd sold twenty-six thousand units.

"You've got to be kidding," he said aloud.

She shot him a glance, trying again to paste on that sneer. "GetTV reaches over eighty million American homes and is the fastest growing and most popular TV shopping network. It's a retail phenomenon."

"Phenomenon? You must mean felony. Because what you're doing is highway robbery."

"This from someone who last night sent over two young men who robbed me of my dignity *and* my cheese fries."

He wanted to snicker, but didn't. "Seriously, doll-face, you're selling some seriously trivial . . . stuff." On the screen, she was presenting the next product, and this time he *had* to snicker. " 'Glammed-up' rubber gloves? I rest my case."

Household gloves, the thick rubber kind that his mother wore when polishing silver. But at the wrists of these pairs were bands of bright-striped fabrics that were then fringed with ruffly lace or pastel pompoms. No longer utilitarian, they were just plain ludicrous. Not to mention that they cost thirty-five bucks, plus shipping and handling.

But something happened as he watched Felicity go through her shtick. She shared a laugh at how far a woman might go to make housework fun. There was an offhand comparison to Cinderella's slippers. Then she giggled as she slid them on and then again as she made the tassels dance while pretending to dust the chair. Without even the smallest warning prick, her enthusiasm infected him.

So when her televised self asked, "Wouldn't your mother or other woman in your life get a kick out of these?" he couldn't help but picture his own mom and her delight in something so whimsical.

Thirty-five bucks wasn't bad for a pair of Cinderella gloves that she'd use *and* smile over every time she did.

That's when it hit him. He turned his head to stare

at Felicity. "You're a witch. I almost pulled out my wallet. *For rubber gloves*."

She smiled, full of smug cheer. "Dressed-up rubber gloves. That's what shopping is all about, you see—identity. More specifically, about transforming it. New lipstick, a special outfit, it's a way of becoming a newer, improved version of ourselves."

"Yeah, but that's just surface—"

"Grammy!" Anna P. suddenly yelled out. "It's the part about Grammy and Uncle Billy."

The—guilty?—expression flashing over Felicity's face refocused Magee's attention to the television. On the screen, she was hawking those flaky light cubes again. In that engaging, between-you-and-me manner of hers, she told the audience that her Aunt Vi had livened up a recent gathering she'd hosted by using them to ice down the drinks—of the members of the George Bernard Shaw Society.

Magee turned his head to look at Felicity, his gaze sweeping past the tall stacks of *People* and *National Enquirer* sitting in a corner, each topped by a tortoise-shell cat. "George Bernard Shaw?"

"A playwright," Felicity answered shortly. "In the first half of the twentieth century."

He was glad he accepted the insult silently, because then he didn't miss hearing that her Uncle Billy had used the lighted cubes in his highball glass to illuminate his way up the wine cellar steps when the cellar's light had burned out.

Magee knew for a fact that the only vintages that interested Billy were the fresh ones from Amstel,

Budweiser, and Busch. What he didn't know was why the hell Felicity had fictionalized her family. But the answer was just minutes away. Though her *Cool Afternoon* ended, the tape kept rolling as she popped out an earpiece and unclipped her microphone.

People crossed back and forth, removing merchandise, wheeling cameras through. Felicity struggled with the earpiece wire caught on the collar of her shirt. Then a man carrying a clipboard strode up to her, the lights gleaming against his blond hair and glinting off his slick-leathered loafers. Richie Rich all grown up.

Oh, now it was clear who Felicity's bogus background was meant to impress.

With the microphone off, Magee had to read the relationship through body language. Richie leaned in, Felicity stilled. The tangle untangled, they stayed close. Richie smiled, Felicity licked her lips. Richie touched her hair, she ducked her head.

Magee wanted to puke.

It was why he hurried out of the house, pausing only to pass on the piece of news he'd brought with him. "By the way, dollface, you'd better give your good friend Richie Rich a call and tell him to postpone your next TV show. You can say your Uncle Billy spent too much time cataloguing his wine collection last night so your car won't be ready this afternoon like he promised."

Felicity returned to the Bivy that night. What else did she have to do with herself? That she was on the lookout for Ben made Aunt Vi feel better, and *that* would

appease Felicity's conscience when she returned to
L.A. the following day.

And if she took Magee out of the picture—and
she'd X'd him out completely!—she had to admit she
got a kick out of the anonymity the place afforded her.
Without her GetTV image to worry over, she was free
to dabble in the hedonistic play of the climbing crowd.

So, knowing that this was her last chance, she
played darts and she played pool. When a man with a
long sideburns and a loopy grin asked her to dance,
she didn't consider refusing.

To the beat of Pink's "Get the Party Started," he
unbuttoned his shirt so that the tattooed snake on his
chest undulated with his movements. Laughing out
loud, she pulled the tails of her own man-tailored shirt
from her tight high school jeans. Then, knotting the
shirt beneath her breasts, she rotated her hips like a
belly dancer.

Her partner fell over, overcome by admiration—
or perhaps too much beer—and stayed flat on the
dance floor until one of his buddies dragged him off
by the shoulders. They exchanged disappointed finger
waves.

In need of fortification, she twirled herself toward
her table on the edge of the small dancing area. Her
glass of water sat where she'd left it, but her plate of
nachos and her glass of wine—both barely touched—
were gone.

The climbers were unabashed moochers.

Shaking her head, she scooped up her purse and
headed toward the bar. Though she'd yet to see

Magee, now she came face-to-face with the bartender, Peter. But even remembering how he'd creeped her out the night before with his near-death talk didn't stop her from smiling at him.

He smiled back. "You look like you're having fun."

"Oh, I am." She slid onto a stool and rested her elbows on the bar. "Leaving Half Palm puts me in a happy mood."

He slid a napkin and a glass of wine in front of her. "Your family will be sorry to see you go."

Her smile faded. "I've done what Aunt Vi asked!" She'd asked people about Ben. Not one had seen him recently, but no one seemed concerned about him, either.

Meaning they knew the Charms as well as she did.

"I'm off the hook," she told Peter, lifting her wine glass. And almost free of them for good, she thought, smiling at her reflection in the mirror over the bar.

Hmm. Her lipstick looked a bit smudged. She started to reach into her purse, then stopped.

Tonight she didn't have to be perfect. Her mood bubbled again.

"Hey, there." A handsome twenty-something stepped up to lean against the bar beside her. "I haven't seen you around here before. I'm Duke."

Felicity took a big swallow of wine and gave him an even bigger smile. "Of course you are. And I'm . . ." She hesitated, glancing over at her smudged-lipsticked, knotted-shirt, and too-tight jeans reflection. "I'm Lissie."

That's exactly who she was tonight. Fun-loving,

wild-living Lissie. Well, not too wild, just wild enough to let darling Duke buy her a drink. And fun-loving enough to let him regale her with boastful accounts of his climbing adventures.

She propped her chin on her fist, devoting her attention to the young man. "Fascinating, just fascinating," she said, her voice booming into a sudden quiet. Looking around, she realized the music had been turned off and that the room's attention was riveted on the TV screen mounted overhead.

Felicity glanced up at it, just as Magee's face appeared there, leaner, stubbled, and sunburned. Then she saw a close-up of Simon, followed by more close-ups, strangers to Felicity, but obviously other members of their climbing team.

The sound of a door banging open jerked everyone's gaze from the TV to the other side of the room. A man stood there, backlit by the overhead lights in what appeared to be a small office. "Turn the goddamn music back on," a hoarse voice—Magee's voice—barked out. Then the door slammed shut.

Bob Marley started up a Jamaican rhythm. Felicity looked back to the TV screen just as the program's title rolled across: *From Daring to Disaster*.

"That's him," Duke said. "The Lucky Bastard."

She flicked a glance back at the slammed door. "Exactly how did he come by that nickname?"

Duke pulled his stool closer to her, as the pounding music drowned out the sound coming from the television. "The way I hear it, if you climbed with the Bastard, you came back alive."

Felicity grimaced as her stomach dipped. "And exactly how dangerous is this sport you people like so much?"

Duke shrugged. "Define danger. We're a wuss culture. There's helmet laws and seat belt laws and laws about how hot to cook hamburgers. Regular soap isn't good enough, now it has to be antibacterial."

Felicity struggled to find something inherently wrong with disease prevention. She was still speechless when Peter rolled up and paused.

"Are you all right?" he asked.

No. She wanted to recapture her earlier mood. She wanted to think of herself shaking the sand of Half Palm off her feet as she sped away from it instead of thinking of that hoarse bark in Magee's voice.

"Just trying to understand this climbing thing," she said. Her gaze drifted up to the television screen, where a line of brightly bundled figures struggled through thick snow. "I don't think I get the appeal."

"It's different for different people," Peter said. "Getting close to nature. The physical challenge."

A head popped around from the other side of Duke. It was the dread-locked guy she'd run into the night before. "And don't forget the chicks, man. The chicks love guys who can kick danger's ass."

Peter grinned. "And then there's the chicks. The chicks love guys who can kick danger's ass."

"Magee said something about the angles and the independence," Felicity remembered.

"He would." Peter nodded. "That's a lot of what it is for him, I suppose."

"How so?" Not that she cared or anything.

"In many ways climbing is a game you play all alone inside your head. As for the angles—that's what Magee is brilliant at. He has a master's in applied mathematics and he looks at the rock like a problem he has to solve."

"Oh." The guy to whom she'd explained chicanery and George Bernard Shaw had an advanced degree in math. Then her mind skittered back to him emerging from that back office. "And, uh, he's not the busboy here, is he?"

Peter's brows rose. "No. We're co-owners of the Bivy. Magee's also a partner in a climbing store—"

"The Wild Side?"

He nodded. "And he has another partnership in a rock gym in Palm Springs."

"Oh." Oh, terrific. She slid off her stool, trying to think how often and how else she might have insulted Mr. Masters-in-Applied-Mathematics. "I think I'll just pop into his office and tell him goodbye."

After she extended a gracious apology. It was the least she could do, right? Then she could leave town in the morning, all loose ends neatly tied up and tied off forever.

The "Come in" he rasped out after she knocked on the door wasn't welcoming. Felicity entered anyway.

At a long wooden desk, he sat with his back to her, his lean body slumped in a black leather chair, his elbows resting on its arms, his chin resting on his fisted hands. His gaze was trained on a small television set sitting on one corner of the desk. The current program: *From Daring to Disaster.*

Somehow she wasn't surprised.

Shutting the door behind her muffled the heavy beat of Shaggy's rap remake of "Angel" and highlighted the thick quiet in the small office. "You're watching with the sound off," she said, because she had to say something. It wasn't clear he was aware she was in the room.

He didn't look around. "I know what happens."

"I don't." She didn't know what made her say that.

But it got his attention. He flicked a glance at her over his shoulder, then went back to staring at the TV screen. "Short version: Eight went up Alaska's Denali—aka Mt. McKinley. Seven made it down."

Not knowing how to respond, she kept her gaze on him and off the television. He watched the program in silence for another moment, then lifted his hands to rub his face. "God, I hate the fucking snow."

Her heart squeezed, and she rushed toward the television. "Then let's turn it off."

He barred her way by simply straightening his leg and resting the heel of one beat-up boot on the desk. "Let's not."

"You said you know what happens." She leaned over his outstretched knee toward the TV's off button.

Twisting the chair toward her, he snagged her around the ribs. When she struggled, he put his foot back on the floor, then pulled her onto his lap, keeping her there with his forearm around her waist.

"But you said *you* didn't know." His breath was hot against her ear as he turned the chair to once more face the TV. "And here's the perfect opportunity to get the whole story, up close and very personal."

"I don't—"

"I watched you on television this morning, didn't I? Turnabout's fair play."

His arm was immovable and his mood angry, but it was clear he couldn't bear to turn the program off. And she wondered if he also couldn't bear watching it alone, and that was why he was holding her against him.

"Here's Simon and I off on our summit bid. Look at those faces. Grins literally frozen on. Simon's blowing kisses to Anna P. and Ashley, in case you can't read lips."

Felicity squirmed, but he just tightened his arm. "Now it's several hours later and here's the team, trying to raise us on our radio phones. The weather's deteriorating and they want to warn us, but we don't respond. It's because I dropped mine and Simon can't reach his—not when he's carrying me because my ankles are broken."

She stilled. "You broke your ankles?"

He continued as if she hadn't spoken. "But Simon makes it back to camp the next morning, see? He'll gather a team to go up and bring me down from the bivy where he left me. There—there I am, about twelve hours later."

He looked like his own corpse, his complexion

gray beneath the sunburn. His lips—his wonderful, thrilling lips—cracked and swollen. Her heart slammed inside her chest and she put both hands over the arm he had around her because she needed to feel that he was warm. Alive. "Magee," she whispered, turning her head toward his.

He tried directing her face forward again. "Look, look. You don't want to miss this, dollface. It's Simon heading down the mountain, while I stay back because I'm barely conscious. See him? He's waving again. That damn Aussie, always trying to hog the limelight."

"Magee." Though his arm had loosened on her waist, she didn't move and she didn't look away from his face. The bad-boy's voice was hoarse and his dark, dangerous eyes were bleak. His gaze never wavered from the television screen.

"Watch, Lissie, because that's the last anyone will ever see of him alive," he said, his voice getting raspier by the second. "Damn Aussie. Goddamn Aussie who shouldn't have saved me. Goddamn fucking Aussie who shouldn't have died."

"Michael . . ." she whispered.

He put his free hand up to his eye.

Right then, someone knocked at the door. As it opened, Felicity moved by instinct. Twisting on Magee's lap to clamber over the chair arm, her knee—intentionally—clipped his groin.

He grunted, bending over.

She made it to her feet, then whirled to face the

newcomers moving into the room. Peter and the Wild Side's Gwen. "He, uh, has something in his eye," she said, motioning toward Magee.

"Like hell," he wheezed out. "She just kneed me in nuts."

Peter winced.

Felicity shrugged, trying to appear apologetic. But he'd been so desperate a moment ago, and though she kept trying to forget about it, she'd seen him desperate before. She knew what happened next, she'd seen that before, too. And knowing him, he wouldn't want to be caught with tears in his eyes.

Now he had an acceptable, macho-guy reason.

He looked up, and his eyes were glittering, all right, but they were glittering with annoyance. At her. "What do you need, Peter?"

It was Gwen who spoke up. "As I was closing up at the Wild Side tonight, a group of three strangers came in. Wearing business suits—ties and everything. They were very polite, and they said they were looking for Ben."

"Did they say why?" Felicity asked.

"They said he owes them money."

Seven

Sitting at his kitchen table, Magee stared at the dregs of his coffee. After three nights of little sleep, his eyes felt as heavy and gritty as the sludge at the bottom of the mug. Last night he'd dreamed again, of climbing.

And it had been a dream of a climb at first, everything coming together as it did on the very best days. Under a perfect sky, his body moved smoothly, a kinesthetic proof of mathematical theorems. Then he was resting on a belay ledge, and someone yelled up to him, "Catch!" A book appeared in his line of vision and he lunged for it, only to fall, a heinous fall, with the book in his hands.

He had plenty of time to page through it as he plunged toward hell. It was the only climbing journal that his tribe was desperate to keep their names out of—the annual publication of *Accidents in North American Mountaineering*.

"Magee!" The little-girl voice and the pitter-patter of Anna P.'s feet on the kitchen floor jerked him back to the present. He had a second to brace before she leaped into his lap and he instinctively grimaced, Felicity's knee jab of the night before just an ache away.

"Morning," Anna P. sang out, and bussed him on the cheek.

He inhaled the scent of baby shampoo as he kissed her in return. Ashley entered the kitchen, and the little girl wiggled away, already demanding Cheerios and toast and orange juice and pancakes and waffles.

Ashley caught Magee's eye and they smiled at each other. "She has her father's appetite," Ashley murmured.

But with her father gone, it was up to Magee to feed her, clothe her, to give her the life, to live the life, that Simon had been planning. He knew that. Watching daughter and mother move about the kitchen, Magee imagined it. Ashley, his wife. Anna P., his, too.

He loved them.

He did.

The time was right to present his plan. He'd meant to a few days before, but then he'd collided with Felicity. There was nothing to stop him now, though, only more pushing him forward, including whatever trouble Ashley's brother Ben had gotten into.

He abruptly stood, the loud scrape of his chair against the floor catching both Ashley's and Anna P.'s attention. Clearing his throat, he wondered how much, exactly, to say.

"I didn't tell you why I went to L.A. a few days ago," he started.

Ashley ducked her head, studying the cereal box in her hand. "No."

"I took Simon's job."

She froze, then looked up. "At Forrester Engineering? That desk job?"

"Yeah."

"Didn't they offer you a position a few years ago?"

"Yeah." The Forresters were wealthy climbing aficionados, and Simon had guided the two men up a few of North America's higher peaks. Magee had been along once as well, and the brothers had used their persuasive powers on him as well as Simon, once they found out they both came out of the same master's program at Cal Berkeley.

"But when they asked you before," Ashley pointed out, "you said no."

Magee shrugged. "Simon said no the first time they asked him, too. But then things were different—after you and after Anna P.—and he changed his mind. Things are different for me now."

Ashley slid her finger under the sealed flap of the cereal box and moved it slowly across without speaking.

Maybe she didn't understand what he was getting at, Magee thought. "I want you to . . ." He cleared his throat again. "I want you and Anna P. to move with me to L.A. We'll find a nice neighborhood with good schools, get a house."

"Mommy?" Anna P. was looking from her mom to him and back again. "Mommy, I like this house."

Ashley looked down at her daughter. "This is Magee's house. If he moves—"

"You go with me," he said.

Anna P. looked up at her mother again. "But—"

"Before every climb I promised I'd take care of you," Magee said, drowning out her protests. "I promised I'd take care of you both if something happened."

Each time he'd made the vow without thinking about it, because he'd been so sure nothing *would* happen. He chose his expeditions and his teams carefully, after all. And maybe he'd begun to believe his own press, too. He was the Lucky Bastard, wasn't he? He could face down anything, and win.

Until that last time.

"It's the right thing, Ash." The only thing that made sense of what had happened. "Simon wanted this, wanted someone for you to lean on."

She looked up then, and in her gentle eyes he saw she understood. Holding her gaze, he walked over to her and tipped up her chin with one finger. Her lashes floated down and he pressed his mouth to hers.

The kiss was as soft and gentle as Ash herself. It might not be a carnal kiss, the Felicity kind that put his soldier at stiff salute, but it tasted of virtue and reparation. It fulfilled the purpose that he'd figured out.

When he lifted his head, he exchanged another long look with Ashley, but he didn't mention marriage.

He didn't have to.

Felicity paced Aunt Vi's living room, stepping over cats and cousins, but never slowing her pace. She'd demanded a family meeting first thing this morning. The calls had been made by her personally, to every family member—with the exception of Ashley, whom Felicity had left off the list for various reasons—but in typical Charm style it was closing on noon and only half a dozen of them had bothered to show up.

Even those who had stirred themselves to get to the house were now draped about the furniture in various states of repose. They petted cats, sipped coffee; one turned the pages of an outdated *People*, while another idly flipped through the TV channels.

Well, she didn't have time to wait for any more of them, not if she was going to make it back to L.A. today as she'd promised herself. This time she wasn't going to let anything stop her from getting out of Half Palm and from getting away from the Charms.

She stomped to the front of the room and spoke over their lazy chatter. "Okay, everyone, here's the deal. We need to call the sheriff's department and ask them to look into Ben's disappearance."

Every Charm head jerked up. A cat yowled, as if a stroking hand had tightened on soft fur. A coffee cup thudded against the old carpet. No one bothered moving to clean up the mess. Instead, they all stared at her as if she'd gone mad.

Felicity held on to her temper and turned to her aunt. "Aunt Vi, you've been worried about Ben from the first. I admit, I didn't think it was anything serious before, but now with these men looking for him . . ."

Felicity still didn't think it was serious. Ben had bugged out of town until he could scrounge up the money he owed some friends. But it gave her a good excuse to pass the problem of her missing cousin on to someone else.

Her aunt responded with the patented Charm helpless-female flutter. "But the *sheriff,* Felicity!"

"Charms don't call the sheriff," her second cousin, Harry declared.

He was in his late teens now, tall and lanky in a pair of expensive slacks, collared knit shirt, and natty white golfing shoes. Aunt Vi had told her the clean-cut-looking kid was "working" around the local courses, Charmspeak for hustling.

"No," Felicity corrected him, "it's that Charms hope someone doesn't call the sheriff on *them*."

Shrugging, he sent her a guileless, engaging grin, probably the very same one he used as he walked away with some CEO's pocketful of petty cash. What would it be? she wondered. Twenty bucks a hole?

"Well, I consulted the Tarot . . ." her cousin Rainbow, aka Roberta, began.

The whole room groaned.

"What? What?" Rainbow/Roberta flung up her many-ringed hands. "Do you want my expert opinion or not? People pay a lot for a consultation with me, I'll have you all know."

"Yeah, yeah, yeah." Uncle Vin, Aunt Vi's and Uncle Billy's brother, spoke up. "And the rest of us are tired of hearing just how much that is. You have a good racket going, I'll give you that, Roberta, but the worst thing you can do is start believing your own baloney."

Rainbow/Roberta objected to that remark, hands and scarves waving in the air to make her point. Then Uncle Vin objected back, and Harry returned to playing with the television controls, while the two oldest relatives launched into a nostalgic reminiscence of previous Charm scams.

Sighing, Felicity picked up one of the cats, holding it against her cheek as it purred, but even the animal's motorboat rumble couldn't drown out that last conversation.

She'd heard it all a million times, because the scams were the stuff of family legend, and each had a colorful moniker. There was "Fruit Loop"—when they'd opened a fruit stand selling the produce they'd stolen from someone else's orchards. That skulduggery had been short-lived, however, since it had entailed doing the actual work of picking the produce.

"Big Chief" was another, when an entire offshoot of the Charm family tree built a teepee in their yard to convince the Bureau of Indian Affairs they were owed a stipend because they were one-quarter Native American instead of one hundred percent lazy. The chain letter from the "Chain Gang" scam had netted next to nothing as well, as far as she knew, but the oldsters still talked about it.

With the argument between Uncle Vin and Rainbow/Roberta showing no signs of ending, Felicity set down the cat and clapped her hands together. She *had* to get the family to agree. "Come on, come on, everybody. We need to wrap this up. Is there a reason, a *real* reason, that I shouldn't call the sheriff?"

The group quieted. They knew what she was asking. Were any of them currently involved in some sort of larceny that would mean real trouble if the sheriff started sniffing around. Heads moved as gazes traveled about the room. No one spoke up.

Scenting freedom, Felicity's heart beat faster. "Okay, then—"

"Wait!" Harry raised the hand holding the TV remote. "We don't know what Ben was up to."

Uncle Vin nodded slowly. "The boy's right. We don't know why these men think Ben owes them money."

Aunt Vi fluttered. "Maybe it's a misunderstanding."

Uncle Vin appeared to consider. "Or maybe it's a misdemeanor."

"Or maybe it's a felony," Rainbow said in ominous tones. "I—"

"Hey, it's Felicity!"

Felicity's shoulders slumped as the last remark distracted the group once again from the point in question. Misunderstandings, misdemeanors, even felonies were forgotten as they all focused on the television. Harry's toying with the remote control had managed to start the VCR playing the GetTV videotape that Anna P. had left inside the day before.

Felicity groaned, but that didn't stop the Charms' fascination with the show. Though she tried to regain their attention a few times, they shushed her as they sat through the cell phone jewelry, the lighted ice cubes, the glamorized rubber gloves, even George Bernard Shaw and the wine cellar.

"You're good," Harry finally said, when the show ended. "Really good."

"Really good," Rainbow echoed. "Looks like a

cushy deal, too, though I bet I still make more money and work less hours than you do."

"Remarkable," someone else added.

Around the room heads nodded, and Felicity now found herself grateful for the latest interruption. *Hah.* The tape was perfect! It was the way to show the family how far she'd come, how far apart she was from them.

She warmed under the murmurs of praise and didn't try redirecting the discussion, even as she sensed someone else come in the room. She wanted every single Charm to see, to know, to realize she'd remade herself into something separate from them.

Then she could walk away from them forever, without a backward glance.

"Excellent," Uncle Vin pronounced, nodding in agreement. He slapped his hands on his thighs and almost cackled. "More than excellent. Eliot? Glenn?"

The two old men looked at each other, then looked at her, their wrinkled faces breaking into proud smiles.

Felicity smiled back at the old darlings.

"A credit to the family," one said.

The first credit, Felicity thought, the first one to break the shameful tradition of petty lying, cheating, and stealing. The newcomer in the room moved, and from the corner of her eye she saw it was Magee.

Fine. She'd not called Ashley about the meeting because her cousin, bless her helpless heart, was part of the dithering half of the Charm family. But she didn't mind Magee hearing this, not at all.

"Yes, yes," the oldest family member repeated. "Felicity, you're a real credit to us."

That's right. A real credit that they'd listen to now about calling in the sheriff.

The co-oldster gave her a thumbs-up. "Undeniable. She's a true Charm through and through."

A true Charm through and through.

Her jaw dropped, the words rendering her speechless. Leaving her nothing to convince them with, which left no point in standing around. Without a backward glance, she escaped.

In his car, Magee followed Felicity as she stomped on foot down the street. After a couple of blocks, when she didn't turn back toward Vi's, he pressed on the gas to catch up with her.

Continuing to walk, she looked over at him. "What do you want?"

He leaned toward the open passenger window. "Whatever it takes." After his breakfast conversation with Ashley, he'd stopped by Vi's to see what he could do to hurry Felicity on her way out of his life. "Do you need a ride somewhere?"

She kept walking. "If you wanted to offer a ride, why were you following me instead?"

"I was keeping a safe distance."

"What? Why?"

"Considering what you did to me the last time we were together . . ."

"Oh. Well. That." She darted him a glance. "That was, you know, a favor."

"Favor, my ass."

"It was!" She glanced over again. "I didn't think you would want anyone to see you with te—"

"I had something in my eye!"

She held up her hands. "And didn't I say that?"

"*After* you gave me a good one to the gonads, dollface."

She smiled, all sweetness. "Shall I kiss it and make it better?"

He stood on the brakes and the car screeched to a stop. "Get in, dollface," he ground out. "Before I take you up on the offer."

With a long-suffering sigh, she marched to the car and jumped in. Then she slid him a look. "I need to make a long-distance phone call. To L.A."

Be still his heart.

Magee drove Felicity to the Bivy, unlocked the front door, then showed her into the back office. After making a quick half-pot of coffee in his personal machine, he poured a full mug, slid some paperwork under his arm, and then left her alone, standing by the phone.

But he didn't go far. So sue him, but he planned on eavesdropping. He had high hopes that this phone call would start the ball—no, Felicity—rolling out of his life. When she'd mentioned "long distance" and "L.A.," he'd concluded she was calling in to work. If that blond boss of hers was as slick as he looked, he'd want Felicity within reach.

Forcing himself to ignore an irritating itch between his shoulder blades, he pulled out a chair to settle himself at one of the small tables on the barroom floor. It was so quiet he could hear Felicity's small sigh and then her fingers tapping the keys on the phone's pad.

From beneath his lashes, he watched her ask to speak with Drew Hartnett. As she waited, she used her free hand to smooth her hair, to tuck in her shirt, to work at her hair again. He'd never seen her primp like that before.

For him, she's fussing for him.

He swallowed some coffee to burn away the annoying thought.

"Drew!" Her posture stiffened, her spine going finishing-school straight. Her voice changed, too, smoothing out to lower, richer, more studied tones. "Drew, it's so good to hear your voice."

Magee wondered if her pleasure sounded as fake to this Drew as it did to him.

"I'm fine, just fine. Still here in Palm Springs. Working, yes. Like I said a couple of days ago, I needed a change of scenery to find some fresh ideas."

Finding fresh ideas? Magee chuckled to himself. So that was her story. He wondered what her boss would think of the fresh ideas the two of them had come up with in the back of his Jeep in a rainstorm.

Felicity was fiddling again, smoothing her shirt into the waistband of her jeans, then reaching up to play with the buttons running down the center. Unbidden, a picture formed in his head. That rain, running down the fogged windows. Her bare breasts, her own hands running over their soft pink nipples.

With his cock hardening against his thigh, he squeezed shut his eyes, trying to close down the screen in his mind. It was Ashley he'd kissed this morning, Ashley who would be his wife. That was his plan, his purpose! Felicity of the feathery hair and fiery mouth was trouble to forget, an obstacle to go around.

And, with any luck, a woman on her way back to L.A.

He refocused on the half of the phone conversation he could hear. "A product conference meeting tomorrow? No, um, hmm. Can't we reschedule that for the uh, week after?"

Damn! That didn't sound like a woman heading back to the job.

"Well, yes, I *could* return today, if you think the meeting tomorrow is necessary. . . ."

She bit her lip and Magee stared at her mouth, willing her to agree and get out of his life. *Dollface, it's necessary!*

As if he'd said it out loud, her gaze found the open doorway and from there latched on to his.

He couldn't look away. It happened again, like it did every frickin' time. Lust, desire, gotta-have-it, gotta-have-*her*, whatever you wanted to call it, swamping over him. Connecting them.

He saw her bottom lip drop as her breath quickened. His cock went harder when he saw her fingers tighten on the top button of her shirt.

She wasn't for him, he reminded himself. He'd changed, and now there were things that mattered to him beyond sensation and thrill. He had a purpose now, a plan to give his life meaning.

But damned if he'd never been so hungry for female skin, for hot, wild, wet sex.

For her female skin.

For her.

Suddenly she started, blinked. *The phone,* he could hear her mind working. *I'm on the phone.* "Drew, yes, yes. Of course, the new scenery is helping out, just as I said it would. Uh-hmm. I have been getting new ideas." She blinked again. "Where? You want to know where I'm getting the ideas?"

Her desperate gaze found Magee again. Now he knew why she'd wanted to reschedule that product meeting. She didn't have any new ideas. But he shook his head, no help to her at all, the firing points of his brain fried by the current sizzling between them.

"From, uh . . . uh . . . from climbers. Climbing." The words stumbled out of her mouth. Rolling her eyes, she half-turned away from him.

He might have felt sorry for her, except she seemed to be getting her concentration back while there was still nothing in his mind but the need to get her naked.

"See, I, um . . ." Her hand snatched a pamphlet off the bulletin board hanging over his desk. "I heard about the National Outdoor Products Trade Show in Palm Springs this coming weekend. That's what, uh, piqued my interest."

Jesus, Magee thought, as she read aloud some particulars off the pamphlet, she was good. Adding words like "splashy" and "playful" to the dry descriptions of some of the products in that sweet, trust-me tone of hers, she made dusty camping equipment sound interesting.

"So that's what I've been doing, Drew," she concluded. "Thinking about GetTV night and day. But you're right, maybe I should come back. . . ." Her voice trailed off as she returned to listening.

Magee inhaled a long breath, feeling that tide of lust start seeping away. Okay. Good. Instead of getting her in the sack, he'd be getting to say his goodbyes.

He wrapped his hand around his still-steaming coffee. Lifting it to his mouth, his grip slipped. The burning brew dumped down the front of his shirt.

"*Hell!*" The fabric seared, blister-hot, against his skin. He leaped to his feet and grabbed the hem of his shirt.

Sorry, mate, but you're both being blithering idiots.

Simon's voice flashed in Magee's mind, but was gone by the time he'd yanked the shirt over his head. He glanced over at Felicity, and found her staring at his bare chest, her mouth hanging open.

Her head bobbed slowly up and down. "Yes, that's right,"she said into the phone. "Believe me, it's hot. It's very, very hot. And those angles—" She broke off. "What? *What?*"

Closing her eyes, she listened for a few more moments, then carefully set the receiver back in its cradle. Still standing in the other room, she glanced over at Magee, glanced away.

"Oh, for goodness' sake, put your shirt back on," she said.

He bristled. "I'll have you know—"

"I'm staying. He wants me to stay."

"What?"

Shaking her head, she walked out of the office. "I was certain he'd tell me to come back. You know, take the decision out of my hands. I was just babbling on about the trade show, trying to justify why I'd stayed this long, and . . ."

"He bought it."

She heard the flat-out disgust in his voice, he figured, because she frowned at him. "I didn't plan—"

"Dollface, *please*." Christ, he felt even more a fool because he'd been this close to thinking that fate knew something they didn't. And he should have known it wasn't mere sexual chemistry. He'd experienced that before, and it had never come along with this sticky connection that felt more than physical.

This had to do with *her*. She'd worked like a charm—hah, hah—on him, hadn't she?

"I'm telling you, I didn't plan—"

"Maybe you don't know just how talented you are," he said, his voice cold. "So let me be the first one to tell you—though really, how couldn't you know? Because it's what you do, isn't it? You're an expert at bullshit. You're an expert at making us believe you have exactly what we need."

Eight

Peter made it up the porch steps of the house that Ashley shared with Magee. Gripping his left crutch hard, he leaned the right one against his side and lifted that hand to knock on the door.

In the distance, he heard the theme song to *Sponge-Bob SquarePants* and quick footsteps. "Who's there?" Ashley's voice.

"It's Peter."

He imagined her surprise. It was Ashley's night off and Peter had the evening free, too. But Magee had a long shift at the Bivy, so Peter had decided to take advantage of that and spend some time with Ashley and her daughter. He hadn't called first.

The front door swung open. Ashley's gaze was trained to wheelchair level, and he saw her little start of confusion before her eyes lifted. "Peter?"

Tingles broke out all over his skin, maybe even on the hollow logs that his legs had become. It had been so long since Ashley had looked *up* at him.

"I'd forgotten how good erect is," he said, grinning at her.

"*What?*"

He laughed, at her startled expression and at how clumsily he'd expressed himself. "I'm sorry, that came out wrong. The crutches and braces are something I've been working on and this is the first time I've tried them outside of my own place."

"Oh." Her gaze swept down his body, bringing another wave of tingles in its wake. "What are you doing here?"

For the first time he realized what she was wearing. Instead of the usual jeans she wore at the Bivy, her long legs were in black pants. With something lacy and feminine on top and her purse under her arm, it was obvious she was preparing to go out.

"Do you have a . . . date tonight?" He hoped to God he looked as if he didn't care. The last thing he wanted was for her to feel sorry for him.

"No. I was going to spend a couple of hours at—" She shook her head. "No place important."

"I don't want to interrupt. . . ."

"No." She looked back as another pair of footsteps clattered toward the front door. "Anna P. will be happy to see you."

But what about you, Ash? He wanted to ask the question, but couldn't. Not yet. First he had to make sure she was seeing him as Peter-the-man, not Peter-in-the-wheelchair.

She stepped out of the way as Anna P. let out a shriek of welcome and scampered toward him. "Petey!"

He rolled his eyes at her mother. "Only for your girl, Ash. I did unspeakable things to my sisters' stuffed animals whenever they called me that."

"Petey!" A small pair of arms wrapped around his knees.

Hell. Locking his elbows, he pushed down on the crutches, struggling to keep his balance. It stabbed his heart, that he couldn't feel the hug, but he'd stab himself before he let it topple him. Sweat broke out on his forehead just as Anna P. stepped back, setting him swaying again.

"Where's your wheels?" She peeked around him, as if she thought he was hiding his chair—his wheels—somewhere.

"I'm moving around this way tonight." Her face fell and he had to grin again. For Anna P., the wheelchair was an incentive, not a detriment, to love. "But to make up for not taking you on any rides tonight, I brought pizza. Maybe you could get it for me?"

She whisked past him, beelining for the open door of his specially equipped van and the pizza box he'd left on the passenger's seat. Juggling the box *and* muscling his next-to-useless legs to the front door had been one of those impossibles that he'd learned to accept after the accident.

"You'd better come on in," Ashley said. "Since it looks like we're having pizza for dinner."

He stood where he was. What would she say of the halting swing-and-shuffle that was his current—even after lengthy practice—version of walking? An image of his father's sneer popped into his head, accompanied by his father's voice. *Men, Peter, don't hesitate*.

Yeah, but they also didn't get B's in biology or go green at the smell of formaldehyde on dead frog skin or flunk out of medical school, either.

He was still stalling when something caught Ashley's attention and she hurried past him toward his car. "Anna P., let me help you with that!"

With her back turned, Peter took his first clumping movement forward and swung over the threshold. As fast as he could manage, he made his way to the living room couch. He was settling onto the cushions just as mother and daughter shut the front door behind them.

Whew. Perfect timing, he thought.

"I'll get plates and napkins," Ashley said. "Do you want something to drink?"

"Water?" Tension had parched his throat, making a beer sound even better, but he wanted to keep his wits about him. Magee had upped his anxiety level with talk about buying him out of their partnership in the bar. Though he hadn't mentioned anything about it since, Peter had his own worries on the subject and he wanted to see what he could find out about how it related to Ashley and the future.

He could still smile, however, as Anna P. clambered up on the sofa beside him. "What kind of pizza is it?"

"The kind you always ask for. Hard-boiled egg and banana."

She laughed, looking so much like Simon that his gaze moved to the collection of framed photos on the wall behind her. There was her dad, Peter's good climbing buddy, standing on the summit of Mt. Whitney, of Annapurna, and of Everest, one arm slung around Peter and one around Magee. The three members of the 3-D Club—Danger, Debauchery, and Demons.

"Here you go." With waitress expertise, Ashley returned to the room balancing all three plates, napkins, and glasses. Noting the direction of his gaze, she looked over her shoulder at the photo-covered wall. "Is something the matter?"

Peter shook his head. "Just reminiscing."

She handed the plates around and took a seat in the chair opposite him. "Private reminisces?" she asked, half-smiling, "Or is this one of those stories I just *have* to hear?"

He laughed. "We put you through that a lot over the years, I guess."

"It's what I treasured most. The three of you safely back from your latest adventure, each of you trying to top the other with the most outrageous story."

"You were always our best girl."

She looked down at the untouched slice of pizza in her hand.

If Peter had a working leg he would have kicked his own ass with it. He didn't want to set himself up as a rival of Simon's—he didn't see himself that way. The truth was, years before Peter had done exactly what his father had always belittled him for. He'd hesitated, and right under his nose it was Simon who had walked—hell, run!—in and snatched Ashley away.

Once upon a time it might have bothered him that she'd loved Simon first. But over that long, bleak night in the crevasse he'd come to know that love was flexible, while his time here on earth was not. He'd take whatever of both he could get from Ashley.

"D'licious," Anna P. piped up, chewing her pizza with obvious relish. "Petey, you're the *best*."

"Thank you, tiger." He reached over and tapped her nose. "If only I'd known before that pizza is the way to a woman's heart. I might not be a single and a lonely man today."

"Are you, Peter?" Ashley glanced over at him, then stared down at her plate as if it fascinated her. "Are you lonely?"

His heart leaped. At the bar the other night, she'd expressed curiosity about his sex life. Now she was asking about his emotional life, surely another hopeful sign.

But tread carefully, pal, he told himself.

He set his slice of pizza on his plate and wiped his mouth and fingers with his napkin. "For the year or so after my accident I was too consumed with rehabilitation and readjusting to feel loneliness. But now . . . well, I'm not sure 'lonely' is the right word."

He ran one palm down the side of his thigh. That he couldn't sense his own touch still jolted him at times, but God, it was damn good to realize that he'd made it past the bouts of bitterness and depression that he'd experienced after the injury. Now he had the energy and enthusiasm to pursue these other feelings that had nothing to do with his disability.

"I come from a big family—you've met two of my five sisters—and because of my dad's medical practice he wasn't home much. My mom coped by letting chaos reign, so I'm accustomed to constant noise and activity and company. When I'm by myself I sometimes feel . . . not exactly lonely, but as if something's missing."

Ashley nodded slowly. "Or someone."

Peter took another stab to the heart. "Ah. You're lonely, Ash?"

Her gaze drifted over to her daughter and she smiled sadly. "I don't think it's fair to complain when I have my Anna P."

"There's a lot that isn't fair, Ashley."

"I try to drown that thought out whenever I can," she said, standing abruptly.

She was towering over him again, like she did when he was in the wheelchair, undermining his confidence. Her hand reached for his plate and his shot out, his fingers closing over her wrist. Her eyes jumped to his and he saw something desperate in them.

"What's wrong, Ash?" he asked. "Something's bothering you."

She shook her head.

"What is it?" he insisted.

Her eyes closed wearily. "You remember how Simon was. Decisive, full of plans, sure of himself."

"He took very good care of you," Peter agreed.

"I counted on that. I miss it. I need it."

Peter didn't know what to say. She was right, Simon had been an unignorable force, and his take-charge personality had overrun the quiet, gentle Ashley. But still, Simon had been gone for months at a stretch on climbing expeditions and during those times she'd managed her own life just fine. Had she forgotten that?

But then, every mountaineer knew that each challenge began as a mental one. You were only as strong as you thought you were.

He released her arm and let his hand drop to one of his dead legs. "I'm sorry, Ash," he said, for want of anything better.

After they finished the pizza, she returned their plates to the kitchen, leaving him to tally up his points in resignation. He might have come in standing like a man, he thought, closing his eyes, but he wasn't certain she was seeing him that way.

A pained cry from the kitchen had his eyes flaring open. He looked at Anna P. "Quick, go check on your mom, tiger," he ordered, reaching for the crutches propped alongside the couch.

It was probably a gimp world record, the speed of his trek down the hallway. He didn't remember it or even think about the ungraceful sight he must have made, bursting into the kitchen with his thump-shuffle-slide.

Ashley stood over the sink, her hand wrapped in a dish towel, Anna P. looking up in concern. "Mommy cut her hand, Petey."

"It's nothing, I just grabbed the wrong end of a knife by mistake." Despite the "nothing," she hunched her shoulder to wipe a tear off her cheek.

"Let me take a look at it," Peter said, his stomach rolling over in his belly. "Anna P., can you bring me some Band-Aids?"

"We got SpongeBob ones, I'll get 'em." She ran off.

Peter dragged himself across the linoleum as Ashley hunched her shoulder again, drying another tear. "Ash, how bad is it?"

When she didn't answer, his stomach rolled again. "*How bad?*"

She shook her head. "It's not."

But she was crying. Reaching her, he leaned his body against the sink and let one crutch fall. He twined his free arm with her hurt one, pulling it against his side and pinning it there with his elbow. Then, holding his breath, he slowly unwrapped the towel from her hand. *Don't be sick, pal. Don't be sick.*

As the towel dropped into the sink, his breath released in a long *whoosh*. "It isn't bad. Not bad at all." It was only a small cut, barely oozing blood.

"I told you."

"Yeah, you did." He was so relieved for both their sakes that he dropped his cheek to the top of her head and rubbed it against her silky blond hair. Her forearm was pressed against his side and his big hand still cupped her smaller one. It felt so good, so comforting and soothing, to hold her like this.

But the man inside his crippled body was clamoring to get out. Peter lifted his head. "Ashley?"

She looked up. He took a moment to appreciate that again, and then he let his mouth descend to hers.

His breath backed up in his chest at the sweet, warm taste of her. He thought *gentlegentlegentle,* because Simon wouldn't have kissed her gently and he didn't want his kiss to be compared to any other man's. Mov-

ing his mouth across her cheek, he heard the faintest
of moans and it drew him back to her lips, drew him
in. *Gentlegentlegentle.* He felt her kiss him back.

His heart expanded, filling his chest, his head, his
hollow legs.

Then, behind the lids of his closed eyes, he saw it
again. He felt it again. That warm, blissful light, that
sense of acceptance and peace, but now accompanied
by a nice kick of earthly sexual arousal. With her
mouth pressing against his, he felt alive. He felt
whole. He felt love.

"Hey, Petey, why you kissin' Mommy?"

He smiled against Ashley's lips then turned his
head. "I like kissin' your Mommy, is why. She kisses
real nice, don't you think?"

Anna P. shrugged. "I guess. Magee must think so,
too. This morning he kissed her, too—and it was even
before breakfast!"

Near closing time, Felicity sat on a stool at the Bivy
for the third night in a row, an icy glass of club soda
on the bar in front of her. It was getting harder and
harder to deny the impulse to drop her face into the
fizzy water and drown.

She spent her days cruising the climbing shop and
fast-food restaurants, hoping to spot Ben. She spent
her nights hanging around the Bivy, waiting for
him—or those men to whom he owed money—to
walk through the door. So far the only rewards for her
diligence were a deepening worry and an addiction to
mini-pretzels.

With his back to her, Magee stood at the cash register several feet away, the canned overhead lights sparking fire in his glossy black hair. She supposed she could ask him to refill her now-empty basket, but she'd avoided direct contact with him since her phone call to Drew and planned to keep it that way.

You make us believe you have exactly what we need.

He'd said that, like it was a bad thing!

And he'd said it out of frustration with their inexplicable, ongoing sexual chemistry. How could she be blamed for the old adage about opposites attracting? But instead of slapping him over it like she wanted to, she'd decided against defending herself. That would have given him the impression she cared a hoot about what he thought.

Which she didn't. He didn't know her or anything about her.

So she'd vowed never to give the scruffy, thrill-banging, bar-owning, good-for-nothing-she-wanted cretin the satisfaction of another cheap shot at her.

Feeling righteous, she glared at his back and the classy sentiment on today's T-shirt choice: *I'm Not Feeling Myself Today . . . May I Feel You?* Then she licked her forefinger to scoop up some of the salt crystals in the bottom of the basket and brought her finger to her mouth to suck them off.

Just then he glanced up, catching sight of her reflection in the mirror. His back stiffened and his eyes narrowed. She thought she saw steam billowing from his ears.

Magee in a slow boil . . . but why?

As he continued giving her the evil eye, and she continued sucking on her finger, it hit her. *He thinks what I'm doing is sexy! He thinks I'm doing it on purpose.*

Hah! This was much more gratifying than slapping the scruffy, thrillbanging, bar-owning, good-for-nothing-she-wanted cretin. She could torture him instead!

Moving lazily, she withdrew her wet finger from her mouth and dipped it back inside the basket. Without breaking his gaze, she slid it inside her mouth again, all the way inside, then slowly slid it back out. Letting her mouth drop open, she rubbed the wet pad back and forth across the inner dampness of her lower lip.

One of his hands jerked, knocking over a bottle, causing Peter, at the other end of the bar, to glance around.

Magee instantly ducked his head. "Peter, get Felicity some more pretzels," he barked out.

At the rough order, Peter's expression hardened. "What?" The angry note in his voice prickled the hairs on the back of Felicity's neck. Ashley, walking toward the bar with a tray filled with dirty glasses, froze as Peter spoke again. "What did you say to me?"

Magee either didn't hear or didn't choose to heed the warning in his friend's tone. "Felicity. Get her pretzels," he repeated.

Peter slung the rag in his hand against the counter with a *thwap* and pivoted his chair to address Magee's back. "What the hell's wrong with you doing it?" he spit out. "Is there something wrong with *your* legs?"

A tense silence descended. The only two other patrons still left in the bar jumped to their feet and hurried out.

When the door shut behind them, Magee turned to face Peter. "All right, what's your beef?" he asked, crossing his arms over his chest. "For the last few days you've been a royal pain in the ass."

"I'll tell you what's wrong. You—"

"Don't." Glass rattled as Ashley, her face pale, dumped her tray on top of the bar.

Peter's jaw clenched and he glanced over at her. "This is between Magee and me, Ash."

"No, it's not." Her hands clutched each other at her waist. "This has nothing to do with you, Peter."

"Ashley—"

"We've been friends for seven years." She was backing toward the exit, her gaze flicking from one man to the other. "All of us. Please, Peter, please, don't spoil . . . things."

He was wheeling his chair to follow her, but she held out her hand to stop him. Felicity saw it was trembling.

"I can't bear it," Ashley said, looking as alone and painful as heartbreak. "I can't bear for something else to go wrong." She whipped around and fled through the door.

Felicity slid off her stool. "I'll go after her."

"No. I will." Peter's biceps bunched as he sped the wheelchair toward the door.

Uncertain, Felicity looked over at Magee. He was slumped against the back counter, his expression unreadable. As the front door slammed shut behind Peter, she found herself walking around the bar.

Magee didn't appear to notice, even when she stopped in front of him. "Are . . . are you all right?" she asked.

His gaze flicked over her face. "Fan-fucking-tastic." He blindly reached to the side, grabbing a bottle from the dozens of call liquors shelved behind him. With his other hand he scooped up a shot glass, poured, swallowed the liquid down. He poured another and swallowed that, too, grimacing in obvious disgust.

"What are you drinking?"

"Well, it ain't no salsa shooter, that's for sure, doll-face." He lifted the bottle and squinted at the label. "Peppermint schnapps. But it'll do." He tossed back another shot, grimaced again.

She put her hand on his forearm, halting him mid-pour. "What's the matter?"

His brows rose. "What's the matter with what—with Ashley or with the whole stinkin' world?"

"With you."

"What could be the matter with me?" The hand with the half-filled shot glass gestured impatiently, and an arc of schnapps flew through the air. He didn't seem to notice. "I'm here, aren't I? I'm the one who made it back, right?"

She didn't know if it was the booze or the late hour and the almost-argument that was responsible for his blackening mood. Wrapping her hand around the bottle, she tried freeing it from his grasp. "Give me this."

He wrenched it away and poured himself another drink. "You won't like it. It tastes like crap."

"I don't want to drink it, and if you don't like the taste, then you shouldn't have any more, either." She reached for it again.

Shaking his head, he cradled the bottle to his chest. "I've decided that I need to get drunk, ugly-dog-drunk."

She sighed. "What if I told you you're already an ugly dog?"

He narrowed his eyes at her. "I wouldn't believe it. You've got the jones for me, dollface, I can tell. Hell of a thing, because I've got the jones for you, too."

"The 'jones'? Personally, I call it the liepshitz, but hey, that's just me."

He toasted her with the liqueur. "Liepshitz, jones. But I have a purpose now, so I'm ignoring the what-ever-you-want-to-call-it. Ignoring the whatever-you-want-to-call-it, that is, not the purpose." Bringing the bottle to his mouth, he bit down on the cork-lined pourer, pulled it out with his teeth, then let it drop to the floor. With the bottle halfway back to his lips, he paused, looking down at her and frowning. "Wait . . . what is the purpose again?"

She shrugged, humoring the idiot. "You tell me."

He blinked at her, his puzzled expression clearing. "Of life, that's it. The purpose of life. The reason why I lived and Simon didn't."

That errant memory: warmth, light, knowledge, blossomed in her mind, but Felicity quickly shut it away. "Don't ask me, Michael."

"We're two of a kind, then. I'm no navel-gazer, either." He looked away. "Lissie, go home."

"Lissie keeps trying to, but—"

"*Felicity* tries to leave," he said, wagging a finger at her. "It's my Lissie who likes to stay and play."

Oh, he had a definite buzz on now. "Well, neither one of us can leave you here. Come on, let me drive you home."

He gave her a smile. "I'll take a cab."

"Hah, hah." Felicity reached for the bottle of peppermint schnapps again, but he was too fast for her.

"Nuh-uh-uh."

She rolled her eyes. "Fine, then. Since you seem to have all the company you need, if you promise not to drive yourself anywhere I'll go find Ashley and make sure she's okay."

"Oh, come on, dollface." Settling his elbows on the counter behind him, he lifted one of his dark eyebrows, a sardonic gesture that sent a sexy shiver down Felicity's back. Even half-drunk, he remained one hundred percent dangerous. "Why set a new precedent?"

She blinked. "I don't know what you mean."

"Simon died eighteen months ago. You weren't worried if Ashley was 'okay' then." His gaze didn't leave hers as he took a drink from the bottle.

"Of course I—"

"Didn't see you at the memorial service, dollface. And I was there, in all my ankles-screwed-together glory."

"It's just that—"

"You would have had to take time off work to do

something for the family that raised you? A day without a rubber glove sale is a day without sunshine, is that it?"

Irritated at his tone, she took a step back. He was hammering at her because he was in a foul mood. Because he missed his friend Simon and because there was tension between him and Ashley and Peter. It wasn't fair, and she didn't deserve it, but she didn't need to defend herself, either.

Remember? That would only give Magee the impression she gave a hoot about what he thought. Which she didn't.

He didn't know her. He didn't know anything about her.

"So I've been thinking, how *are* you going to get rid of your Charm relatives?"

Her gaze jerked up to his. "What?"

"It's obvious your pretty-boy producer has swallowed your fairy tale about the Charm wine cellar and the Charm sponsorship of the George Bernard Shaw Society." His eyes were hard and most of the drunkenness had disappeared, leaving only the danger behind. "Just as it's obvious you're angling to become Mrs. Pretty Boy."

Her face heated. *Don't explain. Don't defend. Magee doesn't know you or anything about you.*

"He's going to want to meet the clan, unless you take them out of the picture first, that is. I'd suggest something dramatic," he went on. "It'll be good for ratings, don't you think? Kill 'em off in a fire. Or how about an earthquake? One big rumble and you're relative-free."

Felicity stared at him. *How could you say such a thing?* she wanted to shout.

It was none of Magee's business what went on between her and Drew. And it was none of his business that she hadn't come clean about the family to her producer, either. The fictional Charms had been a part of her life for so long, since boarding school, that they *were*—nearly, anyway—real to her. She'd never given a thought to telling Drew the truth.

No man knew the truth about her.

Her heart jittered.

Except one.

Her heart jittered again.

She looked at him, at his faded jeans and his rude T-shirt, at his stubbled chin, too-long hair, and dark, inscrutable eyes. He lifted the bottle of schnapps with two fingers and chugged down another swallow, then wiped his mouth with the back of his hand.

How could this have happened? Him? *Him?* She felt like crying.

Because facts were facts. The only man who truly knew Felicity Charm was the scruffy, thrillbanging, bar-owning, good-for-nothing-she-wanted Michael Magee.

A sob rose in her throat, and to escape it—and Magee—she ran for the door.

Magee slammed the bottle onto the countertop as Felicity rushed out of the bar. He was an ugly dog, all right, picking on Felicity instead of picking at his own damn wounds.

A headache already pounding at his temples, he grabbed a mug and poured the last of the evening's coffee inside it. Then he drained the mug, filled it with water, and drained that down, too.

Making his way toward the front door to lock it, he decided to spend the night on the couch in the office. He'd wake up with a crick in his neck, but just in case he bypassed the hangover he so richly deserved, at least it would be one punishment.

With his fingers on the door handle, he paused. Then he swung it open, just to check that Felicity's car had started.

To his surprise, instead of tearing down the road away from the Bivy, she was tearing across the parking lot toward him.

He braced for another knee in the nuts. Instead, she leaped into his arms, her legs wrapping around his waist.

Nine

The casino doors swung shut behind her, allowing Ashley her first full breath since running out of the Bivy. She closed her eyes for a moment, appreciating the sense of well-being already wrapping around her like a warm blanket. Though she'd promised herself a month ago not to return, after stepping into that brewing clash between Magee and Peter she deserved a little fun.

Making her way to the nearby cashier's cage, she dug her tip money out of her jeans pocket. It had been a quiet night, so there wasn't much. That was fine. Her tips would be her limit. Once she played through them, she'd leave.

The young woman behind the bars looked up and smiled as Ashley pushed her cash across the counter. "Hey! We've missed you. How's your little girl?"

"She's great. Keeping me busy." Ashley smiled back. "Quarter tokens, please, Meg. How's your mom's carpal tunnel?"

Meg slid a yellow plastic cup with the Easy Money

Casino insignia to Ashley and grimaced. "She has to wear those wrist guards now. But she'll tell you all about it herself. She has the shift after this one."

"The next shift?" Ashley wrapped her hands around the plastic cup, assessing the heft of the tokens inside. "I don't think these will last . . . oh, what the hey. Give me another forty dollars' worth."

As she reached inside her purse for her wallet, the other woman dragged her stool closer to the counter-top. "And where's your cute little brother Ben been hiding himself lately?"

Ashley's mouth dried, and she grabbed an additional twenty from her wallet. "He's somewhere around." The second cup of shiny tokens made it easier to swallow.

With the tokens resting comfortably in the crook of her arm, she grabbed up her purse and rounded the corner toward her favorite slot machine. A little sigh of contentment escaped her when she saw that it was free. Lengthening her stride, she moved quickly to claim it.

"It's me," she whispered, patting the Silver Lady's gleaming chrome side. "I'm back."

She settled into a high-backed cushioned chair, as the Lady's jewel-toned lights winked back at her. Then Ashley dug into one of the yellow cups. A token slid coolly through her fingers and into the machine. *Clickety-click-clack*. She lifted her hand to the Lady's arm—she figured it burned a few more calories to pull the arm instead of pushing the roll button—and drew it down.

The Lady's lights twinkled, her gears purred. A

melodic ping sounded as each tumbler halted. Cherry, cherry, orange, grapes. Ashley fished for another token.

> *clickety-click-clack,* twinkle, purr, ping ping ping ping
> *clickety-click-clack,* twinkle, purr, ping ping ping ping
> *clickety-click-clack,* twinkle, purr, ping ping ping ping

Within minutes, the stranglehold that tension had on her neck eased. "Thank you," she said, as the machine sipped another token from her fingers. She drew the Lady's arm down gently, even as she reached her other hand for her favorite iced tea—with extra lemon—that the barmaid brought by without being asked.

"Thanks, Joanne." Ashley passed over a tip just as the Lady lit up, beaming in all her glory like a woman for a lover.

> *ding ding ding ding ding ding ding ding ding ding ding ding*

Ten dollars in token credit ticked onto the digital counter.

Yes! Ashley relaxed back into her seat. Every win meant a few more minutes in this peaceful paradise where nothing—no worries, no grief, no confrontations—intruded. She reached for another token.

Once down to the ice in her iced tea, Ashley admitted to herself she couldn't put off a pit stop any longer. "I'll be right back," she whispered to the Lady, then looked over a couple of machines, relieved to see someone she knew.

"Ted!" When the older man glanced over, she smiled. "Watch my machine for a minute?"

He nodded in understanding, then turned back to his own play.

Ashley beelined for the restroom and hurried through the necessary activities. As she stepped back onto the casino floor, her gaze went immediately to her machine. A figure was sitting in front of it, backlit by the Lady's bright lights.

"Wait a minute!" she muttered to herself. "That's *my* machine." She stalked toward the usurper, anger threatening to spoil her good mood.

Don't let it, she admonished herself, taking a deep breath. *Don't let anything disturb your peace.*

It was then that she realized who the intruder was.

Peter.

He pivoted his wheelchair toward her as she approached. There was a cup of tokens in his lap.

She swallowed. "I didn't know you, um, came here."

"First time."

Angling his chair, he gave her room to get back to her stool. She returned her token cups into the holders, then gestured toward the Lady. "I'm, uh, playing here."

"I know. You were heading for the restroom when I

wheeled up. Your friend over there let me know this machine was taken."

She nodded, dropping into her chair. "We do that for each other."

"We?"

Instead of looking at Peter, she looked at the Lady. "People around here who know each other." Her fingers itched to grab a token, to start her play again and let the lights, the sounds, the Lady herself, soothe the nerves that were starting to fray. But with him watching, she felt her usual helplessness.

What did he want? What if he wanted to talk about that kiss? She couldn't do it, she just couldn't, because that would lead to a confrontation between herself and Peter and probably another between Peter and Magee and —

To quiet the turmoil inside her, Ashley reached for a token and quickly fed it to the Lady.

clickety-click-clack, twinkle, purr, ping ping ping
   ping

From the corner of her eye, to her relief, she saw Peter position himself in front of the machine on her left. Without another word, he inserted his first token.

Relieved, Ashley blew out a silent sigh and dipped back into her own plastic cup.

clickety-click-clack, twinkle, purr, ping ping ping
   ping

clickety-click-clack, twinkle, purr, ping ping ping
   ping

Soon, the hypnotic sound began smoothing out all
the edges that Peter had roughed up. As the silence
between them continued, she was able to pretend it
was a stranger beside her and she slouched down in
her chair and lost herself in the gambling.

"Relaxed?"

At the sudden sound of Peter's voice, Ashley bolted
upright in her chair. Tokens rattled against plastic.
"Huh? What?"

"You seemed upset when you left the Bivy. Feeling
better now?"

"Yes." She poured the last tokens from her first cup
into one hand and rubbed them between her palms.
"You know I don't like arguments."

She could feel his eyes on her, but she pretended
she didn't and slipped another coin into the slot. But
the twinkle, the purr, the ping ping ping ping, none
could take her away like she wanted when Peter was
looking at her. Still, she deposited another token and
reached for the Lady's arm.

"I know a lot about you, Ash."

The low, sexy note in his voice caused her hand to
miss. It fell into her lap. She stared at it, remembering
that when he'd kissed her it was the same hand that
had curled behind his head to hold him close to her.
She'd been helpless against the urge to keep him near.

Helpless.

The word shivered through her mind again and she

didn't want to think about it, to think about the two of them together—certainly not *kissing*!

"We've known each other a long time." Her hand rose toward the Lady again, but she didn't have the strength to pull on the arm. Instead, Ashley pressed the roll button. The lights flashed, the cherries and oranges and grapes whizzed around. She hoped they would whisk her back to that insulated, peaceful place. "Seven years."

It was her own words that kept her out now, though. *Seven years,* and suddenly she was recalling their first date. Peter had been the first climber she'd ever gone out with. The only climber before Simon, the only climber other than Simon. And though it was Simon she'd married five years ago, she'd always considered Peter as hers. Not in a romantic way, but in the way of . . . of . . .

She looked over at him. "You're one of my best friends."

He smiled. It was a roguish, boyish smile. In her mind's eye she saw once again that roguish, boyish young man who'd had her briefly, then let her get away.

"Why didn't you fight harder for me?" she asked, then clapped her hand to her mouth, astonished that she'd voiced the thought.

"Ah, Ash." Peter's smile died. "I—"

"No, no." She shook her head. "I don't know why I said that, what I was thinking." Reaching out, she stroked the cool, solid case of the Lady, trying to steady her nervous insides.

In desperation, she started feeding the Lady token

after token after token. She didn't want to think of the past, the future, the present, anything.

"Ash, Ash. Stop, Ash." Peter grabbed her hand and held it tightly. "Listen to me."

Ashley couldn't meet his eyes, so she stared down at their linked hands instead. He had climber's hands, the fingers long and limber, the knuckles scarred. Simon's had been similar, but bigger, so much bigger, that when he'd touched her she'd felt so safe.

Peter's touch frightened her.

She tried to pull away, but he hung on. "Ashley, I was a screwup when we first met. My father had accused me of it since the day I was born, so I'd spent over twenty years proving him right."

She shook her head. "You were never a screwup."

His voice softened. "You've always been so damn loyal. It's one of your very best qualities, you know. But if I wasn't a screwup, I *was* careless. With the people around me, with what I wanted for my life, with my own physical safety. Magee and Simon knew that. It's why they stopped climbing with me. It's why I wasn't with either of them when I had my accident."

Now she was hanging on to him, because thinking of him in that crevasse, broken and alone, made her feel shivery and scared again. *Helpless*.

"So I don't know if you got away because of my stupidity or if I never had a chance against Simon, Ash, but I know this. I know you loved him."

She nodded. Grief over his death had knocked her to her knees. That's when the casino had become her haven.

"But Ash . . . maybe our time is now."

Her head jerked up. No, no. "*No*."

"Whatever's going on between you and Magee—"

"He makes me feel safe." Like Simon. Magee didn't need her. Magee didn't need anything from her. So she couldn't mess it up. She couldn't fail him in any way.

"I don't care. I won't let you go so easily this time. I've changed, Ash."

"Peter, you've got to understand. You *are* changed, and—" The expression that overtook his face halted her. He looked stunned. Hurt.

"Oh." *Oh, Peter*. He thought she meant he was changed because of his paralysis.

His hand released hers. "I understand."

"You don't—"

"I do!" He rubbed his palms over his thighs, his voice tight. "What was I thinking? Why would you want to be with half a man?"

Oh, my God. Her throat burning and her heart aching, she reached out to caress the Lady like a touchstone. What she wouldn't give to be so solid and so powerful. If she was, then it wouldn't matter that Peter was half a man at all. She rattled the tokens in her cup, hoping that he would leave soon and that they and the Lady would be enough to deaden this new pain.

Because she knew who the real screwup was. It was her. She was a weak woman, so weak that she'd been prepared to deny the truth that Peter had seen.

But he was right. She could never be with Peter.

She could never be with half a man.

* * *

Magee's arms automatically closed around Felicity's back as she gripped his waist between her thighs. His heart slammed against his chest as he scanned the parking lot, looking for a threat. "What is it? What the hell is it?"

For an answer, she took his face between her hands. Something crackled beside his ear as she leaned in to buss him a big one on the mouth. "Ben's okay!"

He shook his head to clear it. "What?"

It was a piece of paper that had crackled, and now she waved it in front his eyes. "A note! He left me a note on the windshield of the car."

"What's it say?"

She squirmed and Magee loosened his hold so she could slide to the ground. "He says he's fine. 'Tell Mom not to worry. Tell her I'll be home in a few days after I take care of some business.'"

Magee narrowed his eyes. "What kind of business?"

Felicity waved the question away. "Doesn't say. Doesn't matter. I'm free! Free!" With a grin, she leaped back at him.

Her impetus sent him stumbling back, but he looped his arms around her again and blinked down at her exuberant smile. "Free, exactly, of what?"

"Conscience-free. Worry-free. Stress-free." Her smile widened. "Take your pick. Tomorrow night, after my obligatory afternoon at the trade show, I'm outta here."

The "for good" she didn't say lingered in the air. It floated around them as she cupped Magee's face once more and moved in for another boisterous smooch. But instead of letting her have her brief, happy smack, he speared one hand in the hair at the back of her head and glued her mouth to his.

She's outta here for good.

The thought making him reckless, he commandeered the kiss. Not letting up, he moved his lips over hers until her mouth softened and he could thrust his tongue into the sweet heat inside. His tongue tangled with hers and then the kiss became reckless, too, each of them wildly angling their heads to find the most pleasurable fit. Sparklers burst in his vision and he broke away to drag in oxygen.

"God, God." He rested his forehead against hers, not sure if he would live.

She replied by raggedly breathing against his mouth. The uneven, humid warmth made him desperate to kiss her all over again. Heat flashed over his skin.

"Let's have sex," he said hoarsely.

Her fingers tightened on his shoulders. "N—"

"Shut up," he interrupted roughly. "Just shut up. We have to have sex." Quick sex, like an inoculation against this fever of lust that spiked anytime she was near.

"What about . . ." Her voice breathless, she swallowed, started again. "What about those rules you mentioned that night in the desert?"

"This is a new day, baby. A new game. Aren't you tired of denying yourself?"

"Yes," she whispered, closing her eyes. "But I don't do—"

"—things like this," he finished for her. Her scent was in his head, her taste on his tongue. She was already in his blood; it seemed only fair that he'd get to be in her body. "I know. But it's not all that difficult to have a one-night stand, I promise. Just follow my lead."

A laugh choked out. "*Magee*. Come on, I have priorities."

"Then let me help you straighten them out." It was the only way, damn it, to get her out of his system. "You're leaving tomorrow. We're alone. Time to do it."

"Well, that's romantic," she complained.

He let her sag in his arms, her body sliding down his until the warm notch between her legs nudged against the head of his hard-on. "Does that feel like *romance* to you, dollface?"

Her eyes closing, she moaned.

His gut muscles tightened and his cock clenched, so damn ready that its pulse was pounding more insistently than his heart. He lifted her a couple of inches and then let her slide back down, his breath hissing in at the wild flash of pleasure as she rubbed over him.

She moaned again, eyes still shut. "What are we doing?" she whispered.

"We don't need to pretend with each other, do we, Lissie?"

Her lashes lifted.

"This is about scratching an itch," he said.

She made a face at him. "You're making me feel like a pest."

"Aren't you?"

Holding his gaze, she rolled her hips, stroking him

with her heat. "Does that feel like *pestiness* to you, Magee?" She rolled her hips again.

He flinched, his fingers digging into her hips. "Be careful, Lissie."

At the name, her eyes glowed and she moved herself over him once again. "Lissie's never careful."

"Huh." Punched by another fierce jab of need, he could only grunt as he stumbled backward to find the door with his groping hand. "Let's do it then."

He staggered inside the Bivy. There was music playing over the speakers, Cake's "Short Skirt/Long Jacket," the stuttering drumbeat mimicking his unsteady heart, the bass line driving just like his overwhelming urge to mate. The first table was as far as he could manage to carry her.

With his forearm, he swept the small surface clean of the bar and appetizer menus, then laid Felicity on her back. He stepped away, ready to tug off her shoes, but she crossed her ankles behind him and pulled him forward again.

"Take off your shirt," she said.

He lifted an eyebrow.

Her nostrils flared. "Take off your shirt. I remember your chest. I want to see it again."

His cock jerking against his belly, he yanked off his T-shirt and tossed it aside. Under her gaze, his pecs swelled. "Now you."

She smiled, and slowly lifted her hands to the row of buttons running down the middle of her blouse.

Damn. He saw why she was wearing that little cat smile of hers. There must be a hundred small buttons, shaped like tiny flowers or some other symbol of sexual torture. The unfastening of each one took an hour off his life.

He'd lost less than half a decade when he couldn't wait any longer. Without bothering to stop her, he shoved at the fabric, pushing her hands away as well as catching his fingers beneath the band of her bra so that it was lifting up and away, too.

She was bare to him, her eyes wide.

The song ended, and in the brief lull before the next came the sound of truck tires on the nearby highway. Her gaze darted for the door. "Did you lock it?"

He cupped his hands around her breasts, the skin hot and soft against his palms. She jerked, her heels snapping him forward so the bulge in his jeans brushed against the intersection of seams at the crotch of her pants. Her eyes widened more; his cock pulsed.

"Did you lock it?" she insisted.

He almost lied. But then he shook his head and pushed against her, steadily increasing the pressure as a flush moved up her neck to her face. "You want me to stop?"

Her head rolled back and forth on the tabletop as he rolled her nipples between his thumbs and forefingers. "Somebody . . . somebody might come in."

"I don't care."

She arched against him as he flicked his thumbs across the raspberry-flushed tips of her breasts. "I do."

"Yeah, sure." He was locked against her by her unyielding inner thigh muscles. "When you let me go, dollface, I'll rush right over there."

Then he distracted her by leaning over to bite at that pink, delectable mouth. She lifted her body to him, her hard nipples branding his chest. His vision was blurring, so he broke the kiss to give them a moment to breathe. Brushing back her feathery, choppy layers of hair, he looked down into her high school sweetheart of a face. Paired with her willing little body, she slayed him.

All at once, something else twined with the lust coursing through his bloodstream. Something treacherous that softened his knees and dizzied his head. His fingers curled into her hair, pulling it a little, punishing her for this new symptom of the disease she'd infected him with. *Candyass,* he accused himself. It was just sex.

"This is going to be fast," he ground out, pushing his pelvis into hers. "Fast and hard."

Her flush deepened. "What?"

There couldn't be tenderness. She might like that, but he didn't want it, couldn't want it. "It's part of the cure."

Her eyes were big again. She was panting. "I . . . like it fast and hard."

He laughed. "I'll bet the Bivy you've never had it fast and hard in your life. With you, a man would plan out soft sheets and champagne and the fricking opera before getting around to fu—excuse me, *making love.*" It sounded like an insult, and that's how it felt to him—the idea of some other man between Felicity's thighs.

Christ, he was making his own illness worse.

Maybe she knew, because she showed mercy and twined her arms around his neck and brought him close for another kiss. Lust took over again, engulfing everything else in his head. He leaned on one elbow and played with her breasts with his free hand, getting her nipples stiff and sensitized for his mouth.

Then he moved lower to suck one between his lips. Her moan vibrated against his mouth. She held his head to her breast, the place between her legs feeling even warmer and damper against his hard-on. He gentled his lips, licking the nipple softly and then pulling back to blow against it, watching with fascination as it lifted chill bumps over the other breast.

He licked his way toward that one, lost in the satin of her skin and the sweet scent of her. "So pretty," he murmured against her flesh, gently stroking his whiskered cheek across her nipple. "So hot and so pretty."

Breath shuddered into her lungs and her hands stroked through his hair. The ends trailed against her skin as he moved to the other breast and rubbed his stubbly chin against that nipple, too. He could see her face, her dark lashes resting against her flushed cheeks. "Look at me, baby," he commanded.

Her eyelids quarter-lifted.

He smiled, wanting to take that sensuous look with him to the grave. "Feeling good?"

Arching against his cock again, she smiled back lazily. "What happened to fast and hard?"

He froze. *Damn!* She'd done it again, diverted his

good—no, bad—intentions! He wrenched back, breaking the vise of her ankles.

"Get your pants off." The order came out harsh and thick. "Get your pants off now."

His jeans were already unfastened and he shoved them and his boxers toward his knees. Without waiting for her to obey, he took her mouth again, fast and hard, and grabbed for her zipper. He missed, his fingers sliding beneath her waistband, and he felt her naked belly against the back of his hand.

He groaned.

Then he heard the distinctive creak of the Bivy's front door. Voices talking, laughing, then breaking off as whoever it was coming in caught sight of, he presumed, his bare ass in its compromising position.

Damn. If he grabbed for his pants, he'd expose Felicity and her naked breasts. *Damn it.* The group didn't sound as if they were turning around and leaving.

"I hope this doesn't mean you're closed for the night?" An amused voice called out.

It was a familiar voice, too, though Magee couldn't place it immediately. Someone he knew, and he'd kill him if he ever mentioned this incident. If he hadn't already croaked himself from whatever Felicity had—or hadn't yet—given him, that is.

"We're definitely closed," he managed to yell out.

Felicity had one hand over her eyes, but, as usual, her lips started flapping. "I'm so sorry you're inconvenienced," she babbled, all sweetness and light and ridiculous lies. "We're, uh, running a test to determine the strength of the bar tables for the, uh, California State Department of Forms and Measures."

"Oh?" said a second voice by the door.

"Exactly," Felicity went on. "I'm a Special Inspector—"

"Of Forms and Measures?" Magee murmured, pressing his naked erection against her body.

She jumped a little, but other than that, ignored him. "And it's my duty to ensure the safety of the, uh, bar patrons of inland Southern California."

The bullshit was so outrageous that for a moment he thought the people at the door bought it.

Then a woman's voice joined the discussion. "Looks like the tables are plenty strong to me. But Magee, keep me in mind next time you want to conduct a 'safety' test, will you?"

Felicity's heels dug into his nakedness and he grunted. He couldn't figure out what had her hackles up, because he was busy coming to grips with one hell of a realization. He didn't have a condom. Mr. Responsible, Mr. Turned-Over-a-New-Leaf had been *this* close to having stranger-sex without a condom.

The fickle finger of fate rose high in his mind. Thank God for the interruption, because he knew he wasn't the Lucky Bastard anymore.

Ten

Despite the untimely interruption, Magee was still desperate to get Felicity out of his system. They were going to have sex, he decided. And this time they were going to have sex someplace where they were guaranteed to be alone. Once the would-be bar customers left, he pulled Felicity across the parking lot, not giving her time to think or protest.

"We're going to a hotel," he told her. "You drive."

He wasn't sure what was going through her mind, but she followed orders readily enough, stopping at the Go-Market he directed her to. When he came out with coffee, condoms, and chocolate bars, she took the styrofoam mega-gulp he offered her without a word.

But then she peered down at what he dumped on the console between them. "Are we preparing for a siege, or sex?"

He ignored her. "Start the car."

Instead of obeying this time, she took in a breath. "Listen, Magee—"

"Don't start with me."

She sighed. "Have you considered this is Fate's way of giving us the opportunity to reconsider?"

"Then Fate should have reconsidered our little bump in the night a few days back." He leaned over and turned the ignition key for her. "I need to get you out of my head." Out from under his skin.

When she still hesitated, he leaned toward her. She expected a persuasive kiss, he could tell because he heard her take a breath like a swimmer about to jump, so he went for surprise. Instead of going for mouth-to-mouth, he ran his tongue across her bottom lip at the same time as he ran his palm up her thigh, from knee to heat.

Then he lifted his head, his hand still insinuated between her legs. He rubbed two fingers along either side of the seam he found there, then pressed them against her, hard.

That wasn't very romantic, either, but she jerked into his palm all the same. In response, his erection lurched against his belly. They stared at each other, both of them already breathing hard. "Decide," he commanded.

The neon *G* in *Go-Market* was busted. It blared red against her face, then shorted out with a *zizz,* only to *zizz* once more, washing her scarlet again. In his ears, his pulse pumped in counterpoint—*thump zizz thump zizz thump zizz thump*—the sound and her indecision stretching his nerves like cheap climbing rope. His fingers twitched.

Her inner thighs clenched against his hand and her

head dropped back against the seat. "Yes," she said. "Okay, yes."

He would have stripped her then and there, but with their luck, in the next instant the Pope would pull in for cookies and latte. Sister Felicity Magdalene's explanations were too painful to even imagine.

As she drove, there was no more talk between them except for his terse directions. He'd downed his coffee and eaten two candy bars by the time she parked outside the check-in office of the Desert Fountains Resort. Once he had the key to a private villa in his hand, he scooted her out of the driver's seat and sped toward it himself.

She went too damn slow.

But once they were standing in the tiled foyer of the Mediterranean-styled cottage, he stilled, incredulous that they were alone. "Is it possible?"

Still suspicious, he reached out and opened the closet door to his left, flipped on its light. Ironing board, iron, wall safe, hangers. The bathroom was next. Thick towels. Two terry robes hanging from a hook. He walked out, shaking his head.

"Not a spider, a relative, a customer, a friend. Nothing. Nobody," he said, stalking toward Felicity. "Just you and me."

She was looking apprehensive again, and he couldn't have that. It made him soft. He snatched her hand—remembered that candyass kissing of it the first night in the desert, damn it—and dragged her up against his body. "Just you and me, Lissie."

The name banished the ghost of anxiety in her

eyes. When he put the arm he held around his neck, she flung the other up to meet it. "Michael," she said, then fisted both hands in the ends of his hair and yanked his mouth down to hers.

Her mouth was hotter than the coffee and ten times as stimulating as the caffeine. He rubbed his body against hers, leading with his clamoring erection, but it wasn't enough. Nothing was going to be enough until he had her, at the door, on the floor, wherever.

Anywhere except the bed, he decided. That would be too soft, too treacherously normal for what he wanted from her.

It was going to be raunchy and crude and she'd probably call him names over it later. He hoped so. He hoped that afterward she'd never want to look him in the face again. That's the way they could end this.

But for now she was sucking on his tongue like she needed it as much as he did and he groaned into her mouth, crowding her against the wall. With his hands on either side of her head, he leaned into her belly, then bent his knees to push against the soft pad of female flesh over her pubic bone.

She pushed back, grinding herself against him.

"I have to get inside you now," he said, wrenching his mouth away from hers. "Don't say no. Don't say anything." He ripped at the fastening of her jeans and shoved them down. He must have caught her panties, too, because she was suddenly, sweetly, naked in his hands.

He cupped the swell of her cheeks in his palms, aware that she was stepping out of her shoes but paralyzed by just how good it felt to be holding her. Then she dragged his head down for another kiss. It went serious in a heartbeat, hot and wet. She teased him with her tongue until he bit down on it, trapping it inside his mouth.

Moaning, she wound one naked leg around his thigh, opening herself to him. He shifted his hand and in one smooth slide thrust his middle finger deep inside her tight, creamy heat.

His cock leaped. He looked down into her flushed face and glittering eyes and felt on the edge of that treacherous internal cave-in. No. *No*.

"You feel so good, dollface," he said roughly, drawing out his finger to the tip. He circled the pad just inside the opening to her body, knowing his rough calluses would stimulate the sensitive skin. "You feel so good, I'm gonna make you come just like this."

He thrust two fingers inside her. She jerked, her shoulders thumping against the wall. The fit was tighter, wetter, and when he drew his fingers back out he stroked them through her soft folds and found her magic button. Her bare heel ground into the back of his thigh and he used it as the barometer to her gathering climax.

"You like that, don't you?" he said, dropping kisses on her cheeks and chin. "Look, it's even better with my thumb there and my fingers right . . . *here*."

The pleasure-filled yet agonized sound she made was *his* magic button. His balls drew up and his cock almost spasmed. A rash of prickles rose on his arms and chest as she dug her heel harder into his leg.

"Michael. Michael." She was tensing up, her hips tilting to allow him better access.

"Right here, baby." He held her in his hand, everything he wanted of her, anyway. She was hot and needy and his to make orgasm at will. He thrust a third finger inside her and pressed the magic button.

She made the kind of half-moan, half-groan that came straight from the belly. Then her head thumped against the wall and her body quaked in waves as the climax rolled through her. Her eyes closed, her cheeks flagged with color, a sheen of sweat broke out on her forehead. It was better than a XXX-rated peep show.

He leaned in to kiss her mouth as her foot slid nervelessly down the back of his leg. She pushed at his wrist and he withdrew from her body and lifted his head. Already she wouldn't look at him—he'd embarrassed her that easily.

His gut tightened, and he reached out to reassure her, then stopped, because her embarrassment was what he wanted! Damn it, he couldn't afford to be tender. He couldn't afford to have actual feelings besides this needy, edgy greed for sex.

"I want you to do it again," he told her, his voice grating and demanding, because it wanted to be gentle and soothing. He grabbed her shoulders and pulled her up to his mouth for a punishing kiss because he wanted so badly to pet her, to stroke her, to coax her back into his arms. "I want you to come for me again."

She ducked her head. "Let me take a shower." Then she slipped out of his grasp and leaped toward the bathroom door.

Just that brief flash of her perfect ass sounded the buzzer on his personal desire-o-meter, and the new jolt of lust steadied him. So he leaned a shoulder against the wall, waited. It was going to be all right, *he* was going to be all right. This was just an everyday case of raging lust.

At the shush of water through the pipes, he did a slow count to ten, then he stripped and strode after her.

The shower was nearly as big as his office at the Bivy. Its glass enclosure was clear, revealing every wet detail of the back of Felicity's body. That buzzer inside him went on and stayed on. For an instant he wondered if it was a warning, but he couldn't care, not when he had to touch her again.

She did the whirl and shriek when he popped open the glass door, but he didn't hesitate. Instead, he continued toward her, fascinated by the rivulets of water sluicing down her breasts and over her nipples. "You give a whole new meaning to the term 'wet dream,'" he murmured.

"What are you doing?" she said, a startled Venus di Milo.

He stopped within a breath of her. The shower's spray misted the hair on his arm as he lifted his hand to push away one of hers and cup her breast. "I'm touching you. I'm going to make you come again."

Her eyes widened and she swallowed. "Magee, no, I mean, well, um . . . there's you and . . ."

"You let me worry about me." This was *all* about him, about getting his wayward libido under control and getting her out of his head and his life. With his other hand, he found the pretty little soap she'd un-wrapped and lathered it between his fingers and palm. "I'm going to make you slippery—everywhere—baby."

Now her eyes dilated. "Magee—*Michael*." His name ended in a moan as he moved the soapy hand over her other breast.

It took no time to bring her to the edge again. It was mutual, he knew that, this greedy need, even though acting on it wasn't so easy for her. He spun her away from him to run his hands over her sleek back and rounded ass.

"Beautiful," he whispered against the back of her neck, tasting water and Felicity with his tongue. "Just looking at you makes me so hard that lately the nights have been endless."

He stroked his hand down one sweet cheek and from there reached between her legs. "I like to sleep on my stomach but the pole you give me makes that impossible."

She gasped, but whether it was at his exploring fingers or raunchy words, he didn't know. He didn't care. "You look so sweet and innocent, don't you, baby, that I bet no man has ever told you how it really is."

One hand between her legs, he covered a breast with his other palm and drew her back against him. Her head lolled against his shoulder as he played in the wet folds of her sex.

"How's it really?" she whispered, her eyes drifting shut. "Tell me."

"When I look at you I want to suck, to lick, to bite.

I want to mark you somehow so that you know you're mine, and then I want to pull off your pants and pull your legs wide to find out all I can about what's between them, with my hands, my mouth, and then my cock."

And just like that, she came again.

It only got wilder after that.

He shut off the shower and then lifted her onto the countertop beside the sink so he could spread her legs and kneel between them. "You taste so good. Luscious. Sweet woman fruit." Her fingers tangled in his hair and she orgasmed in pulses against his tongue.

She was still unsteady on her feet, so she braced herself with her hands on the counter when he thrust into her from behind. He groaned. "So tight, so hot and tight and wet. I love this. I could live thrust up inside you."

She shuddered, goosebumps breaking over her skin.

At the sight, his cock jumped inside her and she moaned sharply. Afraid it was all going to be over, he pulled out and dragged her into the bedroom. There, he grabbed a straight chair and sat down. "Straddle me, sweetheart," he directed, caressing her breasts as persuasion. "Take me for a ride."

Oh, she did. She took him all the way home and back.

But he still hadn't had his fill of her. So he drew her down to the carpet and learned everything he wanted to about every square inch of her body. He placed kisses on her hip bones, ran the flat of his tongue down her spine, surrendered to temptation and took a bite of one peachy cheek.

"I'm hard again, Lissie," he said, flipping her over. "Look what you do to me. Look where I'm going." He pushed her knees apart and thrust into her. "And look how easy this is, how easy I fit, because you're so wet and you're so willing."

The rhythm got out of his control and he felt himself climbing, climbing. "So wet," he said, pushing a hand between them to press her magic button again and send her falling.

She was milking his body, draining him of this unprecedented, unwelcome lust. Thank God. "So willing," he murmured, just as he was about to come. "So mine."

Magee woke up some time later, still lying on the plush carpet. Felicity was nearby, facing away from him, her back curved into a lonely *C*. He heard her steady, deep breaths as she slept the sleep of the well and truly fucked.

Reaching up, he snagged the bedspread and pulled it off the bed. Then he tucked it carefully around Felicity, unwilling to disturb her.

But he was disturbed, as images of the two of them piled up in his mind. To stop their exquisite torture, he pushed the heels of his hands against his eyes. What had he done?

He'd learned her secret.

Damn it, his raunchy routine had backfired, because she'd responded to it, hotter than he could have imagined.

What he'd thought would turn her away had only turned her on.

* * *

It was all Richie Sambora's fault.

That's the first thing Felicity thought when she woke the next morning to find herself on the floor, covered by a bedspread. Certainly the man dead asleep on the rug beside her shared some of the blame, but it had all started with Richie. One of the girls at school had smuggled into the prep school dormitory a couple of Bon Jovi CDs.

The nuns at Our Lady of Poverty didn't approve of rock music, and the band members' untamed hair and painted-on pants would have scandalized them, making their music only more appealing to the students. In secret, Felicity's dormmates had poured over the liner notes, drooled over the photos, passed around the headphones, and gone headlong into puberty to the thudding pulse of songs like "One Wild Night" and "Slippery When Wet."

Felicity had been right there alongside them—except in one respect. While her friends had been boy-crazy for the long-tressed blond beauty of lead singer Jon Bon Jovi, his pretty, almost androgynous look hadn't intrigued her in the least. No, it was bass-player Richie who'd made her quiver. Dark-haired, dark-eyed, and smoldering Richie Sambora, who looked like he'd say and do all manner of dangerous things.

Like the things that Magee had said and done to her last night.

Felicity shot him a sidelong look. He was still in dreamland, but relaxation didn't add a whit of little-boy vulnerability to his features. After a night of debauchery, a sleeping Jon Bon Jovi would look lost-angel sweet. But Magee . . . even with his lashes resting against his cheeks, their thick bristle paired with that black stubble on his chin and around his full mouth made him an unrepentant gunslinger—passed out after a night of whiskey and women.

She had to get away from him. He threatened the image—the All-American, girl-next-door Felicity—she'd worked on for years. Conscience pricking her, she admitted to herself that she'd been overdoing the blame game. It wasn't Richie's fault. It wasn't Magee's sole fault, either. The two of them together created a synergy that stripped away her inhibitions and scratched out all her mental lists of Mr. Right qualities.

Which didn't change the fact that she had to get away from him.

Commanding herself to stay quiet, she made a surreptitious slide and nearly yelped out loud. Her backside hurt! More gingerly, she moved again, managing to rise to her feet without a sound. In the mirror over the room's long dresser she saw the cause of her discomfort.

She had a rug burn. Felicity Charm, the Sweetheart of Sales, had a rug-burned behind. And then there were the sore inner thigh muscles, the tender flesh between them, and . . . as she swung around to face her reflection, she stiffened in shock.

Oh. My. God.

Now, *this,* this *was* his fault. And she was going to make him sorry for it.

Temper flaring, she stomped to the bathroom to grab a robe, then slid it on as she marched back to the bedside table. Opening the drawer, she found what she was after. First, a thick, binder-bound guidebook. Next, an even thicker phone book. Finally, a hefty copy of the Gideon's Bible. With a ping of Catholic schoolgirl guilt, she stacked it on top of the other two books and then strode over to stand behind the naked, depraved monster still sacked out on the carpet. Raising her arms high, she let the heavy books fall to the floor, three inches from Magee's glossy mess of hair.

He jolted awake, his eyes wild. His attention jumped to the bedspread she'd been under and his hands patted at it frantically. "Dollface? Are you okay? Felicity!" He shot to a sitting position. "*Lissie!* Where'd you go?"

"How could you?" she ground out.

"There you are." Sounding relieved, he twisted around, his glance sweeping past the books up to her face, then back to the books again. "What the hell happened? You smush a spider under there or something?"

When she didn't answer, he looked up again, and stilled, seeming to take in her mood. With his gaze glued to her face, he slowly reached over and pulled the bedspread across his naked lap.

"A wise precaution," she said.

He cleared his throat. "So. You're mad about something, right?"

She rolled her eyes.

"Okay, okay. Give me a second, I was just rudely awakened." He scrubbed his face with his hand and then ran it through his hair. "You're mad about some-thing and it's . . . it's . . . is it that the in-room coffe-maker isn't working?"

"No."

He gave her a hopeful half-smile. "Then there's co—?" The word broke off as she took a step toward him. "Fine, fine. No coffee. You're mad, and what you're mad about is . . . uh . . . uh . . ."

She started tapping her toe.

He started talking faster. ". . . is all the wasted years?"

Her foot froze. "Wasted years? What wasted years?"

"Without knowing you're multi-orgasmic." He had the arrogance, the audacity, to look smug.

Her vision narrowed and the edges turned red. "I didn't need you to tell me that! I'm perfectly aware of what I'm capable of. For your information, I happen to be deci-orgasmic, milli-orgasmic! What I'm mad about—and 'mad' is too tame a word—what I'm *homicidal* about is this!" Aghast all over again, she wrenched apart the lapels of the terry robe, exposing her nakedness to the waist.

The smirk fell from his face, to be replaced with something else entirely. Something serious—maybe even tender. "Oh, Lissie. You're so pretty."

She experienced a moment of girlish softening, then, flushing, she whipped the robe back over her-self. "I'm talking about the hickeys, Magee."

Blinking, he rose to his feet, hitching the bedspread around his waist. "Hickeys? You have hickeys?"

Slapping him sounded good. "How could you have missed them? I can hide the ones on my breasts, but the one on my neck makes me look as if I've been making out with a junior high schooler."

"Show me again," he said, his voice gentle.

Though she felt more heat rush over her skin, she slowly parted the edges of the robe again. "Look. What am I supposed to do about them?"

There were five hickeys altogether. On each breast, there was one on both the upper and lower curves. And then the last one, the biggest one, was marking the skin at the side of her neck.

The rise and fall of his chest quickened as he looked her over. She felt his gaze on each of the marks in turn, bringing back searing memories of the night before. His mouth, so hot on her breasts. Her fingers, tangled in his damp hair, holding him to her as her voice begged for more.

Then Magee standing behind her in the shower, his big body curved around hers, his lips on her neck as his clever hands proved that she was—indeed—multi-orgasmic.

Now his gaze lifted from her body to her face. "I don't know what to say, dollface. I don't regret it, do you?"

Regret it? Of course she regretted it! She regretted everything that had happened since she'd made the impetuous decision to come back to Half Palm in order to prove something to the Charms. But the only thing she'd proven last night was that she could make irresponsible, shameless decisions like the rest of them. What else would explain the most decadent, wanton night in her life?

Somewhere, somewhere deep inside, she must be truly depraved, too, because God, how else could it feel so right with someone so wrong?

It was anger that made the corners of her eyes prick with tears. "You're right," she said, spinning and then rushing toward the bathroom so he wouldn't see them. "You're right. I suppose I can't regret my chance for a real thrillbang from the Master Thrillbanger himself."

How could she make him sorry when it was so impossible to feel sorry about it herself?

The next person who brought up that thrillbanging crap was going to wish he hadn't, Magee fumed as he drove them out of the resort. It made him sound unprincipled and . . . and unfeeling, damn it!

He had plenty of feelings. Plenty for Felicity, too. She ticked him off, she twisted him up, she shredded him with her pretty skin and those possessive marks he'd put there.

But hell, was it his fault she bruised so easily? If he wanted to, he could make her admit that she'd loved what he'd done to her. That had been his surprise—that she'd been with him all the way.

He didn't know why he was feeling so unsettled. The whole damn night had been for both of them to release the sexual steam that had been building up for days.

He glanced over at her. She was staring out the side window, her expression unreadable, and he wished he could shake her up like she'd shaken him. But her posture was relaxed and calm, except for the one small hand half-hiding that truly spectacular love bite he'd managed to lay on her. Okay, so it was puerile of him, but just thinking about it made him hard.

"Stop! Stop right now!"

"Jesus, Felicity!" She was reading minds now. "I can't help it." He was a man, wasn't he?

But she wasn't looking at him. "Pull over. Right here."

He did what she said, pulling over in front of one of the walled and gated residences so popular in the chichi desert communities. "What's going on?"

"This is where I went to school."

Now he noticed a bronzed sign reading *Our Lady of Poverty Prepatory Day and Boarding School* on the stucco wall. His hand rubbed over his whiskered chin. "Did you want to visit?"

She shook her head, her posture tense. "I want to remember."

He didn't like her new mood. "The old alma mater, huh?"

"From sixth grade through twelfth. I lived here year-round."

"Nice place." From the little he could see of it. The fancy desert cities subscribed to the "less is more" theory. The less you saw of a place, the more expensive it was.

"Only girls of the very finest families attend OLPP." The way she said it sounded as if she'd memorized the phrase of a recruitment brochure.

"Did you say you lived here year-round?" Something was starting to click here.

She nodded, her gaze still trained on the iron-gated entrance and the lush grass and massive flower beds on either side of it.

"It says it's a day school, too. Why didn't you save a few bucks and get a ride in from Half Palm?"

"I had a scholarship." Her head turned toward him and then she repeated that recruitment-brochure phrase again, with the same calm conviction. "Only girls of the very finest families attend OLPP."

She said it as if it were an answer to his question, which, he was beginning to understand, it was.

Her gaze returned to the OLPP gates. "I made myself there," she murmured.

He didn't know why he hated the sound of that so much. "Yeah, and it's where you started *re*making the Charms." Because that's what her brochure phrase made clear. She'd turned her back on her real family and chosen her hoity-toity school over Half Palm and the people who'd raised her. Felicity Charm was an image-conscious, artificial snob.

Who was obviously reminding herself that she'd been slumming by doing the nasty with someone like him.

He burned an inch of rubber off the tires getting the car back into traffic. His mood only turned darker as they left the luxury desert cities behind and neared Half Palm and the Bivy. He didn't know why that was. He should be happy. Once he got back to the bar, he was never going to see her again.

Taste her again.

Touch her again.

"I guess this will be goodbye," she said. "We won't be seeing each other anymore."

She was back to reading his mind, damn her. And he hated the way she sounded so cheerful. For God's sake, they'd just had the best sex in memory—his memory anyway—and she was acting as if she were saying goodbye to . . . to some distant relative!

And then it hit him. Something he'd managed to push out of his mind for days. They might not be so distant from each other after all. He whipped into the Bivy's parking lot, the undercarriage of the car grating against the sharply angled driveway. "I don't know about that, dollface. We might be running into each other sooner than you think."

That got her attention. "What are you talking about?"

"I'm moving your way."

She didn't even bother trying not to look horrified. *What are you talking about?*

"That night we met, I'd just accepted a new job. In L.A., as a matter of fact." He smiled at her. A mean, nasty smile. "I start next month."

"I don't get it."

"I'm taking a job. A real, eight-to-five job in a big engineering firm. I'm going to be part of the ordinary working class, dollface. Just think, maybe we'll be neighbors."

Her mouth moved, but no sound came out. She looked away from him and out the window, as if trying to fathom this latest piece of news. Then she suddenly reached over and clawed at his arm with one hand. The other flew up to cover the hickey on her neck. "No. No, no, no, no, no."

"What?" He followed her gaze to an unfamiliar car parked beside the Bivy's entrance. He'd wanted to shake her up, but the expression on her face was making *him* uneasy. "Who is it?"

"It's Drew," she said. "Drew Hartnett, my . . . my boss."

Eleven

"Boss, my ass," Peter heard Magee mutter as he stepped around him to reach the coffeemaker.

"And a hello, how's it going to you, too," Peter replied, though it wasn't clear that Magee even realized he was there, let alone was speaking to him. All his friend's attention was focused on the other end of the bar, where Felicity was cozied up to a country-club type who had walked in a few minutes before and introduced himself as Drew Hartnett.

"Did the pretty boy say why he's here?" Magee asked.

Peter continued to stock the undercounter refrigerator from the case of beer on his lap. "For Felicity. She told him about the place, I guess. He must be interested in climbing, because he came in with that stack of *Climber* and *Rock & Ice* magazines they're poring over."

"Interested in climbing, my ass. He's too wimpy to scale a sidewalk curb."

Peter recognized the raw edge to Magee's voice as jealousy—and recognized the emotion, too.

"And she's just as bad," he went on in a disgusted tone. "Troweled on the makeup before she dared come inside. Couldn't let pretty boy see her without the whole buff and polish job. Now look at her. It's like she's a different person, don't you—"

"Ashley's fine, in case you're wondering," Peter put in.

Magee froze, scrubbed a hand over his face, then looked down at Peter. "Jesus, I'd forgotten how she ran out of here last night. You found her? You cheered her up?"

He almost laughed. "I wouldn't say that exactly."

"Damn." Magee scrubbed his face again. "I should have . . . but, see, Felicity heard from Ben. He left her a note that said he's all right. That should make Ash feel better, don't you think?"

"I don't know how to make her feel better." He couldn't hide his bitterness.

Magee's eyes narrowed. "What's going on, Peter? I remember you were in a shitty mood last night, and now you look like hell."

He felt like hell, even though he'd spent the hours since leaving the casino trying to come to grips with Ashley's rejection. But when Magee and Felicity had walked into the bar just minutes apart, it had been obvious what they'd been up to. And now it made Peter furious. Last night, while Ashley had been turning from him, Magee had been turning to someone else.

Peter took a calming breath. "And you look like you camped out on the floor all night."

Magee glanced at his reflection in the mirror over the bar and winced. "You're right." Then, at a bubble of bright female laughter, his gaze jumped to Felicity again. "So how come she looks like a fresh, dewy daisy?" he muttered.

"I'm right, then." But perhaps he should be glad of it, Peter thought. If Magee wasn't available to give Ashley that safety net she needed, maybe she'd decide that half a man was better than none at all. "You slept with Felicity."

Magee shot him a sidelong look. "It didn't mean anything."

Another rush of acid surged through Peter's gut, and his hands curled into fists. Oh, what he'd give to knock that cool expression off his friend's face. How could Magee so coldly dismiss Felicity when Peter couldn't do the same to Ashley?

"Hell, Magee, I thought you'd pledged no more danger, no more debauchery?" he demanded. Though God knew his own demons were still hovering, even closer than usual. *You're a failure, Peter.* That voice from the past roughened his own. "I thought it was you who denounced the 3-D Club."

"Shut up, okay?" Magee suddenly sounded angry, too. "I told you. It doesn't mean anything. I'm never seeing Felicity again."

Peter shook his head in frustration. "What the hell are you doing, Magee?"

"The right thing." He poured a mug of coffee and chugged it down. "I'm going to do the right thing, okay? What I promised. I just had to get her out of my system."

"That's possible?"

Magee's gaze wandered to the other end of the bar again. "Everything's going to be all right. Believe me."

Peter opened his mouth to protest, but at that moment Felicity called out to Magee. Peter watched his friend saunter slowly toward her. He held out his hand when he was introduced to Felicity's "pretty boy" and even widened his mouth in a genial smile.

From the neutral expression on Magee's face, Peter believed his friend. Magee was intent on doing the right thing, which meant not involving himself any further with Felicity. Which also meant he would be giving Ashley what she needed—a man to make her feel safe.

Peter continued stocking the cooler, the anger seeping out of him. He loved Ashley enough to want that for her, too. Her friendship would have to be enough for him.

By the time he wheeled into the storeroom for another case of beer, he could draw slow, even breaths. The last of which was startled out of him when Magee bolted into the room.

"Damn woman. She could sell camels to eskimos."

"What? Who?"

Magee rolled his eyes. "Who? The who is that Evil Sorceress of Sales. Pretty Boy is going to the trade show with her this afternoon—apparently Felicity's

BS about climbing as cutting-edge sparked his interest. They'll be trolling for more products to push on the unsuspecting public."

"So?"

"So, Pretty Boy likes what's put out by Mountain Logic." As if he had to work off the bottled energy inside him, Magee stalked back to the doorway and reached up to grab the bar installed across the top of the frame.

"And you're a spokesman for Mountain Logic."

Magee racked up two dozen pull-ups from a dead drop before he answered. "Yeah, and I'll be in their booth this afternoon and the rest of the weekend. Damn woman knew that." He did the next dozen with his right arm alone, and then the next dozen with his left.

"So now the three of us are having dinner tonight," he finally muttered.

The expression on Magee's face hinted at the rest of the story. "Whose idea was that?" Peter asked.

Magee dropped to the ground. "She wasn't being herself, okay? It made me nuts, watching her acting all prissy and syrupy-sweet, even while she's watching *me* as if she thinks any minute I'm going to start belching or scratching my balls. I just wanted to poke at her, that's all. Make her squirm a little."

"So tonight you'll poke her again. Make her squirm a little more."

Magee shot him a glance. "Not in the way you're implying. I told you, Peter, it's over. And that every—"

"—thing will be all right. Yeah, yeah, yeah." Peter wheeled past him, back into the bar.

His gaze clashed with Ashley's, who was just letting herself in the front door. They stared at each other a moment. "It's my afternoon to work on the books," she offered.

"Yeah." *Everything's going to be all right*. That reminded him of the news about Ben, but instead of telling her himself, he directed her to Magee. With a last, unreadable look for him, she headed for the storeroom.

The rest of the afternoon was quiet. Magee left for the trade show. In the office, Ashley sat at the computer to work on the books. He turned on the stereo and queued up a few CDs while he went about his own tasks.

At four P.M., he unlocked the doors and the usual crowd trickled in, asking for the usual drinks and working up to their usual level of rowdiness. Ashley switched roles from accountant to waitress and they fell into their usual routines.

Everything's going to be all right. He continued trying to believe it.

The usual gossip was passed along, too. Who was planning to tackle what climb, who would never tackle any climb rated higher than 5.10, who was likely to be too hungover the next morning to show up at the designated meeting place to go bouldering.

"Did you hear about Linc?" someone asked Peter.

He put a face to the name. Young kid, he'd carded him the first few times he'd come into the Bivy, checking over his ID carefully. Skinny and blond, he looked a lot like Ashley's brother Ben. "What about him?" he said, sliding the mug of beer across the bar.

"Got himself beat up."

"What? You mean he took a fall?"

"Nope. Took a few fists. It was a group of slick, city-looking guys. Three of 'em. He came out of that bar right outside Joshua Tree. They called him over and then slugged him a few times in the parking lot. Demanded money. Said he owed them."

Peter froze. "Does he? Owe them money?"

The guy telling the story shook his head. "Nope. They grabbed his wallet, took a look at it, then stopped whaling on him. Case of mistaken identity, they said. Gave him a hundred bucks and said they were sorry."

"Very polite," he murmured, remembering what Gwen had said about the men who'd come into the Wild Side. Telling himself it was just a coincidence, he still searched for Ashley among the tables. *Everything's going to be all right.*

When his gaze settled on her, her head whipped toward him as if she felt it. Then just as quickly it whipped away.

Everything's going to be all right.

Magee wasn't going to touch Felicity again.

Ashley wasn't going to let what happened at the casino get in the way of their friendship.

Ben wasn't in any kind of real trouble.

The floor of the trade show was open until seven P.M., but the crowds didn't clear out until after seven-thirty.

When Magee managed to end his conversation with a buyer for a chain of sporting goods stores in Colorado, he turned to find Felicity sunk in one of the cushioned chairs the Mountain Logic people used during deal-making. Her head was tilted against its back and she flicked him a glance as he half-sat against its thick arm.

With her chin, she gestured to the massive wall hanging that was the focal point of the booth. "Very impressive."

He didn't bother looking at it. "I have six more months on my endorsement contract. They gotta make me look good." It was a photo of him climbing Half Dome in Yosemite, with him in Mountain Logic wear, using Mountain Logic gear.

For a moment, he let himself remember the day. He'd been in a flow state, what other athletes might call "the zone," where the difficult had seemed easy, the impossible just a handhold away. Tuned in to himself and in to the environment, he'd felt powerful, focused, unconquerable.

"Speaking of looking good," Felicity said, flicking him another glance, "you clean up well."

"Gee, thanks." Apparently she thought his wardrobe consisted of jeans and questionable T-shirts, which, of course, mostly it did. But his mother had raised him right. He knew when to put on pleated slacks, polished shoes, a dress shirt. "I even remembered to brush my teeth and comb my hair. Now if only my table manners won't embarrass you in front of your Boy Scout boss at dinner tonight."

She waved a hand. "No dinner."

"For God's sake," he bit out, insulted all over again. "I may not be a stuffed shirt like your pretty boy Drool, but I *do* happen to be aware I shouldn't eat my peas with a knife."

"His name is Drew, not Drool, as you very well know. And he's gone back to L.A. Thank God."

"Why gone back?" *And why "thank God"?*

Her eyes drifted shut. "Didn't you hear? He cut a deal with Mountain Logic. Some of their products will be part of our Spring Spotlight. We think the jackets and especially the rock shoes will be hot sellers. He needed to get back to work his end."

Magee wondered what kind of work her boss did on Felicity. Right now it appeared as if she needed help getting out of that chair, though she looked properly Charm-ing in a champagne-colored suit that had a tight, knee-length skirt ending in a girlie ruffle. On her feet were a pair of matching needle-heeled shoes that looked sexy as hell as well as hellishly uncomfortable.

Somewhere under the high-necked blouse she wore were the hickeys he'd given her.

Though he shoved the thought from his mind, he couldn't stop himself from running his fingertips over the feathery ends of her hair. "When are you going back to L.A.? You look too tired to drive, doll-face."

She gave another little wave of her hand. "Not tonight."

"Good." He played with her hair again. "So . . . where shall I take you to dinner?"

Her eyes opened. "You don't need to take me to dinner."

Of course he didn't. Maybe he shouldn't, but then she'd guess he'd only extended the invitation so he could tweak her in front of Drool. That petty last memory didn't sit well with him. So he'd take her to dinner to smooth things out between them, and to smoothly say goodbye.

But just to get her goat, he leered down at her. "You're wearing my hickeys, aren't you? The least I can do is buy you a meal."

That woke her up. Her eyes sparked and she straightened. "You shouldn't remind me of the hickeys," she said through her teeth, her fingers going to the high collar of her blouse. "But now that you have, it's going to cost you. I haven't eaten all day. I want Italian food. Lots of expensive Italian food."

He grinned. "Italian food's my favorite." He'd take her out for a nice dinner, give her a goodbye kiss on the cheek, and then smoothly erase her out of his mind. He'd promised Peter that everything was going to be all right, and it was. It was all going to proceed as planned. New job. New wife. New life.

Friday night meant there was a line out the door of Il Calore just to put a name on the list for a table. But even from the sidewalk the smells of garlic and herbs had Felicity swooning, and they decided to wait. He used his shoulders to wedge them a place inside the packed bar, so crowded that when he tilted his bottle of beer to take a swallow, it clipped her forehead.

"Sorry." Grimacing, he stroked his thumb over the spot. "Guess I should've fed you last night before I boffed you. Thursdays aren't so crowded."

Her jaw dropped. There was a moment of offended silence, then she squinted her eyes at him. "You do that on purpose, don't you? You're deliberately crude to annoy me."

He couldn't bite back his grin. By the end of the trade show he'd been tired, too, but three minutes in Felicity's company gave him the energy of a school-boy intent upon pulling a certain little girl's pigtails. "You're reading me like a book, dollface."

Which was okay. He knew her, too. Standing this close to her made him half-hard—he'd been expecting too much to imagine that a few explosive orgasms could neuter him or neutralize her sex appeal—but his lust for her was under control. Last night he'd plumbed her physical depths, and this morning, outside OLPP and then again when Drool had appeared on the scene, he'd discovered how truly shallow she was.

She'd be easy enough to forget.

It was as if that very thought turned a spotlight on her. A thirtyish woman at Felicity's elbow jostled her and while making an automatic apology, the stranger's eyes widened. "Felicity!" the person said. "Felicity Charm!"

Magee saw her stiffen, but then she beamed over a relaxed and friendly smile. "Hello," she said. "How are you tonight?"

As if they'd known each other since childhood, the woman smiled back. "I'm better, now that my fiancé's mother-in-law flew home to Minnesota." Then she leaned closer to Felicity, peering into her wine glass. "Is that Chardonnay or Pinot Grigio?"

The crowd shuffled a bit when a name was called out and Magee saw the exact moment when Felicity was recognized again. A man with a touch of gray at the temples nudged his very pretty, very young wife. She turned and then almost hopped in excitement. "Felicity!"

Felicity didn't bat an eyelash. She smiled, she chatted, she admired how pretty the bracelet looked on the woman—the bracelet the woman claimed Felicity had sold to her. It was clear she felt that Felicity had personally selected it just for her.

As the older man drew his wife away, Magee caught the little sigh that washed out of Felicity. "Are you all right?" he murmured into her ear.

But there was already another stranger edging nearer. "I'm lovely," she said cheerfully, turning toward the newcomer. "And how are you?"

By the time they made it to their table, it took more than two hands to count the number of times she'd been spoken to or at least obviously recognized. She breezed through it all like a pro—until the moment the hostess pulled out Felicity's chair at their table.

"What's new with Aunt Vi?" the young woman asked.

The name acted on Felicity like a doctor's mallet to a knee. Her body jerked, one hand flying out to knock over her empty wineglass. Magee caught it as it rolled off the edge of the tiny table.

Felicity had recovered and was giving away that pretty smile again. "Aunt Vi's her usual self."

"How did her charity luncheon turn out?"

"Perfect. A viewer in Louisiana called in with her mother's iced tea punch recipe that tasted delicious. Thanks for asking."

The hostess handed Magee the wine list, but spoke again to Felicity. "I just love hearing about your life and family."

Magee watched Felicity's smile thin, though the wattage remained high. "Thanks, I appreciate that."

Then the hostess left them alone and Felicity slumped back against her chair. "I'd almost forgotten what it's like."

Now that her public wasn't clamoring for her attention, he could see how her performances had rubbed away some of her usual sparkle. "What do you mean?"

But his question got lost as the sommelier dropped by their table. Apparently his college-age niece was another of Felicity's fans. Without losing a beat, she revived the twinkle and then wasn't able to relax again until the entrees were served.

"Jesus, Felicity, how can you possibly get a charge out of all that?" he said, as their waiter walked off. He sounded critical, he knew it, but the interruptions had annoyed him. He wanted a quiet dinner as their final goodbye.

She looked up from her pasta. "I like the people. I

like it that they like me. Talking to them is what I'm good at."

"Lying to them, you mean," he muttered. "Aunt Vi and her charity luncheon. Please."

She straightened in her chair, bristling, then slumped back again. "Okay, fine. I admit that the Aunt Vi part has had me on edge all day. We're too close to Half Palm. During the trade show, I kept imagining someone walking up and blowing my cover in front of Drew."

Magee stared at her, anger sparking again. "So the lies themselves aren't bothering you, huh? Just that Drool's image of you might shatter."

A flush rushed onto her cheeks—of temper, not shame, he was sure.

"You don't know anything about it."

"I know you're full of shit."

"Just a min—" Stopping herself, she set down her fork and folded her hands in her lap. "Tell me about your family, Magee. Who they are. What they do."

"What does that have to do with—"

"Just tell me," she insisted.

She was out to make some point, but he couldn't figure the angle he should take to deflect it. "Dad's a professor at Washington State University. My mother works in the alumni office there part-time—she's a fundraiser. I have an older brother."

Felicity laughed. "I couldn't have invented anything more sitcom suburban if I'd tried."

"Why is that sounding like an insult?"

She shook her head. "It's not meant to be. Your

family is one I would have chosen myself. Stable, un-complicated, people to be proud of."

He shook his head. "It's not as simple as you think."

She shrugged. "I'll have to take your word for it. But when I started at OLPP, what I wanted seemed very simple. Nobody knew me, so nobody knew dif-ferently when I spun a harmless little fantasy about who I wanted the Charms to be. I didn't pretend to be a sheikh's daughter—though two were my class-mates. I didn't co-op the past of the Beverly Hills jun-ior high dropout that was my first roommate. I merely took Aunt Vi and Uncle Billy and made them . . ."

Fake. He nearly said it out loud. "And then you took your harmless little fantasy to TV."

"I didn't intend to." She picked up her fork and fid-dled with her food, making designs in the sauce. "My first week on GetTV, we had Reese Witherspoon as a celebrity guest. One minute we were talking about her line of luxury pet carriers and the next, she asked me about my family. The past I'd made up for myself when I was eleven years old just popped out."

He stared. "*Luxury pet carriers?*" It was hard to get past that.

She made a face at him. "What I'm trying to say is that it was an accident. It just . . . happened."

As she'd just happened to remake the Charms.

He still didn't get it. He still didn't get her. But, damn it, every time he thought he had her pegged, she twisted on him.

She picked up her fork and held it, staring down at

her plate, her eyelashes casting feathery shadows on her cheeks. Her voice was tired. "But don't you worry. I pay for it. Every day I'm afraid that someone will see through it. I'm afraid someone will see through *me*."

Oh, hell. Every time he thought he had her pegged, she twisted his heart. He wanted to remember her as a shallow sham of a woman.

"It's a good thing you're leaving in the morning," he muttered. Because his smooth goodbye was already in jeopardy.

She glanced up. "Leaving?"

"In the morning."

An expression crossed her face. An expression that made him uneasy, that made him remember every painful piece of ill luck that he'd had in the last year and a half and that he was paying for every good piece he'd had in all the years before that.

"You don't know?"

He shook his head. "What?"

She lifted one shoulder in a casual shrug. "I thought maybe those Mountain Logic people would have mentioned it to you. We're doing a live shoot from this area next week and taping some teaser segments to run during the spring. I'll be hanging around until then, scouting locations."

She let a beat go by, then smiled a smile so full of sweet innocence that it sent a shudder worming down his spine. "So this isn't goodbye after all."

Twelve

Magee was staring at her from across the table as if she'd gone mad. Felicity let her smile widen, enjoying the idea that she'd dropped the news into his unsuspecting lap. She'd agreed to dinner because . . . because she was hungry, not realizing it presented such a prime opportunity to get the upper hand with him.

She liked unbalancing him for once. Last night . . . But she wasn't going to think about last night. If she couldn't regret her lapse in clear thinking, then she refused to remember it.

Magee finally found his voice. "But you said you were leaving."

She noted the muscle ticking beneath the dark stubble developing along his jawline. "What can I say? I'm the proverbial bad penny."

His frown deepened. "Bad pennies keep turning up. *You* won't go away."

As if it was her fault. "C'mon, Magee—"

A couple—more fans of GetTV—paused by their table, interrupting her point. Even though she felt

Magee fuming over his plate of fettucine, she drew out her conversation with them. Darling man, his frustration only increased her confidence. She could handle him.

The instant the two people wandered off, he leaned across the table. "Look, we have to talk," he said, his voice tight. "I need to tell you something."

"You're getting Alfredo sauce on your shirtfront," she pointed out.

"I don't ca—"

But the restaurant hostess was back, with a helper from the kitchen in tow. Felicity turned her attention to the shy young man, chatting with him in her halting Spanish, leaving Magee to dip his napkin into his water glass and dab gingerly at his shirt.

With an inward smile, she managed to signal his predicament to their hostess, and they finished the meal with frequent visits from the young woman, their waiter, and the restaurant manager, all checking in on either Felicity, their food, or the status of the stain the hostess herself had doctored with a fresh napkin and club soda.

Magee's steely fingertips didn't leave the small of Felicity's back as they left Il Calore to the tune of the dark-eyed hostess's gushing, "*Arrivederci.*"

"It appears you made a new conquest," Felicity said as he prodded her in the direction of his car.

He didn't glance back. "We have to talk," he repeated. "I need to tell you something."

"So talk."

His head swiveled, taking in the crowded sidewalk. "When we're alone."

Once they were both sitting inside his Jeep, he gripped the steering wheel without looking at her. Tension radiated off him like heat and she half-expected the car's interior to melt. Her thin blouse and silk suit started to itch like woolly tweed.

What could be so difficult to tell her? Her fingers fumbled a little as they moved to unfasten the first few buttons of her blouse. But she was under perfect control, she reminded herself. *He* was the one whose equilibrium was upset.

"You don't have a weird communicable disease or something, do you?" she finally ventured.

"No. It's that . . ." He glanced over. "Jesus! Do up your shirt, will you?"

She looked down, light from the nearby streetlamp confirming there wasn't anything uncovered that warranted his reaction. "What's your problem?"

He was staring at the dashboard again. "It's the hickey, okay? I can't think straight when I can see that damn hickey on your neck."

"Oh." Served him right for sucking on her. But she refastened the buttons anyway. "There."

He cast a sideways glance. She felt it flick over her buttons, then up to her face. When their gazes met, her pulse leaped and her blood rushed to the surface of her skin. The hickeys on her neck and her breasts throbbed. Last night his mouth had been—

No! She wasn't going to think about last night.

Folding her arms over her chest, she tried forcing her brain onto something else. The alphabet. The alphabet backward. $Z \ldots y \ldots x \ldots$

Cursing, he started the car with a jerky motion.

"What now?" Felicity choked out.

He stayed focused on the road. "We need to talk alone, alone but around other people, all right?"

She should tell him not to worry about it, that she wasn't about to let her physical impulses overrule her mental reasoning again. Instead, she spent the next few minutes breathing.

By the time they'd traveled a few traffic-congested blocks and pulled into a parking space, she'd regained her cool confidence. Let him rail, let him argue, but there was nothing she could do about leaving the area until her work for GetTV was completed. Her job came first, before anything.

He grabbed her hand and pulled her down the street, tugging her through a door. Dark, quiet night switched to fluorescent-lighted, drumbeat-thumping day.

She blinked. "What is this place?" She had to raise her voice over the loud rap beat of a Nelly song.

"Rock gym."

A gymnasium, she realized, a cavernous, three-story-high structure, with walls that looked like sometimes-craggy and sometimes-smooth rock studded with small circles of different-colored plastic. The floor space was broken up by monolithic boulders made of the same material as the walls. Climbers in bright-colored sportswear crawled over the surfaces like insects while others watched from the ground.

"Why are we here?" Felicity asked.

"Nobody will know you."

He dragged her around one boulder and along half a wall before pushing her through another door. It was a small café, with a few tables, a juice/espresso bar, and a wall of glass that offered a view of the people moving over the gym's perpendicular surfaces.

Magee pulled out two chairs at a table along the glass wall and pushed her into one of them. "Want something?" He gestured toward the bar.

Though she shook her head, he came back a few moments later with a bottle of sparkling mineral water for each of them.

"So," he said, settling into his seat. "You gotta get out of town. Go back. Go away."

She sighed. "Magee, you're being unreasonable. I have a job to do."

His mouth flattened and he took the top off his water with a vicious twist. "We're trouble for each other. You've gotta know that after the sex last night."

She made a big play of rolling her eyes, to show him who was boss. "Speak for yourself. As far as I'm concerned, we took care of the trouble last night. It's over now. Done. *Finis. Finito. Terminado.* Inishedfay."

He'd waited patiently through her speech, not even cracking a smile at her pig latin. "Are you going to be staying at your aunt's?"

"Well, um . . . I haven't really thought . . ." But she

had. In that old bed, wrapped in quilts so worn that their batting was mere memory, and lulled by the motorboat purrs of many cats, she'd been sleeping like she hadn't slept since she was eleven years old. She'd already decided to remain in her old room until the rest of the GetTV crew rolled into town.

She lifted a shoulder. "Aunt Vi will expect it."

"Then we have a problem." His gaze bore into hers. "We won't be able to keep apart. At least admit that much. Within a few miles of each other and we become a magnet and metal filings."

Twisting off her own bottle top, she reminded herself that *she* wasn't metal or a magnet or anything other than an ambitious woman who could forget the past when it was necessary. "I don't agree," she said coolly. "I can control myself."

One of his eyebrows lifted. "Maybe I can't."

"Oh, please." She just barely resisted the urge to lean over and bite him. "Magee—"

"Do you know what I've been thinking about since I woke up this morning? The way your body is so soft and wet. The way it opens for my fingers, then grips them, hard, when I slide inside of you."

Her stomach hiccuped. Heat swarmed over her body. *Don't think about it, don't think about it, don't think about it.* She tried the alphabet backward thing again. *Z . . . y . . . x . . .* It wasn't working. "You just say things . . . things like that to aggravate me."

Sighing, he shook his head. "Aggravate you? No, dollface, if I wanted to aggravate you, I'd tell you the truth. I'd tell you—"

A thunderous knock on that glass wall just inches away startled them both. A man on the other side directed a series of hand gestures and eyebrow signals at Magee. Though he tried waving the other man off, though he tried an irritated "Get lost," though he even tried turning his back, the other man was having none of it. In obvious challenge, he shook a coiled rope in Magee's face and grinned.

With a groan, Magee rose out of his chair. "He won't leave me alone until I take care of this."

For her part, she could kiss the guy for giving her some time to recover. When Magee returned, she'd get him to take her back to her car. From there she'd go home, crawl under the quilts, pull a cat or two over her eyes, and use sleep to restore her battered self-control.

After all, one night of wanton, reckless sex with the wrong kind of man didn't mean she'd taken an irrevocable turn. She'd remade herself and sex with Michael Magee didn't mean her image was permanently marred or her life plan irrevocably changed. Closing her eyes, she thought of the Joanie as she'd seen it on the dais in that Las Vegas ballroom. Cool, gleaming, golden feet firmly rooted onto golden ground.

"Hey, Lissie! Don't you want to see Magee airwalk?"

Felicity's eyes popped opened. It was Gwen from the climbing shop, her head poking through the café's door, her dozen braids quivering.

"What?"

"He's going up on the tightrope."

Tightrope? Curious, she followed Gwen into the gym. At the far end, climbers were huddled beneath two giant boulders that were twenty-five feet high and twenty feet apart. A figure on top of each mammoth rock was busy knotting down a line between them. One of the figures was Magee.

Felicity felt her eyes bulge. "*What* is going on?"

Gwen's gaze was glued to the activity above them. "It's called tightroping a slack line."

"Slack?" Felicity squeaked. Slack did not sound good.

Gwen nodded. "Circus ropes are tight, helps with balance. But Magee and my brother won't have that much tension on the rope."

"Before they walk on it." She was still squeaking.

The girl sent her an impatient glance. "Don't be such a sissy. I've seen Magee walk a line a hundred feet off the ground. All it takes is incredible balance and *juevos grande*."

Felicity's stomach churned. "Oh. Well." Were these people crazy? "If that's all."

"I knew you couldn't appreciate a man like Magee."

The you're-not-one-of-the-tribe dismissal from this tomboyish little twit made Felicity want to whack her with a high heel and then spray her silly with a particularly cloying eau de toilette. "Explain him to me, then."

"Magee's put new routes up some of the toughest mountains in the world. But he gets off all the same, he says, on a boulder or a cliff that's been climbed a hundred times before. He just looks between the regular routes and finds one even hairier, even sicker." She shrugged. "And then he does it."

"It's a math thing," Felicity murmured. "A math problem."

Gwen's head turned around to stare at her. "You *do* know him."

She didn't. Because he claimed to be giving up the very thing that so very clearly defined him. But there was no time to puzzle out why when one of the men—Gwen's brother, she was told—clipped a short lead from his harness to the line strung between the boulders. With a grin for the crowd gathered below, and then another for Magee, he started across.

At his first wide-armed step, the rope sank and Felicity gasped. "Something's wrong."

"Nah," Gwen replied. "Climbing ropes are designed to stretch a foot or two when under stress."

Tension! Stress! Apparently these people didn't know the meaning of the word, because they were all watching the man wobble and dip with a nonchalance that had Felicity ready to scream. And then she did, just a short, choked-off one, when, halfway across, Gwen's brother lost his balance. His fall was a quick, downward jerk as if an invisible Jaws lurked in the ocean of air beneath him.

At the same instant, the lead clipped at the man's waist pulled taut and his fist closed over the line. Hanging by one arm, he wryly grinned at the spattering of applause from those below. Then he walked himself, hand over hand, to the boulder he'd started from and scrambled back on top.

At his go-ahead gesture, Felicity realized it was Magee's turn.

He'd removed his shirt and shoes. His naked torso gleamed under the fluorescent lights. In contrast to his pleated dress slacks and polished leather belt, his ripped pectorals and sculpted abdominal muscles appeared even more powerful and primitive.

Folding her arms tight against her chest, Felicity reminded herself she liked civilized, cerebral men. Her gaze stuck on Magee, though, as he called out something insulting to his challenger, then approached the tightrope and clipped on his own safety leash from the slack line to the harness around his hips.

Even from two and a half stories below, she could see the new light in his eyes and feel the heat of the daredevil rising in his blood. He glanced down at her and grinned.

She couldn't help herself. She grinned back. He looked so young, so free, so full of energy that it didn't matter, suddenly, how "sick" and how "hairy" the tightrope walk appeared to her. His confidence was infectious. If at that moment he'd told her he was going to fly, she'd have believed him.

He took his first step, and the climbing rope sagged.

After that, Felicity didn't blink. She just dug in, her feet to the floor, her fingernails into her palms, and watched Michael Magee stroll across air.

Oh, my Lord.

It was beautiful. *He* was beautiful. He held his head

slightly back so that his dark, bad-boy hair brushed the spine between his shoulder blades. A slight sheen of sweat glistened on his sculpted chest and arms as he moved with relaxed grace. Her heart contracted, but it was fascination, not fear, that squeezed from it.

Her breath caught as he approached the halfway point—the point where the other man had fallen. But she wasn't worried about Magee. He would have no trouble surviving this.

She wasn't so sure about herself.

Because each step of his animal-prowl brought her nearer to the brink of her own giant chasm. She sensed it yawning in front of her, she could feel it in the panicked fluttering in her belly and the pounding of her fist-tight heart. Each of his moves brought her nearer to the ledge.

Another step. Then another.

Magee didn't wobble, didn't strain, didn't hesitate.

One step more.

He glanced down, his gaze touching Felicity's face. As his bare foot reached the boulder on the other side, his intense, rawly male expression transformed into a boyish, look-what-I-can-do! smile.

Just like that, Felicity felt herself falling, her feet scrabbling on nothing, her stomach elevator-*whooshing,* and—

—then she remembered what had been written on the T-shirt he'd been wearing the night before. *WANTED: A Meaningful Overnight Relationship.*

With one massive, metaphorical effort, she slung up an imaginary arm and gripped the ledge's edge. It

only took recalling another of his T-shirt slogans—
I'm The One Your Mother Warned You About—to haul
herself back onto solid ground.

To the tune of the crowd's applause, Felicity turned
away from the tightrope, cursing herself. How could
she have put herself at so much risk?

Sure, watching him air-walk had given her the final
nudge, but she'd been flirting with disaster since the
first time she'd set eyes on him and felt that odd tug of
recognition. But falling in love with Magee would
have been flat-out ridiculous.

"Sheesh," she muttered aloud. "What a near nitwit
miss."

"Are you talking to me?"

She swung around to confront Magee. Regarding
her with a bemused smile, he slipped his arms into his
shirtsleeves. Her gaze moved from his mouth and settled on the slice of golden chest between the unbuttoned edges. This time, when her heart squeezed, her
inner thigh muscles followed suit.

"Charm-ish," she added. "Embarrassing, irresponsible, and shameless." He wasn't her type. His T-shirts
weren't her type. The uncivilized way he went about
sex wasn't the way she liked it at all.

"Oh, *God*." She closed her eyes. *Don't think about
the sex*. Don't think about the control he had over his
body in order to walk across that rope.

"You're trembling." Magee's voice lowered. "Are
you all right?"

"I'm fine." She couldn't let him guess she was anything but, because she was stuck in the area a few

days longer. If his magnet-and-metal-filings theory was true, she'd have to get real good at ignoring her inconvenient urges and at staying away from that looming ledge. "But I'm tired. Just get me out of here, please."

Back in his car, she shut out him and his disturbing presence by closing her eyes and huddling into the hard plastic seat. *Hold on,* she told herself. In minutes she'd be alone in her own car and leaving him behind.

Without warning, he swerved, then braked.

Startled, her eyes popped open and then she was startled all over again. She must have dozed off, because outside the windshield was dark desert night and a black ribbon of road surrounded by scrub-covered sand.

"Where are we?" she demanded.

Stupid question. They were nowhere! "Take me back to the convention center. Take me to my car."

"We haven't had that talk. Look, Felicity . . ." He turned in his seat to face her and placed a gentle hand on her knee.

She nearly jumped out of her skin. It was the late hour, the dark, the desert. It was him and how her reckless, wicked body responded to him.

He frowned. "You're trembling again. Is it the air-walk? I didn't mean to scare you." Reassuring and friendly, he squeezed her knee.

The top of her head almost hit the roof of the car, but this time she managed to find her voice. "Of course you didn't scare me. Nothing about you scares me. I could never be scared by you or anything to do

with you. As a matter of fact, you so not scare me
that . . ."

Argh, she thought, edging her leg out from under
his palm. On the scale of denials, what she'd let loose
was much closer to Babbling Defense than Emphatic
Truth.

He stayed silent a moment, then prodded her again.
"That what? What is it?"

In search of inspiration, she shifted her gaze away
from his dangerous, gorgeous face toward the bleak
desert landscape. *Find something.* Telling him that
she wanted him so much it was scaring her wasn't a
smart move. *Find something else.*

"Um . . . spiders, all right? I was thinking about
spiders."

His eyes narrowed as if GRASPING AT STRAWS were
written on her forehead in big block letters. "Spiders."
Oh, yeah, he sounded dubious. "Just thinking of them
makes your bones rattle."

"Yes." That part was true. "Ask anybody. Ask
Ashley."

His jaw tightened and he straightened in his seat.
"Felicity, about Ashley—"

"She'll tell you! So let's go back to Half Palm, let's
go back right now, and she'll tell you all about it."

Magee's eyes narrowed again, and it was obvious
her eagerness to get away from him was reigniting his
suspicions. "You tell me."

She hesitated. Damn, she'd painted herself into a
corner. He wasn't going to be satisfied without a confession, and the only other one that felt ready to trip

off her tongue was drastically close to the David Cassidy variety. And she'd rip out her tongue—not to mention her heart—before she leaped onto the seat and belted out, "I Think I Love You."

Because it wasn't true.

It would never be true.

"Felicity?" He switched on the overhead light.

She blinked to adjust her eyes to the dazzle. "Freud would have a field day with the spiders, okay?"

Magee raised an eyebrow. "You're telling *me* you're nuts? I've seen those rubber gloves you sell."

She smiled a little. "And almost bought them, too."

"Okay, so we're both a little crazy." He stretched out his legs in the large space between their seats and crossed his ankles. "Go on."

"The spider thing, well . . ." She'd toss it out there and then he'd take her back home. "We—me and a bunch of cousins—were camping out in Aunt Vi's back yard. I was little—four years old. My parents were spending the weekend in Las Vegas."

As usual, she closed her eyes, trying to conjure them up, and for a moment, for the first time ever, she thought she . . . But no. Opening her eyes again, she looked up at Magee. "It was tarantula migration season. When the grown-ups came to tell me my mom and dad had died in a car accident, they had these big flashlights that lit up the tent. And crawling all over it were . . . were the—"

She broke off, shuddering as she remembered the huge shadows creeping along the outside of the musty-smelling canvas—the hairy-legged embodiment of the bad news waiting to pounce on her. She'd always felt as if the tarantulas had carried away her security as well as her parents.

With a grimace, she lifted her hands. "Go ahead, laugh. Tell me I'm a basket case."

Shaking his head, he reached out to tangle the fingers of one hand with hers. "Everybody has their kink or two. My brother, he hates the taste, even just the smell, of Tootsie Pops."

She shouldn't let Magee touch her again. But his hand was so warm. Not sexy at the moment, but . . . strong. "I didn't know Tootsie Pops *had* a smell," she murmured, fascinated by the interlocking fit of their linked fingers.

"Like your spiders, Tootsie Pops remind him of a bad time."

After a silent moment, she looked over, tugging on his hand. "Hey. You can't leave it like that. What 'bad time'?"

He frowned. "Maybe I shouldn't—"

She shifted closer so she could swat at his shoulder with her free hand. "C'mon! I told you about the tarantulas!"

"Yeah, and thanks to you I'm going to spend the rest of my life listening for their long fangs clackety-clacking and their fat hairy legs rub-a-dub-dubbing."

Now he *was* laughing at her. Diving toward him for another swat, in her over enthusiasm she half-slid off her seat. Magee caught her, pulling her toward him to keep her from the floor. In a blink, she was sitting on his lap.

From inches away, they stared at each other. Her heart started that fist-thumping against her breastbone again as she breathed in the scent of him. Were there enough words in the world to talk herself out of this strange sense of comfort and connection? "Magee, I . . . I . . ."

As if he were afraid of what she was on the verge of saying—something she didn't know herself—Magee started talking. "They gave my brother—he's my half-brother—a bag of Tootsie Pops at the police station after his father's murder."

She blinked. "What?"

Magee's arms tightened around her. "His father was shot, almost right in front of him. He remembers unwrapping and eating those Tootsie Pops, every single one, while he waited for our mom and my dad to come get him."

The shocking information should have acted like a dash of cold water. It should have had her hopping back into her seat and demanding he return her home. But his heart was thudding against her shoulder and his breath was warm against her cheek and the intimacy of their conversation made it hard to think clearly.

She ran her fingers over his glossy bangs and down the side of his face, lingering along his cheek so that his stubble scratched her palm. "Your poor brother," she said.

Magee gave a little shrug. "So, see? You're not the only person with weird childhood shit."

She brushed his hair back, watching as the slippery

strands drifted through her fingers. "What about you, Magee?"

His gaze was focused on her mouth. "What about me?"

"What's your kink?"

He tensed for a moment, then relaxed, smiling as he lifted one finger to start tracing her top lip. "You. I think my kink just might be you."

She grabbed at the finger. "No ducking. C'mon, I gave you spiders. You give me one real kink."

In a single smooth movement, he straightened up in his seat and flipped the interior light off. She was now in the dark, and though she was still on his lap, his thighs were stiff and hard beneath her and his voice was stiff and hard, too.

"I don't have a right to any kink, okay? You said it, I grew up in sitcom suburbia. My parents are still married, they're still happy. I come from the most conventional, the most fucking functional family I know."

Hmmm. And yet he possessed one little quirk that pushed him into climbing tough mountains and air-walking across slack ropes. That last thought set her shivering again as she thought of his gleaming torso, those rippling abs, his glossy hair playing over the wide shoulders of his muscled back.

Don't think about sex, don't think about sex, don't think about sex. Trying to rein in her wayward thoughts, she restarted her mental exercise. *Z . . . y . . . x . . .*

"Lissie?" His big hand ran up her spine.

At his touch, she quivered again, this time the shiver starting inside and moving outward. Oh, God, she wanted—

No! Z . . . y . . . x . . . e . . . s . . .

X . . . e . . . s. S-e-x. She couldn't get away from it, she thought, panicking.

But wait! It was s-e-x, not l-o-v-e. In this particular instance, s-e-x was good. S-e-x was safe.

He was right, they were a magnet and metal filings, but the bonus to acting on their potent physical attraction was that having sex with Magee didn't leave room for gooey, ephemeral emotions and notions that might try moving into her heart.

Rough-and-tumble. Hot and earthy. When she was having sex with him she couldn't think of the cool, golden statue. And she couldn't think of anything terrifying and long-term like love, either. With him it wasn't emotional or spiritual. It was all about being Lissie, with greedy, animal urges. Lissie, who wanted to roll on the floor, to scratch and bite the greedy animal inside Magee.

She wound her arms around his neck, pressing her upper body into his and sinking her teeth into his bottom lip. "You need a kink then, Magee? I accept. Let your kink be me."

Thirteen

At her words, Felicity felt Magee jerk and his voice lowered in warning. "Lissie—"

She was already working on the buttons of his shirt. "C'mon, Magee, let me give *you* the thrill this time."

He stilled. "What are you up to?"

She'd made it to the buckle of the slick leather belt. It gave way, leaving only a zipper between her and her goal of mindless, heartless, down-and-dirty sex. What would her fans from GetTV think about that?

The naughty idea put a sexy little throatiness into her voice. "The real question is," she said, undoing the top button, then tugging on the little metal tab, "exactly how many inches are you up to, hmm?"

But the metal tab wasn't budging. She gripped it tighter between her thumb and forefinger and yanked. Her fingers slipped off. Setting her jaw, she went after the zipper again, but its metal teeth were clenched as tightly as her own.

She sucked in a fast, deep breath through her nose. This was clothing, damn it. She was good with cloth-

ing. She sold clothing, extolled the virtues of clothing, made people *yearn* for clothing. A simple fas-
tener of fabric would *not* get the best of her.

With a small growl, she attacked.

And failed again.

No. She wanted sex! She wanted to feel that flood
of heated passion, that flood that would drive everything dangerous and frightening out of the way. She
wanted that Erica Jong moment when the clothes
peeled away. That anonymous, zipless fuck. Her eyes
stung. But she couldn't even get the stupid clothes to
cooperate! No wonder Erica Jong had called it a *zipless* fuck.

"Can I help you with anything down there?" asked
a bemused male voice.

Magee. In her tempestuous passion and almost-
panic, she'd nearly forgotten all about him.

Impatient, she tried to explain what she wanted.
"It's Jong—"

"You've said that before, dollface, and I appreciate
your noticing," he said modestly.

She shook her head. "No, really. *Jong.*"

"Thanks. Really long, I know."

It made her laugh. She wasn't sure if he was teasing
or if it even mattered, because laughing reminded her
not to take this so seriously. It wasn't life-or-death. It
wasn't heart-whole or heartbreak. It was the opposite
of all that. It was wanting sex with *Magee,* the most
casual of all men.

So she took each open edge of his dress shirt in a

fist. "Listen up," she said. "I want earthy, raw, bad-to-the-bone sex, and I want it right now."

He groaned. "Hell, Lissie, what am I supposed to say to that?"   .

She slid off his lap, settling onto her knees on the metal floorboards between the two seats. From between his splayed thighs, she looked up at him and smiled. "You're supposed to say yes, and the nastier you say it, the better."

Now the zipper parted like butter. Inside it, he was hard, hot, and smooth. She took a bracing breath, then began indulging herself on his body, running her mouth up his sex and beyond, tickling his navel, licking one nipple, then rubbing her cheek over the lean, taut pad of pec muscle to find the other. It puckered against her tongue and her womb clenched.

He was murmuring something—cursing, maybe—but she couldn't tell because her sense of hearing was subjugated to her other senses—the ones that were relishing the salty-citrus taste of him, the sleek, firm feel of him, the heated scent of the both of them together.

Making her way back down his chest, her lips bumped over his fascinating male topography. She wished she was a painter, able to capture all his hard, muscled beauty on a canvas, but she settled for making her tongue into a brush and stroking over every inch, rendering the image in her mind.

Her mouth found his erection again. It was hotter now, harder. As she bent over him, he speared his fingers in her hair, the urgency of the gesture driving up her own need. Her blood was humming with it, singing. This was what she wanted, the flavor of desire in her mouth and the flame of it burning through her body.

Earthy, raw, bad-to-the-bone sex.

Her pulse jumped higher and she took him deeper, taking herself deeper into mindless sex. Heartless sex.

His fingers bit into her scalp, then he grabbed her by the upper arms. She found herself being pulled free of him, off her knees and back into his arms. They tightened when she squirmed, wanting to dive back into that heavy, throbbing place of desire.

"Don't move," he choked out. "You're killing me, Lissie. Give me a minute. Just a minute."

But nothing was going to stand between her and her need for earthy, zipless sex. She twisted against him and found his mouth, plunging her tongue inside. He groaned, the sound a buzz against her tongue and against her breastbone, plastered to his. He slid his hand between them to make quick work of her buttons. In short order he had her blouse undone, the front clasp of her bra unfastened, her garments spread to expose her breasts to his gaze.

He held her upper body away from him to look at her, and she watched his breath rasp in and out of his chest. With his nostrils flared and his hair mussed, he looked like trouble—a reckless, hot-blooded lover who was going to take her down with him.

She couldn't wait.

"Magee. Magee, please."

He glanced up at her, and she saw what she wanted

in his eyes. Risk and defiance and heated intent. He
wouldn't care if he marred her polish. He wouldn't
worry about fingerprints or scratches. He was the
bad-boy, tempting devil of all her gotta-be-a-good-
girl fantasies and he was going to give it to her hard
and fast.

He smiled, slow and seductive. His voice was dark
and bad. "I've got your number now, Lissie."

She shivered.

"You're the one who they trusted to work in the at-
tendance office, aren't you? But you'd help out guys
like me, wouldn't you? Cut class? Go see Lissie.
She'll fix it for you."

The skin between her breasts prickled as he drew
an idle pattern there. "You'd be my biology partner,
too. The old fart who taught the class hoped that a
sweet thing like you would keep me in line. But you'd
do all the work yourself and then put my name on it,
right next to yours."

She tensed as his wandering finger edged toward
her nipple. It was aching, hurting for his touch, but he
was still talking, teasing her, telling just like it was.

"And you're the one, Lissie," he continued, "the
one with the sweetheart image by day but who by
night unlocked her bedroom window and let the
scruffy boy with the motorcycle crawl into her room
and into her bed."

Her breath stuttered into her lungs. Yes. *Yes*. She'd
never done any of those things, but she'd wanted to.
Oh, how she'd always wanted to.

His fingers closed gently over the throbbing tip of

her breast. But it wasn't enough. Not enough. She squirmed on his lap and he lightened his touch. She stilled, moaning.

His forefinger and thumb clasped her nipple again and he laughed, a rough, threatening, delicious sound. "Oh, yeah. There's no doubt about it. You, Lissie, are a very, very bad girl." And then he squeezed.

Every muscle clenched. She arched toward him, wanting more of that not-quite-painful touch, wanting him to unleash every bad-girl craving burning inside of her. As his head dipped toward her bare breasts, she managed to shuck her suit jacket, blouse, and bra.

"I'm ready," she whispered to him as his wet mouth latched on to her. The devil could have his way with her.

But then something happened. Somewhere between the rasp of his tongue on her hard nipples and the shedding of the rest of their clothes, the devil and the bad girl slowed down. Urgency thrummed beneath her skin, but he stoked her fire with soothing strokes, lingering here, playing there.

Even when she found herself sitting sideways on the passenger seat, with Magee kneeling, her thighs over his shoulders, his mouth was gentle, his tongue not taking her anywhere, but exploring her *everywhere*. It was raw and it was earthy and it was . . .

Not.

It was Lissie and Michael—she kept calling out that

name, over and over. It was passionate, but when he made her come the first time she had tears in her eyes.

It was everything that Erica Jong described in *Fear of Flying*—passionate and exciting—except it wasn't anonymous. Because as Michael entered her, his gaze didn't leave hers.

"Lissie, Lissie, Lissie," he whispered. "Oh, sweetheart. You are so, so bad."

And he was so, so good. Hard and strong and parting through the folds of her body with the same sureness as when he'd parted the veils covering her secret self.

Just as she reached for her pleasure, just as she knew it would take only a few strokes more, three, two, she closed her eyes. A haze of golden warmth spread behind her eyelids, reminding her of something. . . . But she was too close to think any longer.

He thrust in, deep, and held there.

"Michael," she cried out, and, pressing herself up against him, convulsed.

Neither spoke as they drove out of the desert and back to her car, parked in the convention center lot. Once there, he turned off the engine and ran his hand over his hair, then rubbed at the back of his neck.

"Well," he said, looking over at her. Unsmiling.

Felicity swallowed. "Well."

"That was—"

"Did you—"

They both broke off.

"Go," he said, gesturing to her with his chin.

She didn't remember what she'd been about to say. "Did . . . did you . . . um, oh, yeah, did you have something you wanted to talk to me about?"

"What?"

She swallowed again. "Earlier, earlier tonight, I think you mentioned . . ."

"Oh. Right. It was . . . it was nothing." He looked away from her, out the windshield, then looked back. "So, you're around a few more days."

She nodded. "Just a few. Scouting locations. Spots where we can get some good shots of climbers."

He rubbed his bristly jaw with the back of his hand. "I can help with that. I'll show you some places."

"Oh. Okay. That . . . that would be great. I guess." She didn't sound enthusiastic, she knew that, but then neither did he.

Her fingers found the door handle.

"Lissie."

She paused. "Yes?"

"You gonna be all right?"

"Truth?"

He hesitated a moment, then nodded. "Yeah."

"My knees are murder."

There was a moment of stunned silence, then he released a bark of laughter. "God, no kidding. Mine are screaming at me."

She nodded in empathetic understanding.

Then he grinned at her—and he looked . . . happy. "We'll take care of that tomorrow, too, dollface. I promise."

Felicity gave him a squiggle-fingered wave and

hopped out. As promises went, it was more than she'd expected from Magee.

The next afternoon, she trudged after him along a dusty path. "Flintstones, meet the Flintstones," she sang beneath her breath.

He glanced over his shoulder. "What's that?"

She gestured at their surroundings. The arid landscape of the "wilderness area" they were walking through was studded with prehistoric-looking, tumbled outcroppings of sandstone boulders, most bigger than houses, many taller than office buildings. "I'm preparing for my introduction to Fred and Wilma. This place is seriously Stone Age."

She paused a moment to study one of the Joshua trees that dotted the area. The twisted branches coming off its equally twisted trunk were tufted with speared leaves. "And these things have always struck me as something Dr. Seuss might have dreamed up."

He grinned. "Welcome to my world, baby."

It *was* his world. Or at least had been, that was clear. Earlier that day he'd taken her by several popular bouldering areas—what they called the sport of climbing the strange sandstone beasts—and she'd been awed by what she'd seen. Women and men scaling walls like Spiderman, their fingers and flexible shoes finding cracks and ledges she couldn't see.

Another group had been doing something straight out of a Marine recruiting film—rappelling down the side of a six-story rock. Farther off, she'd glimpsed specks on top of the tallest boulder yet—a skyscraper!—her gaze landing on them just as one of the tiny figures tossed a coiled rope over the side.

Magee appeared to know everyone and everything about what they were doing, from their equipment to their routes to their chances for success. At their last stop, a climber in a bandanna 'do-rag and a ragged *Yosemite Mountaineering School* T-shirt had offered Magee a waist harness and a rope, but he'd shaken his head.

"I don't climb anymore," he'd declared, his expression closing off.

Mr. Bandanna hadn't questioned any further. In silence, Magee had stalked back to the Jeep.

As he'd started driving again, she'd tried to probe what was going on inside his head. "So why does anyone do it? Climb, I mean. Why did you?"

He was quiet a moment, then answered. "There are as many whys as there are climbers. To appreciate nature. As a physical or mental challenge. To leave stuff like money troubles or the asshole at work behind—ordinary, everyday worries—because they don't matter when your life depends on the very next step or the very next move."

He'd subsided into a brooding silence again, and she'd let it go, though she suspected she wasn't any closer to *his* why than she'd been before.

But now, as his strides ate up the ground in front of them, he appeared to be distancing himself from his dark mood. Hurrying after him, she was forced into a trot. Beads of sweat rolled down her temple, clearing a sticky path through the layer of gritty dust covering her skin, and she grimaced.

"Hey, listen. I've seen plenty already," she called out. "Really."

The other locations he'd taken her to had been camping or picnicking sites as well, but this area appeared deserted. Felicity glanced over her shoulder. They'd left the Jeep behind ten minutes ago but thanks to a rise they'd headed up, then over, she'd lost sight of the vehicle. "Do you have the creepy feeling that we might be the last two people left on earth?"

He took a sharp right and beelined toward another one of those primeval outcroppings. She hurried behind, but lost sight of him as he threaded through the jumble of massive boulders. "Magee?" Her voice was *not* warbling, she could almost swear it wasn't, even though she was preoccupied by thoughts of spiders and snakes and why she hadn't insisted on keeping the car keys in *her* pocket. "*Magee?*"

"This way."

She followed the sound of his voice, embarrassed by how relieved she felt when she edged around another boulder and caught sight of his boots.

His empty boots.

Beside a dusty pile of his empty clothes.

A panicked thought speared her. He'd been abducted by aliens. Maybe that's what had happened to Ben!

"*Michael?*"

"I'm over here."

She whirled, found herself facing a vee'd notch of space between two huge boulders. Stepping through it, she found him. Her feet stumbled to a stop, toes of her sneakers splashing in water at the outer edge of a natural pool, about as big as a hot tub for six. Magee lounged in it, naked.

"What are you doing?"

"Soaking my knees." He grinned at her. "I promised relief, didn't I? The water's just right, not too hot and not too cold. C'mon, get in."

Her eyes widened. "No!"

"Why not?"

She glanced around. "Because—"

"Someone might see you?" One of his eyebrows arched in a challenge. "There's only me, and I've already looked my fill, right?"

A shiver shimmied down her back. "Yes, but—"

"Someone might come along? I doubt it, but let's drum up one of your infamous excuses, just in case." He stretched both arms along the lip of the pool and tilted his head, as if in thought. "I know. You're a park ranger, with a sworn duty to protect all natural pools from . . . foreign bodies. If anyone shows, I'll affect a Ukrainian accent and you can frisk me for my passport."

"Don't scoff."

"Please. You're the only scoffee in my life and I'm beginning to enjoy it."

She stuck out her tongue at him.

"Ah, you're just mad because I wore my *I'm With Stupid* T-shirt today."

That made her smile, because the phrase was on the back of the shirt and she'd just happened to have a Sharpie marker with her. At their first stop, under the pretext of removing some burrs, she'd held the fabric away from his body and penned out the *With*.

He crooked his finger at her. "C'mere. You know you want to."

Oh, she did. Because she was hot. Because her knees *did* ache. Because she'd woken up giddy at the idea of spending the day with him and she didn't want their time together to end.

Yet, she added. Not *yet*.

Her fingers went to the hem of her shirt. "Don't look."

Of course the devil didn't even bother pretending he didn't. But feeling naughty and daring, she threw off her clothes anyway and slipped into the water on the other side of the pool. But then his smug expression made her self-conscious, so she closed her eyes to enjoy the sensation of warm air and tepid water.

"Beautiful day," he said.

She nodded. Desert daytime temperatures in winter usually wavered between the pleasant seventies and eighties. Her eyes drifted open and she took in the stark blue of the dry, smog-free air. "Not beautiful in the summer, though."

"It's not that bad."

She waved a hand at him. "So says you, with your air-conditioning and your secret springs. At Aunt Vi's house we had an old swamp cooler that broke down the afternoon school let out in June and stayed broken until past Labor Day. My cousins and I used to scrounge for change every day to buy our way into the community pool to cool off."

"Yeah, but then you left all that behind for Our Lady of Prim and Proper."

"Our Lady of *Poverty*."

"Sorry. Our Lady of *Poverty*."

She frowned at him, trying to determine if he was scoffing at her again, or worse, judging her. But she couldn't read the expression on his face and then he closed his eyes and rested the back of his head against the ledge of the pool.

Still, in the silence that followed she couldn't shake the notion that he was thinking the words that no one else had ever said to her. Not Aunt Vi, not Ashley, not any of the Charms. She tried pushing the thought away, but it loomed too large in her mind, spoiling the day, the relaxed atmosphere, these moments with this man who had begun to be a kind of . . . of friend to her.

She swallowed, trying to sound calm. "You have no idea what it's like to be me."

"You're right," he answered, without opening his eyes.

She waited for him to keep talking. To ask her to explain herself. But he did nothing more than stay still and silent.

"OLPP was a great educational opportunity," she finally said.

He grunted.

"I made friends with important people." She bit her lip. "Influential people." God, that sounded worse.

She rubbed her forehead with a wet hand. "One of them recommended me to her alma mater. I went to the University of Southern California on a full-ride academic scholarship."

His mouth curved up. "Go, Trojans."

He wasn't getting it. She wanted him to understand, she wanted him to like her. People always liked her! They'd been getting along so well and it was—it was important to her that he, in particular, didn't think less of her.

She waded through the water toward him. "Look, I couldn't stay at my old school."

In a slow movement he straightened and opened his eyes. "No?"

"No. The summer before I changed schools, I . . . I had an incident with the principal, Mrs. Myers."

"What did you do? Try to sell her some light-up ice cubes?"

"She caught me trying to scam her husband."

His eyebrows arched. "Scamming him how?"

"I told you how we used to scrounge for the entrance fee to get into the pool."

His gaze never leaving hers, he nodded.

"We had a con. My cousins and I. My oldest cousin, Mark, would take us to the shopping center in the next town. We had brochures for a kids' with cancer summer camp in Idyllwild and Polaroids of ourselves taken with our five-year-old neighbor who had a really bad buzz haircut." Her voice lowered to a near-whisper and heat rushed up her neck. "We approached shoppers in the parking lot and said we were collecting money so our sick little brother could attend the camp."

"Then one fine day you gave your pitch to the principal's husband."

She nodded. "And when he was digging out his wallet, she walked out of the store."

"I suppose she knew you didn't have a little brother with cancer."

"Yes. She knew the Charm family well. So she snatched the photograph and the brochure out of my hand and ripped them up."

He let a beat go by. "And then?"

She blinked. " 'And then'?"

"And then did she call security? Did she grab hold of your earlobe and haul you home? Did she threaten to blackball you from the elementary school's honor roll?"

Felicity felt another burning wave of heat washing over her face. "She told me I should be ashamed. Of myself. Of the Charms." The words croaked out. "And then I was, Magee. I was ashamed to my very soul."

Magee pulled Felicity's wet little body into his arms, even as he told himself he should be running from her. She'd been trying to kill him from the beginning. First with her car, then with sex, but now the attempts had turned serious.

That summer camp story had nearly finished him

off. He could picture it so easily, the little orphaned kid criticized for the only family she had left in the world.

He kissed her. There was nothing he could do to stop himself. Despite his unspoken agreement with Ashley, after the knee-bruising with Felicity in his car last night, he'd given up on staying away from her. The way he figured it, their affair could last until she left town. Then he'd return to the straight and narrow, a last 3-D Club fling behind him.

"Magee—"

He kissed his name off her lips. That name. Magee had other obligations. Felicity, ashamed of her family, had left them behind and now sold stuff on TV.

It was Michael and Lissie who made love.

Later, as he drove back toward Half Palm, he glanced over at her. Her eyes looked drowsy, her mouth swollen. If they weren't careful, someone was bound to guess what they'd been up to.

He knew he should feel guilty about it, but he supposed Denali hadn't scoured the hedonist out of him altogether.

Ah, don't be such a yobbo! It's all going to come good.

The Aussie accent, the Aussie words startled him. He glanced over at Felicity again. "Did you say something, dollface?"

She turned her head toward him and frowned. "Was I thinking out loud?"

He shrugged. "What were you thinking?"

"About Ben." She sighed. "I'm still worried about

him—a little, anyway. I was wishing he'd followed my advice."

"What advice is that?" Magee reached over to brush a lock of her soft, feathery hair off her cheek.

"I called Aunt Vi a month or so ago and he answered. During our conversation, he mentioned he was short on cash. I told him to get a job."

Magee smiled. "I've told him the same thing myself a time or two."

"I even had a good lead. I suggested he go see the Carusos."

Magee's heart gave one heavy *thwomp* and stopped. He coughed, trying to get it beating again, trying to find his voice. "The *Carusos*? You told him to go to the *Carusos* for money?"

She didn't appear to notice he was having trouble breathing. "I went to OLPP with the Caruso girls. The family grows and packages foods for the gourmet market. I'm sure you've seen the La Vita Buona plant outside of Palm Desert. They call old Mr. Caruso, the grandfather, the Sun-Dried Tomato King."

"Godfather," Magee choked out. "They also call him Godfather."

"What?" Felicity blinked at him. "What are you saying?"

He wanted to say he was certain now that he wasn't going to survive knowing her. But instead, he turned off toward the Bivy, where he'd have a phone and privacy. "I'm going to call my brother. He lives in Las Vegas. He'll know for sure."

"Know what?"

"If I'm right that the people you sent your cousin to have their fingers in something other than tomatoes—like loan-sharking. The way I've heard it, the Carusos are the first family of the California Mafia."

The Bivy had just opened when they arrived. He jogged to the office, leaving Felicity to make excuses or explanations to Peter and Ashley. It wasn't clear which she'd offered up when he emerged. She was standing near the bar, quietly talking with the other two.

She read the answer on his face, her eyes going big and her hand creeping over her stomach. "Magee?"

"Mafia, all right," he said to her. "If Ben went to the Carusos for money, he could be in real trouble."

"No," she whispered. "Can it be?"

"Yes." It was Ashley who said the word.

Their heads swiveled toward her. Magee wondered if perhaps one of Felicity's earlier attempts on his life had affected his hearing.

"He did," Ashley went on, louder. "He went to the Carusos for me."

Fourteen

Of the three stunned people staring at her, Ashley could meet the eyes of only one. "I didn't ask Ben to," she told Magee. "I wish he hadn't."

Would any of them understand? Felicity wouldn't. Felicity had been born standing on her own two feet. She'd lost her parents, she'd moved away from Half Palm, she'd gone about making a life for herself, by herself.

Still, Ashley had to try to make them see.

"After Simon died, one night . . . one night a girl-friend took me to the Easy Money Casino outside Half Palm." Even now she could remember how the flashing lights and ding-ding-ding of the machines had dazzled her, distracting her head and her heart from the weight of grief and the realities of single parenthood. "I . . ." She shrugged. "Liked it."

Magee scrubbed his face with his hands, then shook his head, as if he were waking up from a bad dream.

"What does that have to do with Ben?" Felicity asked, her voice gentle.

Ashley risked a glance at her. Her younger cousin didn't look angry or even aghast any longer. There was a wrinkle of concern on her forehead and puzzlement in her eyes.

"Once I started playing more often, I . . . I took out cash advances on my credit cards. Big advances. When I started having trouble making the minimum payments, I told Ben—"

"Why didn't you tell me?" Magee was frowning now, but like Felicity, he looked more troubled than mad.

Ashley shrugged. "You were already doing so much. . . ." From the corner of her eye she took a peek at Peter. But he'd half-pivoted his chair away from her so that she couldn't gauge his expression.

She looked down at her hands, clenched together at her waist. Peter *would* understand. He probably already did. He was one of her best friends, she assured herself. Maybe her very best friend. Despite the recent tension between them, she could count on his sympathy and support.

"So Ben decided to help you, is that it, Ash?" Felicity sounded gentle still.

"He thought he could come up with some cash to help me out. So he started going to the casino, too."

Magee cursed beneath his breath.

"I told him not to play the slots," Ashley said quickly. "I made him promise he wouldn't. He was sure he'd do all right betting on sports."

Magee muttered another curse. Felicity guessed what happened next. "But he didn't do all right. So he went to the Carusos to—what? Bail you out? Bail himself out at the casino?"

Shaking her head, Ashley wrapped her arms around herself. "The casino wouldn't give the Charms any credit. But I still owed all that money on my cards and Ben was flat broke. A few days before he disappeared, he told me he'd gotten his hands on some more cash. He was going to use it as his stake to win big for both of us."

Now Magee groaned, but Felicity ignored him. "So you don't know for sure that he went to the Carusos," she pointed out.

"No . . . not for sure. But he may have mentioned the name."

The long silence following that said everything Magee and Felicity didn't.

"I know, I know," Ashley said. "I should have told Mom when he didn't come home. I should have told you, Magee, or you, Felicity, when you came to town. But I . . . I didn't want to sound a false alarm. Not when I wasn't exactly sure what had happened."

Even to her own ears, her excuses sounded helpless. Pitiful. Which was exactly how she felt.

Felicity turned to Magee. "Okay, let's think. What have we got? Ben possibly taking a loan from the Carusos. Some men looking for Ben who say he owes them money."

"Men who mean business." Peter spoke for the first time, but Ashley couldn't detect his mood from his voice. "I heard a story about three slick guys who picked on a Ben look-alike outside another bar a few nights ago. They demanded the money he owed them and slugged him a few times before they checked his ID and realized their mistake."

The fear Ashley had been running from caught up with her now, grabbing her around the back of the neck like an icy hand. "But there's the note," she whispered. "The one Ben left on the car saying he's okay."

"*Was* okay," Felicity corrected. "Maybe by now they've found him and—wait, wait, *wait*." She rounded on Magee. "I don't believe what I'm saying. Are you sure about this? The Carusos grow produce, that's a fact. The girls went to OLPP with me, and I heard that one of them now has her own interior design business. Their grandfather is the Sun-dried Tomato King!"

Magee drummed his fingers against his thigh. "I know. They do own legitimate businesses."

Felicity sighed. "I think we need another Charm family meeting."

Family. The icy hand on Ashley's neck squeezed. "Felicity, do me a favor? Please? Go straight to Mom's. Anna P. is there with her. You and Magee stay with them until I'm off work."

The door to the Bivy opened and a raucous group of dusty climbers pushed in. "Hey where's the music?" one yelled.

"I need a beer," ordered another.

Barstool legs screeched against the floor. "Make that three beers!"

Magee shot a look at Peter. "I can stay. Help out."

But the other man shook his head. "Do what Ash wants. Jim's on in an hour to tend the other half of the bar. We'll be fine."

Wearing that worried wrinkle between her eyebrows again, Felicity reached over to rub Ashley's upper arm. "Why don't we trade places for the evening, Ash? I'll play waitress. You go home to Anna P."

"No." It was Peter again. "Ashley's on tonight and Ashley will do her job."

No? To Ashley, getting her daughter and then going home and pulling the covers over her head sounded like all she could handle right now. She opened her mouth to say so, just as Peter lifted his gaze to hers, meeting her eyes for the very first time since her confession.

The frigid anger that she saw in them froze the words in her throat. Speechless, she accepted a consoling hug from Felicity and a shoulder squeeze from Magee before the two of them headed off, leaving her to face Peter, the one person she thought would have accepted her mistakes.

The one person who looked as if he wanted to burn her at the stake.

She decided to avoid him as much as possible, which wasn't difficult, since the evening was busy. He passed her orders over the bar, but other than that he didn't send her so much as a smile—but neither did he send another harsh word or cold glance. As the night wore on, she began to wonder if she'd imagined his earlier reaction.

That was it! He'd been surprised by what she'd said about Ben and about her gambling . . . situation, but Peter wouldn't desert her. He knew she was the kind of woman who depended on the men in her life.

He took a break at eleven, calling out he'd only be ten minutes. Waving a hand in acknowledgment, she let herself relax a little more. By the time he returned, the bar would be quieter. They could have a few minutes of their usual, comfortable conversation.

She needed the usual. She needed the comfortable.

Fifteen minutes passed. Then twenty. She cast a glance toward the door to the combined storeroom/break room, but it didn't budge. A little niggle of concern tickled her spine, but she didn't have a spare second to act on it when a rowdy party wandered in.

Once she'd settled them with their beverages, Peter had been out on break nearly thirty minutes. Signaling to the other bartender that she'd only be gone a second, she dashed for the break room.

"Peter?" she called as she opened the door.

"Go away."

His voice sounded strained, but she couldn't see him or into the small break area—essentially a folding table and a couple of chairs—because of some tall stacks of cased beer. "Is everything all right?"

"I'll be out soon. *Go away.*"

For a moment she considered it. But there was something in his voice . . .

She took a slow step around the stacks of beer. Then, seeing him bent over in his chair, she rushed forward. "Peter! What happened?"

"Damn it." His shoulders hunched and he twisted away from her. "I told you to get out of here."

The harsh tone of his voice was enough to make her hesitate, but not enough to get rid of her. "Is something the matter? Do you want Jim instead of me?"

"No, I don't want Jim instead of you. I don't want anyone."

She'd come up behind him. "You've hurt yourself!" He was cradling his left hand in his lap. Now she could see there was a broken bottle on the floor, that his hand was wrapped in a crimson-stained towel, and that Peter's face had gone chalky.

Her eyes widened and she backed up a step. "I'll call an ambulance. You must have lost a lot of blood."

Peter swayed in his chair. "No!" he choked out. "Not a lot of blood."

Puzzled, she strode back to him and peered into his lap again. "You need to show me."

With a disgusted sound, he turned his face away and lifted the towel.

He was right. There wasn't all that much blood. The cut was hardly bigger than the one she'd gotten on her finger the other day in her kitchen. "Then what's the matter?"

"Makes me sick," he muttered, throwing the towel back over the injury. "The sight of blood makes me sick. Now go away."

She stared at him. "You're afraid of blood?"

He made that disgusted sound again. "For God's sake, yes. Terrified. Horrified. Makes-me-want-to-barf scared. Okay? Are you satisfied?"

Keeping a cautious eye on him, she headed for the first-aid kit mounted on the nearby wall. Then, with the antiseptic and a wide adhesive bandage in hand, she crossed back to Peter. It only took a second or two to take care of the cut, but even after it was done, he wouldn't look at her.

She disposed of the stained towel then went about sweeping up the broken glass. "I had no idea you were afraid of anything."

He mumbled something.

The pieces of glass clattered to the bottom of the metal trash can. "What did you say?"

"I said, 'To hell with it.'"

Startled, she looked over at him. "Peter?"

His face was set, his eyes glittering. "I said, 'To hell with it.' Why should I worry about hiding my weaknesses from you anymore? You don't want me, so what's the big deal about another flaw or two?"

"It's not a flaw—"

"And why you should be critical of *me,* I don't know. Jesus Christ, Ashley, you get into gambling and into credit card debt and your way of dealing with it is to tell your dumbass of a baby brother?"

"I wanted to take care of it myself—"

"Give me a break, Ash." He pushed his chair toward the door. "Calling in Ben to bail you out is not taking care of it yourself."

She flushed in shame. Peter was right about that. "Well, you know I'm not good at—"

"And don't give me that, either. That crap about needing a strong man." He spun the chair to face her, his expression furious. "That's a bullshit excuse. Bullshit! You let Simon roll over you when he was alive. You let Magee baby you after Simon was dead. But you forget that I've seen you when both of them weren't around. Simon would be gone for weeks at a time, and you were fine then, Ash, and good at taking care of yourself, your job, your home, Anna P. You'd be fine again if you'd can the clinging vine act."

He spun around and wheeled toward the door again. "Take the advice of someone stuck sitting down, Ash, the advice of someone who'd trade years off his life to be able to do what you should. Put your own two feet on the floor and stand the fuck *up*."

Ashley trailed Magee, who carried Anna P. over his shoulder, through the dark house. She followed him into her daughter's room and watched as he laid the little girl on her pillow. Ashley drew up the covers.

On the bedside table, next to the framed photo of Simon, was Anna P.'s favorite stuffed animal. Magee lifted the fleece llama and tucked it beneath Anna P.'s chin. Then he took Ashley's hand in his warm one and led her out.

In the living room, he left her to flip on the nearby lamp. She stood where she was, her heartbeat sluggish, her mind numb.

Magee turned and studied her for a moment. Then he crossed to her again, once more taking her hand. His fingers were so warm and strong. She let her hand rest in his.

"I've let you down, Ash," Magee said. "I'm sorry."

She should shake her head. She shouldn't let him take any blame. But that took so much energy and she was so, so cold.

"It's not going to happen again," Magee continued.

He took a deep breath and Ashley envied him the ability. The conversation with Peter in the bar's break room earlier that night had stolen hers.

Magee's fingers tightened on her hand. "Ashley, look at me."

Strong men made everything so easy. She did as he asked.

"I should have been clearer about this before, Ash," he said. "I want you to marry me. Marry me and let me look after you and Anna P., just like Simon would."

Simon. Ashley latched on to the thought of him. Brash, loud, larger-than-life Simon. The one who always knew what she should do. He *would* want that. He would want her and Anna P. to have someone like Magee to lean on.

"Say yes, Ash," Magee urged.

Once again, she obeyed.

Aunt Vi's cats were underfoot, the TV was droning, Charms were wandering between the kitchen and the living room. The only family member who appeared to feel any urgency, Felicity thought, grinding her back teeth, was herself.

"Ben may have gotten into trouble with the *Mafia*," she said again. "Don't you think that requires some action?" The family fidgeted. Knees shifted, coffee cups rattled, someone passed out old copies of *Us* magazine.

Only Aunt Vi appeared to hear her. "Ashley and Magee aren't here yet. Maybe we should wait—"

"It's Ashley that got Ben into this mess!" It was out before she could stop it. And then, worse, she sensed movement behind her.

Aunt Vi fluttered. "Good morning, you two. Can I get you anything?"

Felicity looked over her shoulder. The late comers, of course. Her gaze slid off Ashley's face and then caught the strange expression on Magee's. He was looking at her with— She couldn't put her finger on it. Disappointment?

She bit her lip, regretting her outburst all over again. "Sorry, Ash," she mumbled. "You're not to blame. After Simon died, I . . . I should have done something. I should have been here for you."

But she'd had a good excuse! Eighteen months ago, her career at GetTV was revving up. Her *All That's Cool Afternoon* had jumped in the ratings and she'd received a personal, glowing memo from Drew's father, the CEO of the company.

"Look, everybody, here's how it stands," she said, rubbing her forehead. "We have the note from Ben. I'm guessing he's fine and lying low somewhere safe.

But we need to find out how much money he owes or find him or both. I'm thinking a visit to the Caruso plant might be a start. And then there's Ashley—"

"I'll take care of that," Magee said, stepping forward. "Ashley, and Ben, too."

Felicity frowned at him. "We don't need your help—"

"You have it anyway." He gazed over her head at Ashley. "Because your cousin and I are engaged."

"What?" Felicity blinked up at him.

"Ashley's going to be my wife."

The room erupted in excitement. Charms pumped Magee's hand. Someone pulled Ashley forward for a round of hugs.

For her part, Felicity focused on one corner of the room and drew a mental camera there. She imagined it in detail, from the omniscient lens to the little red light on top that signaled it as the camera to play to. And then she gave it her sweet, appealing best, determined that the audience would never know that her smiles and good wishes were anything less than sincere.

Surprise. Betrayal. Humiliation.

They stayed well hidden behind her smooth, professional veneer. After a few minutes she took a little stroll into the kitchen, looking for . . . for . . . something. Her gaze snagged on her Joanie, sitting on the countertop, and she lunged for it, her knee connecting with an ajar cupboard door.

Pain bloomed over the tender skin she'd gotten from kneeling in Magee's car.

Which triggered yet another wave of humiliation.

Her hand tightened on the Joanie, and its abraded exterior scratched her palm. She looked down, staring into its still-serene gaze. "We're getting out of here," she promised.

Fifteen

Magee knew the instant Felicity left the living room. Half-relieved and half-sick at how he'd sprung the news on her, he kept watch for her return. He owed her an explanation.

The hell of it was, he didn't have a good one.

Damn it! She'd sped out of the night and blindsided *him*! He hadn't planned what happened after, not any of it. But because he couldn't keep his dick in his pants he'd screwed up. Screwed her.

But what a thrill. She was right about that.

At the screech of peeling rubber, one of the young Charms, dressed for a round of golf, glanced out the window. "Felicity," he announced. "Driving off like the cops are after her."

Magee stilled.

Vi leaned over to pick up a cat, then stroked it, a slight frown on her face. "I wonder why?"

Magee wondered where. Had she run off for L.A. without a goodbye? Without another try—and with very good reason this time—at running him over or running him through?

Maybe. He'd said he'd take care of Ashley and Ben.

We don't need your help. She'd sounded adamant about that—before, of course, he'd announced the engagement.

But hadn't she mentioned something about a visit to the Caruso plant . . . ?

The hairs on the back of his neck sprang up. Damn stupid, stubborn, crazy woman! His hand slid into his pocket and closed over his keys. He hoped he didn't know her as well as he thought he did.

Felicity pushed out of the double doors of the corporate offices of La Vita Buona Foods and right into Magee's chest. She gasped in surprise. "How did you find me?"

He grabbed her wrists. "It wasn't that hard. Now, what the hell are you doing?"

She wrenched her arms from his fingers. "What the hell I *did*," she said through her teeth, trying to keep her voice low and calm, "is meet with a representative of the Caruso family."

"You've got to be kidding. You had, what? A fifteen-minute head start on me?"

She lifted her shoulder in a nonchalant shrug. "I work fast." Then she made to step around him, intent on hurrying down the wide steps and hurrying away from Magee before she blew her cool.

He blocked her way. "We need to talk."

No! "I don't have time." She sidestepped again.

Her shoulder bumped his as she rushed down the wide steps of the office building.

He caught her elbow at the bottom of the short flight. "Where do you think you're going?"

Anywhere you're not. But she couldn't say that out loud, not and keep her pride. She couldn't let him guess what a blow it had been to hear him say he was marrying Ashley and how ashamed she was to be proven just another one of the women he'd slept with, just another one of his thrillbangs.

"Where do you think you're going?" he asked again.

Determined to appear unmoved, she looked up and met his gaze. "I'm going across the parking lot to that little store right over there, where I'll be selecting some Caruso gourmet products."

"Jesus. Shopping." He spit the last word out.

Vile, traitorous, rude man!

"It's shopping that's saving Ben's behind," she hissed, leaning toward him. Then she pulled back, frantically smoothing out her expression. *Don't let him see you're hurt.*

With quick strides she headed toward the small store, hoping his disdain for her and dislike of shopping would take him away. Far away. But he dogged her footsteps, frustration fanning from him like smoke.

"We still need to have that talk," he said.

Instead of replying, she grabbed the store's door handle. He slapped his palm against the plate glass to keep it closed. Her spine stiffened.

"Speak," he said.

"Arf, arf. Now let me go inside."

His hands landed on her shoulder and he spun her toward him. "*Felicity*. Don't be such a smart-mouth."

She glared up at him. "I have to get on with this, Magee. I need to pick out some products, then I need to call Drew and use my smart mouth to give a kick-butt pitch that convinces him they'll be sure winners for GetTV. That's the deal I made to bail out Ben."

"Jesus, Felicity. You weren't kidding? You walked into the Caruso corporate offices and brought up their mob dealings?" His fingers convulsed on her shoulders and he gave her a quick shake. "What the hell were you thinking?"

"It worked."

His expression turned furious and he shook her again. "I didn't save your goddamn life so that you could end up wearing a pair of high-heeled cement sandals."

"Your karmic spitwad isn't as stupid as all that. I told the front desk I was stopping by on the chance that the product manager was free because I was scouting new items for the shopping channel. That got me into a plush office for a private meeting. Once there, I mentioned that my cousin Ben was having some financial difficulties that the Carusos might know about. A phone call later, we were making a mutually beneficial deal."

His hands had loosened on her shoulders and she used the opportunity to twist free and slip inside the store. A bell rang, announcing her entrance, and she took her first breath of delicious smells—tomato, garlic, onion, and herbs. Stocked like a gourmet shop, the store had floor-to-ceiling shelves of bottled Caruso sauces and imported Italian products. One corner held a refrigerated unit stacked with fresh pastas. Nearby, a small wheeled bar with overhead heating lights displayed a mouthwatering selection of free samples.

Her stomach growled, the sound covered as the front bell rang again. Pretending not to notice the surly newcomer, Felicity turned toward the freebies and filled a small paper plate with ravioli, penne in a marinara sauce, and a side dish made with white beans and herbs.

"We're not through," Magee ground out from behind her.

She used a plastic utensil to fork up a big bite and stuff it in her mouth. Better to chew than chew him out over the end of an affair that had been doomed from the very beginning.

"Ignoring me? Don't be such a baby, Felicity."

She stabbed a ravioli. Fine, maybe she was a baby. Maybe she was a big, spoiled baby and that's why his defection mattered. *She* was a successful businesswoman, the It Girl of Electronic Retail. *He* was a scruffy, bar-owning, good-for-nothing-she-wanted cretin. She studied his reflection in the stainless steel roof that housed the food bar's overhead lights. Hair too long. Faded jeans. A T-shirt—she couldn't read what it said—that probably insulted her intelligence, her sex, or both.

Why, *she* should have been the one to dump *him*. Driven away with a casual wave of her hand, back to her good life and the civilized, successful kind of men who appreciated her. The kind of men who—

—had never known her like Magee.

The ravioli stuck in her throat, a dry lump. He'd known her. He'd made her laugh. He'd found his way past her facade to that raw, physical passion she hadn't even been aware was inside herself.

"Felicity."

She turned. It was all there, all that appealed to that secret side of her. Rough-cut hair, rough stubble of whiskers, rough, rangy man who could make her wet with just the touch of his rough, callused fingertip. Her pulse tripped, then started thrumming again, hummingbird wings at her throat, and at her wrists, and under the prim, knee-length skirt she'd pulled on that morning.

She remembered their first meeting. How she'd opened her eyes to find the man of her most deeply buried fantasies standing over her and how there'd been an almost cosmic, magical connection between them.

"Damn it, Felicity, tell me more about this business deal."

She started. So much for connections, cosmic or otherwise. He'd already moved on and his only remaining interest in her was a practical one. Frowning, she glanced around the room. There wasn't a clerk or any other shopper in sight. Still, she kept her voice at a whisper.

"The man I met with made a call to old Mr. Caruso. That's who he asked his secretary to get on the phone, anyway, Cosimo Caruso. He left the room when it came through, but once he was back we made our agreement. My *All That's Cool Afternoon* does a prominent, month-long sell of Caruso products in the late spring, and Ben's debt is forgiven."

Magee's eyes narrowed. "That was actually promised?"

"In so many words. As a matter of fact, the debt is erased as of right now. To show my good faith, I'll be previewing a few items of the Caruso line during the show we do here at the end of the week."

"I don't like it," he said, shaking his head.

She gritted her teeth. "Give me some credit, okay? For your information, there are sharks in L.A., too. I know how to negotiate."

"I don't like it that *you* are involved." His hand reached out and he stroked his fingertips along the curve of her cheek.

She held herself still, though she was unable to stop the goosebumps sliding down the side of her neck, toward the site of that silly, sexy, junior high hickey he'd given her.

He let out a soft groan as if he remembered it, too. "Lissie . . ."

Those prickly bumps rushed up her thighs, between them. She took a step toward him. Undeniable, that connection between them. Unignorable and . . . im-

portant. If she kissed him maybe she could understand it. If she kissed him, maybe he'd forget all about
Ashley and be—

"I'm sorry," a female said from the other side of the
room. "I didn't hear anyone come in. We were in the
back and— Magee!"

The last two syllables were rife with delight.

As one, Felicity and Magee turned toward the
voice. In a pair of black pants, a white shirt, and a red-
checked apron around her waist, a young woman was
gazing on him with a smile in her eyes and on her full
pink lips. As she rounded the sales counter, her
bouncy blond curls, twisted at the back of her head
and then pinned in a tousled top knot at her crown, jig-
gled with the same enthusiasm as her full breasts.

"Magee," she said again, coming to a stop in front
of him. She put a palm on both of his lean cheeks and
brought his mouth down for a juicy, noisy kiss. As he
lifted his head, the woman smiled at him again.
"That's because I'm glad to see you."

Smiling wider, she reached around and gave him a
lusty pinch on his perfect butt. "And that's because
you broke my heart!"

Magee shook his head, a smile tugging at his
mouth. "It's been too long . . ." He hesitated, his gaze
dropping to the tag pinned over her voluptuous right
breast. "Tracy."

Felicity rolled her eyes, cursing herself for ever
imagining *she'd* had anything special with Magee.
This woman had probably thought the same, and the
jerk couldn't even recall her name! Give him a

month—a week!—and Felicity would be just another of his hazy memories.

While she'd remember him the rest of her life.

"Magee!" A second delighted, trilling voice echoed in the small shop. A second young woman wearing a red-checked apron danced toward him.

Not a *second* young woman. A *twin*.

Felicity's jaw dropped. The whole scene played out again, the kiss, the pinch, the "You broke my heart," followed by Magee's sheepish smile, except this time it starred Tanya, not Tracy.

As he slipped an arm around each of them, Felicity backed toward the door. Twins. Twins!

Even the wild sex he'd shared with Felicity had probably seemed like a day at kindergarten to him. What had been exotic and erotic to her had been ho-hum, run-of-the-mill for Magee.

Tracy and Tanya were chattering away as Felicity slipped out. She'd get her Caruso products elsewhere.

Anywhere away from Magee.

She made it only as far as her car.

"Damn it, Felicity," he said, striding toward her. "Don't think you're going to duck the rest of this conversation."

She rolled her eyes. "Why not? Your actions speak for themselves."

He frowned. "And what do you mean by that?"

"Twins," she muttered.

"So that's what has your panties in such a tight twist."

She shot him a look. "Admit it. You're a deviant."

"And that's exactly what you like about me."

She froze. Then, damn it all, she laughed. Leaning against the side of her car, she crossed her arms over her stomach and let the helpless laughter bubble out. What could she do? The man did know her *much* too well.

But it was time for her to move on, too.

"I suppose I do like you," she finally managed to get out. "However . . ." Straightening up and then lifting to tiptoe, she grabbed his face between her hands and transferred a noisy, juicy kiss to his mouth—a kiss just like the twins'.

"That's because I'll be glad to see the last of you," she said, striking a friendly, it-was-fun-but-now-I'm-done tone. Then, as she beamed up a carefree smile, her hand shot around his hip to administer her own cheeky pinch. "And that's because you broke my heart."

Her sassy smile died. *And that's because you broke my heart*, replayed in her head. Oh, God, no.

No.

Magee's gaze swept over her naked face. "Lissie," he whispered, as if what he saw pained him. "Sweetheart . . ."

She spun away, fishing through her purse with her back to him. "Leave me alone," she croaked out, desperate for her car keys.

"Lissie—"

"*Leave me alone.*"

Only then could she convince herself she hadn't just spoken the truth.

* * *

Magee knew the exact instant Felicity realized he was following her car. The Thunderbird slowed for a second, then the vehicle jumped forward.

Crazy woman. As if he could leave her alone after seeing her stricken expression. Was he responsible . . . ?

No. He couldn't have *hurt* her, not really. Not Felicity Charm, with her L.A.-sized ego and her short, strict list of acceptable men. For God's sake, she would have been crossing him off herself in less than a week. Her annoyance came from the fact that the situation with Ashley meant he'd beaten her to it.

Still, he had to make her understand why he didn't wait for her to leave him.

Between the Caruso offices and wherever the hell she was heading was the turnoff for the wilderness area they'd visited the day before. At the last second, she surprised him by taking it, the back end of her car fishtailing.

"Shit!" He shot past, then braked. Cursing again, he shoved the Jeep in reverse, then forward, his gaze trained on her speeding car and the rooster tail of dust she was kicking behind her. She had a hell of a head start on him now—and she was barreling toward unforgiving desert that didn't house a single sign of civilization.

In minutes he went from pissed to near-panicked. But then he found her car where they'd parked yesterday, and then he found her footsteps, and then, finally, he found her. In the distance he saw her moving along

Devil's Torch, the name of the path leading to the top of Devil's Peak. Though the area was rarely visited, the Boy Scouts had established and maintained a decent route. It wasn't much more than a moderate hike—unless, that is, you were wearing a skirt and city sandals and were without a hat and water.

Or common sense.

To hell with explaining himself and why he was marrying Ashley. Felicity better have a good reason for this stunt!

With a water bottle and the ball cap he kept stashed in the Jeep, he set off after her. When he reached the trailhead, he could see she was moving steadily upward, making decent progress. But any second could mean a turned ankle—a sprain or a break—not to mention the rattlers and scorpions that would find nothing between their teeth or stingers and her sweet, soft skin.

His anxiety rising, he abandoned the idea of following her along the switchbacked route, and hurried toward the perpendicular slab of rock that would be his shortcut. Getting up it meant he could intercept her well before she made it to the top of the peak.

He clapped the ball cap on his head, shoved the water bottle in the waistband at the back of his jeans, then bent to dust his hands in the powdery dirt at his feet. Without a chalk bag it was the best he could do.

He took a moment to study the slab's features, his gaze leapfrogging from one likely hold to another. Then he bent his knees and jumped. As if it had been eighteen hours instead of eighteen months, his fingers crimped down and the toes of his running shoes wedged into a crack. Just like that, he was once again playing kissy face with warm, solid rock.

It smelled like he remembered—salty and clean—and he closed his eyes a moment, savoring the scent. Then he reached up for his next hold. Climbing in his Nikes sucked, but he was concerned for Felicity's safety, not his own.

That became his focus during the climb, the particular fear that he stared down this time. In minutes, he lifted himself over the slab's lip, just as Felicity came around the next bend in the path.

Catching sight of him, she *eeked,* her feet stuttering to a stop. But her slick leather soles lost purchase on the loose dirt and her legs went out from under her. She landed with a plop on her butt.

"You okay?" he asked, flexing his fingers as he advanced on her. The muscles in his forearms burned like a bitch, but now that Felicity was safe, he relished the way the blood was pumping through his body. Only one other activity made him feel more alive.

She pressed her knees together and pulled down on the hem of her stretchy skirt. "II-how did you get up here?"

"You saw me. I climbed." He held out his hand to help her up.

She ignored it, scrambling to her feet on her own. With her bulging purse secured under her arm, she approached the trail edge and peered over. Her eyes were wide as she glanced back at him. "You don't have any equipment!"

"Neither do you, dollface." His temper reigniting, he whipped out the water bottle from his jeans and waved it back and forth. "*Never* go traipsing through the desert without this."

When she didn't respond, he moved toward her. "What the hell were you thinking?"

Instead of answering, she grabbed the water bottle from him and used her teeth to pop open the stopper. Then she squeezed the bottle, and the thick stream of liquid caught her unawares. While she got some of it down, a mouthful or two dribbled over her bottom lip to her chin and from there ran down her neck.

Her tongue came out to swipe at the moisture on her lip. "I thought you didn't climb anymore."

His gaze dropped from the wetness of her mouth to the now-transparent spot the dampness made in the thin knit at the throat of her white shirt. "I don't climb anymore."

She unfastened the buttons right over that wet mark. Lifting the clinging fabric away from her skin, she glanced over the edge of the path again. "That sounds like a good idea to me, since it appears you can't be bothered to take even the simplest safety precautions."

He snorted, and forced himself to stop staring at the pulse he could see thrumming at the notch of her throat. "Safety precautions aren't guarantees."

She shot another squirt of water into her mouth. "I suppose that's the point, though, right? You want risk and you don't want guarantees. That's why you climb—or *used* to climb."

"Sorry, but it's my turn for questions, dollface," he

said, swiping the water bottle back. "Why are you out here?"

She lifted her eyebrows. "I don't owe you anything, Magee. Least of all an explanation of *my* behavior."

"Bullshit, you—" He broke off, the anger he'd been using to disguise his guilt evaporating. "Oh, hell, fine. You're right. I do owe you an explanation."

"I'm listening."

Sucking in a long breath, he glanced away from her face, then forced himself to meet her gaze. "Last night, after finding out about the gambling, when I . . . talked to Ashley, I wasn't thinking about you."

"Oh, well," Felicity said, her voice dry. "Now I feel so much better."

"C'mon. You can see Ashley needs someone." He tried to reason with her. "And we both know what we had was a temporary fling—"

"Which you ended in a manner straight out of an episode of *The Jerry Springer Show*."

She was pissing him off again. "I never claimed to be perfect," he muttered.

"Oh, please." She glared at him. "Imperfect is dropping towels on the bathroom floor or putting the empty ice-cream carton back in the freezer. You, Magee, are such a perfect degenerate that while you were having sex with me you got yourself engaged to my cousin!"

"I promised Simon."

"Not only that, but—" Her mouth closed on the rest of what she was going to say and she stared at him. "You what?"

"Don't think that it means I don't actually care about Ashley and Anna P. I do, very much. They've always been like family, which is why I promised Simon before every climb that if something happened to him I would take care of them."

Felicity's legs folded beneath her and she sat down on the dirt, hard. "But marriage—"

"I promised that I would take care of them just as he would." Magee dropped beside her, but he couldn't look at Felicity's appealing, astonished face any longer, so he transferred his gaze to the sweeping desert vista that spread out just inches from their feet. "It's why I'm taking the job that was supposed to be his, too. He was planning on giving up climbing, so I'm giving up climbing. He was moving himself and his family to L.A., so I'm doing that. I owe him that much."

She was silent a long moment, and then she sighed. "You owe him your life."

His gaze jumped to hers. "Yes. You get it."

She shrugged. "The night we watched the documentary together you made it very clear."

In his mind's eye, he saw Simon's grinning face on the TV in the Bivy's office. Brash, brilliant Simon, the best friend a man could have. There was a big hole in Magee's chest that he was certain would never be filled. "Damn Aussie," he muttered, shaking his head.

Felicity looked out over the view. "The night I met him, he made me laugh so hard I cried. We got to the restaurant at six, and it was after one A.M. when they threw us out. By that time our waiter and the manager were sitting with us. I think the only reason they made us leave was because the cleaning crew showed up."

Magee found himself smiling. "He could tell a damn good story."

"I remember one about a friend who called three separate women from the summit of Mt. Whitney and told each of them he'd climbed it just for her."

"The dog."

She laughed.

Then they sat in silence, but it wasn't tense or angry. Memories of Simon welled up and Magee let them, more at ease with the bitter sweetness they left behind. Probably, he thought, because he'd finally made the commitment to Ashley that Simon had wanted.

You're such a dipstick.

"Did you say something?" Felicity asked.

"No." He poured a stream of water down his throat, then offered her the bottle. "Are we okay now?"

She sighed again. "I suppose I . . . understand."

He let more beats of silence go by, then he bumped her shoulder with his. There was still something he wanted to know. "So tell me why you came up here."

She shook her head.

"C'mon." He bumped her again. "Why?"

Another sigh leaked out of her. "If you really want to know . . ." Her level gaze met his. "It was for a burial."

At his shocked look, she laughed again. "Not of myself, if that's what you're thinking, Mr. Never-Ending Ego. I was looking for a final resting place for this." She reached into the purse she'd set on the ground beside her and pulled out that statue she'd defended on the first day in her aunt's kitchen.

He took it, cupping the beat-up figurine in both hands to study it. "I can see why you'd want to put it out of its misery, dollface. It's butt-ugly."

"It's not! At least it wasn't." She reached across to stroke a fingertip over its dinged finish. "And it *will* be perfect again. I lost sight of that for a minute. But once I get back to L.A., I'll find someone who can tell me how to smooth it out and give it a new finish."

"Someone like your boss Drool?" He didn't know what made him bring the man up.

Shooting him a dirty look, she grabbed for the statue. For some reason he was feeling mean, so he leaned away from her. Half-rising, this time she lunged, and managed to wrench the figurine away. But her fingers must have slipped, because it bobbled in her hand, struck a rock, bounced up, and then it was falling—over the edge of the mountain.

In slow motion, she dove for it, and he dove for her. His hands closed over her waist and heaved. They fell back onto terra firma, with him belly-up and Felicity sprawled on top.

It probably wasn't that close a call, but try telling his heart that. It was slamming so hard and fast against the wall of his chest that he thought he might be sick. Needing something—something? needing *her*—he held Felicity so that her face was pressed against the bare skin of his neck and his was buried in her hair.

For just a second it had been the night they'd met

all over again, including the wrenching possibility of a world without her in it. When he could breathe again, he pressed a silent, imperceptible kiss on the top of her head.

"Did you save it?" he asked, his eyes closed.

"No," she croaked out. "It was too late."

She rolled off him and lifted her hands. They were shaking, but each held a piece of that goddamn statue—in one was the shabby-looking figure, and in the other, the pedestal it had stood upon.

Worse, though, was the tragic expression on Felicity's face. "Broken," she said, blinking at the tears in her eyes. "It's broken."

That wasn't the only thing broken, he realized, as he held back from pulling her into his arms again. He wanted to comfort her too much. He wanted *her* too much. But the promises he'd made meant the two of them were separated forever.

Sixteen

Two days after her Joanie had nearly been lost, Felicity battled her restlessness by alternately playing with the cats and going through the drawers in her old bedroom. As she watched one of the ragged beasts leap off the faded quilt to chase another out the door, she sighed and turned to the old painted dresser under the window. With only one drawer left to occupy her attention, it was a good thing she had to meet the GetTV crew in a few hours. They'd selected a nature amphitheater in a nearby state park as the location for the live feed of her *All That's Cool Afternoon* the next day.

Her time in Half Palm was almost up. The trouble almost behind her.

Though Ben had yet to show his face—they figured he was still hiding, unaware the heat had blown over—he was debt-free, thanks to her agreement with the Carusos and Drew's enthusiasm for their sauces as future products for GetTV. Her production crew had arrived at the crack of dawn and Felicity would meet them there later to prepare for the show. Once her live sell was over tomorrow, they'd shoot some preview spots in other locations in the area.

Once *that* was over, she'd return to L.A.

The dresser's bottom drawer stuck; it always had, she remembered. She yanked, the wood-on-wood screech like fingernails on a chalkboard. Her skin crawled at the sound, and then prickled when her next yank fully revealed the contents of the wooden drawer. Photos. And the one right on top was of Felicity's mother and father. Though the clothes they wore in it appeared strangely familiar, she knew she'd never seen it before. All her parental memorabilia, stored in a locked, fireproof box, had moved with her to USC and then every place she'd lived since.

Picking up the single photograph, Felicity eyed the remainder and judged them to be from later times and of more far-flung family members. Curious about this photo, she wandered out of her bedroom. "Aunt Vi?"

It was Peter she found first, however, with Anna P. on his lap. The little girl was pushing open the front door with the heels of her feet as the man wheeled them through the entry.

Felicity hurried over to help.

"We can do it," Anna P. said, smiling her sunny smile at her. "Petey and I can do anything other people can."

"You got that right, tiger," Peter said.

He glanced up at Felicity and she saw lines around his eyes and mouth that she hadn't noticed before. He was either in pain or hadn't been sleeping, or both. "Are you all right?" she asked. "Can I get you something?"

"If only you could . . ." he murmured, but then he smiled, a shadow of his usual grin. "However, I've earned my gold star for the day. Anna P. needed a ride to Grandma's house and I obliged."

"Mommy said I'd have more fun here. She's doing papers and money and stuff with Magee." Anna P. rolled her eyes as if she were fifteen instead of not quite four. "Boring."

"Grandma's somewhere around," Felicity said. "Maybe out back?"

The little girl slid to the floor. "I'll find her."

Felicity watched her run off and then turned to Peter. " 'Papers and money and stuff'? I hope that means he's taking charge of Ashley's financial situation."

"I wouldn't know." His gaze dropped from hers. "But, to tell you the truth, I hope not. Ashley can do her own taking-charge."

Felicity lifted her eyebrows, thinking of gambling and huge credit card balances. "Well . . ."

"Not you, too." Peter shook his head in obvious disgust. "Have you forgotten she has a degree in accounting?"

A degree in accounting? Felicity blinked. "I—I didn't know. I remember she was going to enroll in some classes at the community college. . . ."

"She finished up her bachelor's degree a week before Anna P. was born. Your aunt and I were at her graduation—Simon and Magee were on an expedition in the Himalayas."

Felicity felt her face flush. Where had she been a week before Anna P.'s birth? She couldn't remember. To avoid Peter's eyes, she glanced down at the photograph in her hand. Her mother and father, in blue jeans and matching satiny flowered shirts of the seventies. Something about the clothes . . .

She rubbed at a sudden ache in her head.

"You don't look as if you've been getting much rest either."

"Me?" She glanced over at him, then looked back at her parents, tracing their smiling faces with her eyes. "I'm . . . I'm just eager to get back home."

"You won't be able to forget what happened to you here so easily," he said quietly. "I remember the light best at night. Do you?"

"Yes." Her answer was automatic. "Sometimes, right before I fall asleep, I feel it again and—" Her head came up and she stared at him.

"And what?" His gaze was steady.

"I don't remember," she answered quickly. "I don't remember anything." It was too weird.

"Maybe it would be easier if I didn't," Peter replied, grimacing. "I hoped if I did things right, made amends where I could, that I'd find that light right here on earth."

She swallowed. "You . . . uh, haven't?"

"Well . . ." He drew the word out, then a small smile curved his mouth. "Maybe . . . maybe in some quiet moments, I have. Magee and I like to play darts before the Bivy opens. One in ten times I let him beat me and I definitely feel the glow then."

She had to laugh.

"Other times, too. When I read a book to Anna P. or tell her a funny story about her dad. And then once in a while I'm behind the bar and I look across the room and see Ashley. It's as if she feels me, because she'll glance up and meet my eyes and then . . . and then she *is* the light."

Felicity's heart squeezed and she sidled toward the kitchen, the conversation making her uneasy. "I should get you a cool drink, or get Aunt Vi. . . ."

At that moment, Aunt Vi herself bustled into the room, Anna P. on her hip. "Get me why?"

"Well, I . . ." As she fumbled for something to say, Felicity's gaze fell again on the photo in her hand. She held it up for her aunt. "I was wondering about this. I've never seen it before."

Aunt Vi frowned. It made her look older, more worn than Felicity had noticed before. "It's Ellie and Ron, of course, but I don't remember the occasion, though it looks like it was taken in front of this house." She pointed to the background. "And that's their red truck. They bought it right before the trip to Las Vegas."

Felicity's fingers tightened on the photograph. It was likely, then, that this was the last picture her parents had ever posed for. Where had she been when it was taken? Playing robbers and cops with her cousins? Watching over the latest of Aunt Vi's kitten-adoptees?

The phone rang and Felicity absently crossed to answer it. The voice on the other end was unfamiliar to her, and sounded muffled. "What? What are you saying?" she responded. "No. That's been taken care of. Yes, it has. Believe me—"

The caller hung up.

Felicity stood frozen. "That was someone who claimed to have . . . that they have . . ." Her gaze latched on to Anna P.'s precious face and she held back her shudder. "B-e-n. They want r-a-n-s-o-m m-o-n-e-y."

Aunt Vi blinked. "What?"

"B-e-n. R-a-n-s-o-m."

Anna P.'s eyes widened. "Is it a secret? About a present for me?"

Felicity pasted on a smile. "Maybe. We'll see." The photo of her parents fluttered out of her hands and she let it fall as she rushed for her purse. "Don't worry about a thing, Aunt Vi. I'm going to find out the problem. I'm going straight to Mr. Caruso."

"Don't," Peter warned. "Let's call Magee, think this through."

Felicity could only think of the renewed worry in Aunt Vi's eyes. "No! It was a business deal, *my* deal, and *I'll* make sure there's not a problem." Maybe it was a mistake, though she'd believed the man on the other end of the phone. "Has anyone seen my sneakers?"

"You can't go visit Mr. Caruso dressed like that," Aunt Vi said.

"What?" Looking for her shoes, Felicity shifted a pile of newspapers off the couch. She was wearing old jeans and on old shirt, but Aunt Vi wasn't one to care about clothes. "Why?"

"If it's business," Aunt Vi said firmly, "then you should dress for business."

Felicity hesitated. "That sounds like something I'd tell my viewers."

"You did," Aunt Vi said. "On the tape you sent me last month. So take a shower. Put some nice clothes on."

Maybe she was right, Felicity thought, looking down at her shabby clothes. She was fairly certain she hadn't brushed her hair since the day Magee had announced his engagement.

She dashed for the bathroom. "I'll be out in seven minutes."

It was little more than that when she walked out of her bedroom wearing the suit she'd worn to the trade show. Thanks to a major case of nerves mixed with anxiety, her ankles felt wobbly in her high heels, but she'd managed to apply a smooth coat of lipstick. "I'm ready," she said when she reentered the living room.

Peter was the only one there. "Felicity, don't go."

She ignored him. "Where's Aunt Vi?"

"Let me go with you. It could be dangerous alone."

Felicity tried on a reassuring smile. "I'll be fine. I met old Mr. Caruso years ago, when I was in school. He was a teddy bear—well, not a teddy bear, exactly, but certainly not the dangerous patriarch of a Mafia family. I'm beginning to think this is all a big hoax."

"Ask Magee if it's a hoax," Peter said. "Ask him who killed Johnny's father."

Her hands went icy, but she backed away from Peter toward the front door. "Tell Aunt Vi I'll call her as soon as I know anything."

Then she hurried out the door, just in time to see a grim-faced Magee pull up in front of the house. He leaned over to throw open the passenger door. "Get in."

She opened her mouth to protest and he cut her off with a gesture.

"Damn it, Felicity, you don't have to take on the whole goddamn world alone."

But she always had and she was accustomed to it. Still, he looked angry and stubborn enough to stop her, so she slid onto the seat.

He left a layer of rubber on the street. "Vi called me," he spit out. "But you should have."

"Why?" she shot back. "You're not my shoulder to lean on. You're not even my lover."

"I care about you."

She rolled her eyes. "I'm fine on my own. No big deal."

"*No big deal?* You're planning to confront a Mafia don in his den and you say it's *no big deal*?"

Her hands went cold again. "Who's Johnny? Peter mentioned the name."

He shot her a look. "My brother."

"And who . . . who killed his father?" she heard herself whisper.

He stayed silent a moment. "The Caruso family," he finally said. "There's no real proof, but it has all the hallmarks of a mob hit."

She swallowed, trying to grasp it in her mind. "It doesn't seem possible . . . and in any case, that was years ago." Her voice got stronger. "There's nothing to worry about."

With a curse, Magee pulled over to the side of the road and braked. "I won't go another inch until you listen. This isn't something to take lightly." He ran his hands through his hair in apparent frustration.

"More than fifteen years after the murder, and the name Caruso still makes my mother break out in a cold sweat. She can hardly speak about the man who was her ex-husband or what happened to him and what Johnny saw when his father was murdered. When I first learned about it—I overheard her talking to my father—her fear scared the hell out of me, because I'd never seen her unable to handle something."

"What did you overhear?"

He looked away, and then back at her. "At the time, I didn't yet know how my brother's father had died, or that he'd witnessed it. But that day the FBI had stopped by the house with some mug shots for Johnny and my mother to look at. She was shaking and crying and terrified that the mob would now come after *us*."

Felicity reached out to clutch his hand. "Were you at risk?"

"I don't think so, now. Professor Magee and family were too far removed from the original circumstances. And Johnny claims to this day he didn't see who shot his father. But my mother lived with that fear for a very long time."

And so had Magee. "What did you do when you found out?"

He blinked at her. "What did I do?"

She nodded.

"Nothing. I was fourteen years old. I heard what my mom said, figured out what had happened to Johnny's father, then I ran off to meet my buddy Brad in our old barn."

"Did you tell him about it?"

Magee disengaged their hands and then turned the key in the ignition. "Tell Brad? I didn't have the chance. We were doing some renovations and there was a two-by-four running across the rafters about twenty feet off the ground. When I got there, Brad had moved a ladder over and the first thing he did when I came in was dare me to walk across that beam."

Felicity studied the blank mask of his face. "Did you?"

"I remember I was shaking, my knees nearly knocking together, but I wanted to."

"And did you?"

"I did." He pulled the car back onto the road. "And when I reached the other end of the two-by-four I wasn't shaking anymore."

They were silent for the rest of the ride, except for when she gave him directions to the Caruso estate. The family had been major benefactors of OLPP and had hosted several school events at their palatial home every year. Felicity remembered everything about it, including the guard in the guardhouse at the bottom of the gated drive.

When Magee braked, she slipped out of the car. "I'll handle him," she said, and hurried to intercept the man before he got too close. The guy was huge, six and a half feet, maybe, and wearing a pale gray suit and matching tie instead of a security uniform. In the dark lenses of his wraparound sunglasses she saw her white face.

But, taking a breath, she donned her Sweetheart of Sales smile. Then she smooth-talked him into getting exactly what she wanted.

Herself inside.

And Magee left out.

Ashley jumped from the couch in the living room when the doorbell rang. Magee? But he wouldn't use the bell. *Ben?*

Throwing open the door brought a quick surge of joy. It was Peter. *Peter*. Then a cold wave of fear doused her.

"Is there news?" she whispered, moving aside to allow Peter to wheel himself inside.

He glanced up. "I wasn't sure you knew."

Ashley flushed. What he meant was that he thought Magee might have protected her from knowing about Ben. "I answered the phone when my mom called over here," Ashley admitted. "She told me."

Peter was probably right, Magee wouldn't have.

"Is there news?" she asked again, trying to sound stronger.

He shook his head. "Not yet. I took off right after Magee picked up Felicity. Don't worry, though, I'm sure they'll handle everything. I came over because I thought . . . I thought you might need a friend."

Friendship. It was what she'd hoped for, even after

that night in the break room—but a hope she'd abandoned the next day, when she'd witnessed the cold expression overtakc Peter's face when Magee informed him they were engaged. But she should have known . . .

Her face broke into a smile and she couldn't help herself from leaning down to hug him. "Thank you, Peter," she whispered, her cheek against his. "Thank you."

One of his arms came around to embrace her, and she closed her eyes to savor the closeness. Beneath her palms, his shoulders were wide and strong. The side of his face was hard, the skin roughened by the slightest stubble, like fine-grained sandpaper. She'd forgotten just how . . . male a man was, and she rubbed her chin against him a little, enjoying the masculine texture and the masculine scent of him.

He pushed her away.

She leaped back, her whole body blushing in embarrassment. "Can I get you some coffee? Let me get you some coffee." Without bothering to look at him or let him answer for himself, she hightailed it for the kitchen.

Dumb, dumb, dumb, she chanted to herself as she prepared two mugs of coffee with hearty dollops of milk and then set them in the microwave for a quick zap. *Peter doesn't want a weakling leaning on him.*

The steaming mugs gave her something to focus on as she walked back into the living room. Peter had positioned his wheelchair beside the couch. She handed him one of the hot coffees, then sat down on the middle cushions—not too close.

An awkward silence—the first she could ever remember with Peter—grew between them. Ashley fidgeted beneath the weight of it, all the things he'd said to her in recent days swirling in her mind.

Why would you want to be with half a man?

You let Simon roll over you when he was alive.

You let Magee baby you after Simon was dead.

"How's your paperwork going?"

His sudden question startled her. "My paperwork?" Peter was looking at the surface of the coffee table in front of the couch, its surface scattered with bills, scratch paper, pencils, and a calculator. "Oh. My paperwork."

A ruddy red colored his cheekbones. "Sorry, it's none of my business."

"No, no!" She must have sounded offended when she'd really been distracted.

You don't want me, so what's the big deal about another flaw or two?

He wasn't the one who was flawed, it was *her*. It had always been her, he must know that.

She tried to sip her coffee, but it was scorching-hot, so she leaned forward to set the mug on top of one of her latest Visa bills. "Now that I've laid everything out and added it all up, the debt is terrible—but not as bad as when I *didn't* add it all up. As of this morning, my credit cards are confetti and I'm going to look for a second job."

Can the clinging vine act. Put your own two feet on the floor. Peter had said that, too. Did he think she was making some progress now?

"You could pick up some more hours at the Bivy, Ash." Steam rose off the surface of his coffee and he blew on it. "Heck, you can have some of mine if you want to tend bar."

Her stomach clenched. At the same time that he'd told Peter about the engagement, Magee had also told him about taking the job in L.A. "We won't be in town much longer, remember? Anna P. and I are moving soon."

Peter looked away. "That's right. You don't have anything to worry about, then. Magee will take care of the money you owe, just like he'll take care of you and Anna P."

"I'll be paying my own debts," she protested.

"Sure you will."

His agreement was so instant it sounded like an insult. It *was* an insult. She glared at him, outrage coming out of nowhere. Well, maybe he was right, maybe she would let Magee help her out of this jam, too.

Peter might not think so, but she needed to be taken care of! Her gaze flicked to the mess of bills on the table. Wasn't that obvious?

She looked back at Peter. He was studying her with those deep, beautiful brown eyes of his, making her feel . . . weak.

No, not weak.

Helpless. Helpless against him.

Which made her angry again. "That's not me," she said from between her teeth. "Who you think I am is *not* me."

He didn't pretend to misunderstand, he just continued looking at her. *You were fine then, Ash, and good at taking care of yourself, your job, your home, Anna P.*

"I'm not that person!"

Desperate to get away from all he wasn't saying, she jumped to her feet. Escape was a quick scoot between his chair and the coffee table. She didn't know exactly how it happened, except that she'd never been graceful under pressure, but as she moved by him her hip jostled his elbow.

His gasp froze her in place.

She whirled. His full mug of hot coffee had spilled down his right leg, leaving a dark stain from thigh to calf. "You're burned!"

He was plucking at the wet denim, his face grim. "I don't know. Since I can't feel it, I've got to get these off. Check the damage."

Damage? Her stomach folded in on itself. "Tell me what to do."

"Ash—"

"Tell me what to do!" But she didn't wait for further instruction. Mothers knew how to undress people. Shoes, then pants. She dropped to her knees and went to work on his running shoes, flipping both off. He was fumbling with the buttons on his fly when she rose, so she brushed his fingers away and took care of them herself.

"Wrap your fingers around the arms of your chair," she ordered. "Now push up." It was how he got in and out of the wheelchair, she'd seen him do it.

As he lifted, she yanked down the jeans. They only moved to the back of his knees, stuck between the seat and his lifeless legs. Ignoring the frightened *whump whump whump* of her heart, she knelt again, lifting one heavy leg at the ankle and then the other so she could strip the pants completely away.

He fell back into the seat. "It doesn't look too bad."

His thigh had gotten the worst of it. Below a pair of wildly printed boxers and beneath golden hairs, the skin was a definite pink. "Cold compress, then 911."

He shook his head. "Just the compress."

"Peter—"

"I hate hospitals, Ash. Please, honey, just the compress."

Honey. He'd done it again, made her feel helpless again, turning her heart into runny, warm honey. She bit her lip, noticing how pale his face had turned and that he was looking anywhere but at her.

"No 911 if you lie down." She looked at the short couch, then back at his long body. "In my bedroom. Can you get yourself on the bed while I make compresses?"

Instead of answering, he wheeled himself toward the hallway.

She ran to the kitchen and filled a big bowl with ice and covered it with water. Then she dumped some kitchen towels inside the bowl and rushed it back to her room, where she saw Peter in the process of muscling himself from wheelchair to mattress. "I'm—"

Her voice must have startled him. His head jerked

and his body twitched toward her, sabotaging the transfer process. With a heavy thump, he fell to the ground between the chair and her bed.

Her heart leaped into her throat, her body leaped toward his.

"Shit!" He was flat on his back on the ground, his eyes squeezed shut. "Shit, shit, shit, shit, shit."

Some instinct told her he hadn't done more damage. "Obviously you didn't bite your tongue," she murmured, coming to stand over him. "Compress first or bed first?"

"First I want the ground to swallow me up," he muttered.

Ashley stilled. Oh. *Oh, Peter.* His cheeks had reddened again.

He didn't want her to see him like this, just as he hadn't wanted her to see him sickened by the sight of his own blood. He didn't want to appear weak and helpless in front of her.

Weak and helpless! In this, she realized, in this they were equals.

Inside her chest, her runny-honey heart swirled, then spread, starting to fill all the scared, empty places that the casino and her slot machine had merely helped her ignore. Equals, she thought again, and the idea filled her with strength.

"Compress," she decided, and dropped to her knees. She squeezed out one of the towels and placed it over his pinkened thigh. Then she set another on his shin.

He yelped both times.

She shook her head at him. "Don't be such a baby. You're paralyzed, remember? You can't feel that."

"Phantom pains."

"Oh." Her sympathy caught, she shifted closer to his face and brushed his golden hair off his forehead. "I'm sorry I hurt you."

His hair slid against her palm, silky and warm.

He reached up and caught her hand. "Go away, Ash."

She blinked. "What?"

"Go away. I don't need you here."

Foolish man. "If I go, I call an ambulance."

He turned his head. "Fine."

Alarm tightened her stomach. She kneed back along the carpet to lift the edge of one dripping compress. The skin beneath looked better already. ASAP, she promised herself, she was going to take some advanced first-aid courses. Maybe there was even something specifically geared for those who . . . who loved paraplegics.

"Go away, Ash."

He was starting to annoy her. "Not until we get you on the bed."

"No!"

His instant denial was certainly interesting. She stared at him. "What's the matter?"

"*We* are not getting me on the bed. Fuck it, Ash, I'm not helpless."

There was that magic word again. She'd never grow tired of hearing him say it, she decided. With a little sigh, she smoothed back his hair. He caught her fingers once more. So she reached out with her free hand, and then he grabbed it with *his* free one. Their gazes locked as they struggled for supremacy.

"I'm stronger than you," he said.

"We'll see about that." Neither of them relaxed a muscle.

"C'mon, Ash," he finally said, trying to cajole her. "This is silly, don't you think?"

She narrowed her eyes. "Silly is you still lying on the carpet because you won't accept my help. Silly is you being afraid to look like half a man in my eyes."

His mouth—full, kissable, and oh, she wanted to—twisted. "Leave me with some dignity. Please."

"Why should I? You've never hesitated to point out my failings." Though he'd reminded her of her strengths as well.

You were fine then, Ash, and good at taking care of yourself, your job, your home, Anna P.

"What do you want?" he asked in a weary voice, closing his eyes.

Oh, my love. So little and yet so much.

"I want to put my own two feet on the floor, Peter. I want to put them on the floor and stand the fuck up."

That got him looking at her.

She smiled at him, at the love that had waited for her, and then ended up with the better her for his patience and for his pride. "And then I want to use my strength to help you stand up with me."

He rose on his elbows, staring at her.

"Let me help you, Peter. Let me sometimes be

your strength, like I know you will sometimes—but only sometimes—be mine. Let me be your weakness, as you are mine. Let me make you helpless, as you make me."

She reached out to brush his cheek with her fingertips. "Let me love you, Peter."

Seventeen

A slender man in another pale-colored suit—this one Armani—met Felicity at the front door of the Caruso manse. Without saying a word, he beckoned to her, then slithered over elegant marble floors that seeped cold through the soles of her shoes. The combination of creepy butler-type and chilly house sent a shiver down her back, but she didn't allow an outward show of it. One of the first things she'd noticed upon entering the foyer was a tiny red light and the unmistakable lens of a security camera mounted in a high corner.

There was likely a network of them. But she was good at playing to an audience.

The Caruso mansion wasn't arranged in the usual sprawl of many desert estates. It was built square and gray, like a fortress, with more tones of gray in the polished stone floors. The Medici Palace, she thought, not Mediterranean warmth.

The silent man passed a massive table with thick, curving legs. On its surface sat a towering Chinese porcelain vase filled with tall stalks of bird-of-paradise. From their lofty height, the orange and blue flowers looked down their sharp beaks at Felicity, like ornamental yet hungry vultures. Everything about the place was designed to intimidate, she decided.

When she'd visited for school events as a girl, the gaggle of excited students and flustered nuns she'd been with had masked that quality—or she'd been too naive to pick up on it.

But she was a woman now, a businesswoman, and intimidation wasn't going to work on her this time, either. She had a deal with the Carusos that she expected them to stick to.

At a door leading out to a courtyard, Pale Suit paused. He turned his dark, reptilian gaze onto her for several long seconds.

Despite her resolve, Felicity's stomach quivered. Didn't this guy ever blink? *It's a ploy,* she told herself, *a ploy to put me on edge.* Still, her stomach made that sick quiver again.

He reached beneath his lapel to his inside jacket pocket.

For a gun? A stiletto? What did the desert Mafia do you in with—cactus spines? Her imagination careening, she focused on that hidden hand and tensed to flee.

Pale Suit pulled out a small leatherbound notepad. She saw the glint of a slim gold pen. "Miss," the man said, his voice as underworld-dark as his demeanor, hair, and eyes.

Felicity swallowed, trying to rein in her wild imagination. Would he ask for the name and number of her next-of-kin? Did a Mafia business meeting require a blood oath beforehand?

He still didn't blink. "My mother . . ."

A nervous giggle bubbled in her throat. *The guy had a mother?* He looked as if he'd hatched out of an egg.

"Could I have your autograph for my mother?"

An autograph. The giggle popped out, making her sound like the nervous twit she'd promised herself not to be. Blame Magee and his talk of cement high heels and mob murders. Blame herself for listening to it.

With a smile, she reached for Pale Suit's pad and pen. Writing "For Nadia" at his direction and then her name gave Felicity time to quiet the last of her jangling nerves. There was nothing to be frightened of. Mr. Cosimo Caruso was her former schoolmates' grandfather. The Caruso family ran a successful, legitimate business.

The loan-sharking and kidnapping were just side ventures.

Another shiver rolled down her back.

But as she was led into the courtyard and saw a well-dressed older gentleman rise to his feet, her anxiety eased again. In silver slacks that matched his abundant head of hair, a white silk shirt, and a soft blue ascot, Mr. Caruso appeared elegant, not intimidating.

Like European royalty, not California Mafia.

"*Buon giorno, buon giorno,*" he said. "Come, please sit down." He beckoned her to join him at a luxurious patio set shaded by a large umbrella.

Before taking a seat, Felicity held out her hand to

him. It was a business meeting, after all. "Mr. Caruso, thank you for seeing me."

He glanced down at her outstretched fingers, hesitating. Then, with a rueful expression, his palm met hers for a firm but gentle shake. "Still I don't get used to this shaking of hands with pretty young women. Pretty young women are for kissing, even to old men like me."

The bit of innocuous flirtation was as graceful and elegant as the man himself. She laughed, as she was expected to, and let him lower her to the cushioned seat. This Old World septuagenarian was the head of a notorious crime family? It didn't seem likely, but she had to hope that at least he could help her find out about Ben.

"Now, what can I offer you?" he asked as he settled into his own chair, with Pale Suit hovering behind him. "I seem to remember that you schoolgirls always liked lemonade."

She smiled. "That would be lovely, thank you. But I'm surprised you remember that I went to OLPP with your granddaughters."

Mr. Caruso crossed one leg over another as Pale Suit slid away—to get the lemonade, she supposed. "When I took the call about your proposition the other day, it came to my mind."

Her tingling shiver returned. So the man at the Caruso company offices *had* phoned Mr. Caruso.

Which must mean the family *was* in the loan-sharking business and Mr. Caruso knew all about it.

The realization apparently showed on her face, because Mr. Caruso smiled. "All sorts of people have a quick need for cash from time to time. You'd be surprised. They're called no-collateral hard loans. There's nothing wrong with them."

She noticed, though, he didn't say there was nothing illegal about them, either. As Pale Suit approached with a tray and two tall glasses of lemonade, she looked Mr. Caruso straight in the eye. "What about kidnapping? Do you see anything wrong with that?"

He stilled and his eyes narrowed under their silver brows. "Explain, *per favore.*"

Pale Suit must have caught on to the mood change, because he hurried over as Felicity outlined the call she'd taken at Aunt Vi's. "The man I spoke with said he would hold Ben until we paid off the loan. I told him it was taken care of, that I had made arrangements, but he just repeated his demands."

Mr. Caruso shot a look at Pale Suit, who strode off. "Give us a moment," the older man said, turning charming and affable again. "I'm sure we can straighten this out for you."

Just as if he were doing *her* a favor, Felicity thought, flabbergasted. She reached for her lemonade and took a sip, giving the reality of the situation some time to sink in. The Mafia had stepped out of Martin Scorcese and Robert DeNiro movies, stepped out of New York and into Palm Springs, and she . . . she *believed* it.

An old desert legend came to mind. The rumor was that Al Capone had escaped the metaphorical heat of Chicago for the physical heat of the Palm Springs area. There was a house, somewhere she couldn't quite recall, where he'd lived for a time. It had been at . . . at . . . Two Bunch Palms.

"Bah!" Mr. Caruso was looking at her, obviously amused. "Capone was never there."

In horror, she realized she'd spoken the name of the place aloud. "Oh. Well . . . I . . ."

Lucky for her, Pale Suit returned and bent to whisper in Mr. Caruso's ear. Felicity's hand tightened on her glass. When the butler-type straightened, Mr. Caruso was quiet for a moment, then he looked over at her.

"I'm afraid there's been a mix-up. *Piccolo*—a small one," he said pinching his thumb and forefinger together. "Some of my associates are young and they go off without thinking, without checking with those older and wiser first."

"But you've straightened it out?"

His hand lifted, made a little wave. "We will."

Will? Felicity cleared her throat. "When?"

He lifted his shoulders and hands in a very Italian shrug. "A few days, no more. We first must find these hotheads. But on my honor, no harm will come to your cousin."

A few days? In less than that she was supposed to be in L.A., putting her past—old and recent—behind her. "But the Caruso products are slated to be previewed on GetTV tomorrow."

He gave another of those elegant shrugs. "What can one do?"

Felicity took a deep breath. "One can say goodbye to a very lucrative deal with the company I work for."

Mr. Caruso's eyebrows rose. "*Sì?*" His voice was quiet, his pose relaxed, but his eyes had gone cold and watchful. She was looking at the Godfather now, Felicity thought, her pulse ticking loudly in her ears, and not the grandfather.

And the Godfather intimidated the heck out of her. But she refused to let him see it, and she pressed her knees together, hard, so they wouldn't rattle. "No Ben, no deal."

"An ultimatum?"

The oh-so-casual inquiry made her palms sweat. She could back off, back away, run for her life to Magee and then race to the sheriff.

It had been her first thought when she'd hung up the phone. But the Charms had to live in the area and live with any trouble she got them into with the Carusos. Going to the sheriff could mean legal complications for Ben. And then there was the small problem of evidence. If she contacted the authorities, what would she have for them? It would be the word of the Charms versus the word of the Carusos.

A notorious family of ne'er-do-wells versus a successful, philanthropic family who brought jobs to the desert.

So she tried sending off her own scary vibes as she looked straight into the Godfather's eyes. "Ben has to be back with his mother, my aunt, by air time tomorrow, or our deal is off."

Mr. Caruso tilted his head, staring at her with those calculating eyes. "Ah, *sì*, it *is* an ultimatum."

Felicity gave her own elegant shrug. "If you like. What I'd say though, is that it's family, and I'll do what I must for them."

A few minutes later she was shown out the front door by Pale Suit. She smiled at him, said, "Give your mother my best," then pointed the pointy toes of her pumps toward the end of the gated drive and the black Jeep waiting on the other side.

Holding back a silly urge to skip, Felicity made her way to Magee. She gave another smile to the security guard and, still wearing it, opened the passenger door.

At the furious look on Magee's face, though, her mouth dried and her heart shuddered. *Whoa.* She was right to have been worried about intimidation—but now she thought she'd been worried about a threat from the completely wrong man.

That Mr. Caruso had promised to get Ben back home—unharmed—within the next twenty-four hours didn't appear to appease Magee's mood. As they drove through the expensive desert communities, Felicity eyed the muscle jumping in his jaw and considered jumping out of the Jeep that was speeding back toward Half Palm.

"I don't see what you're so angry about," she finally said.

He shot her a look. "The goon at the gate pulled a gun on me when I tried to follow you in, Felicity."

"You're kidding." She shook her head, connecting *crime family* and the Caruso family was still not easy. "No wonder you're upset."

He cursed beneath his breath. "I'm upset because you went inside the house without me. Did you stop to think I might be worried as hell?"

She'd thought about making sure Magee didn't have the opportunity to do something stupid like bring up an old, unsolved murder. And she'd thought about making it clear to him they were two separate entities who could get engaged or get on with business without informing the other.

"*Well?*"

"Look," she said. "You don't *need* to worry about me. I can manage myself. I'm not Ashley. I'm not anything like her."

Everything went quiet.

Felicity pinched her thigh as punishment and turned her head away from him as if she had a sudden need to count palm trees or luxury cars. Why had she said it? She'd promised herself not to say anything more, *not one thing,* about her cousin or about the engagement.

"I do care about you."

Oh, Lord. He'd said it before. Could there be a more tepid declaration? She tried to laugh off its sting. "Please, Magee. If you want to coax me back into your bed, you'll have to do better than that." Not that they'd ever been *in* a bed, come to think of it.

In the short city block they drove along, she added up twenty-one date palms before he broke the silence.

"Our . . . affair shouldn't have happened, I'm aware of that. And I'm sorry."

No! She didn't want him apologizing. Worse, she didn't want him wishing away one moment of the time they'd had together.

"But now that I've asked Ashley to marry me . . ." He stopped for a red light.

In need of fresh air, Felicity unrolled the window and stuck her head out. The wind rustled the fronds of the palms overhead, creating a shimmery sound like a drummer's brush against cymbals.

Magee raised his voice against the noise. ". . . I want you to know that I'll be faithful to her."

God, how she hated that she believed him. It would be easier on her to still think of him as the debauched Thrillbanger, instead of a man whose worst fault was how seriously he took his promises. "I don't know if you're noble or just plain nuts," she muttered.

"Noble?" He glanced over at her, frowning. "What the hell makes you say that?"

"You don't like noble? Fine." The light turned green, he accelerated, and she was forced to pull her head inside or risk eggbeater hair. "Then feeling obligated to marry your best friend's wife is nuts."

"I love Ashley and Anna P. I told you that."

Thinking of him galloping the little girl up Aunt Vi's sidewalk, Felicity believed that, too. It wasn't any of her business, though—it wasn't as if *she* wanted to marry the man—so she kept her mouth shut.

He shot her another frustrated look. "You don't understand."

The car turned, leaving behind the carefully groomed excess of the desert estates—excess grass, palms, water, wealth—and moving toward the de facto desert that was dusty scrub and twisted cactus . . . as well as amazing skyscraper rocks and hidden, natural pools.

"Damn it, Felicity!" His harsh voice snapped her attention away from the scenery and back to him. "Can you imagine how close you get to someone you trust with the other end of your rope? We were more than climbing partners, we were like brothers."

"All right."

"No, it's *not* all right." Everything she said and anything she didn't say seemed to increase his foul mood. "You need to understand that I should have died when I broke my ankles that day. Simon should have left me there. But instead he saved me."

She remembered the night Magee had saved *her*. Once the realization had sunk in, she'd wanted to celebrate her breath, her beating heart, each drop of blood that pulsed through her veins. "You must have been relieved. Euphoric."

"Euphoric? Relieved? I was barely conscious on the way down. When I was lucid again, they broke the news to me that Simon was dead."

Meaning he'd skipped right over rejoicing and moved straight into mourning. "But . . . but you'd lived. That had to mean something to you."

"What, exactly? I've thought about it for months, and I can only conclude that I must have been spared for a reason."

And it was clear what Magee thought that reason was. He'd been saved to live out the rest of Simon's life. It was what gave him purpose—she remembered him mumbling about it when he was half-drunk the night they'd first made love.

And he was almost right. Looking into the light she'd understood—

No. Felicity shut down that train of thought. It was weird. Creepy. And it made her . . . doubt.

Her sanity, she told herself.

"Magee, take me to the amphitheater, not back to Aunt Vi's," she said, her voice urgent. "The GetTV crew should be there by now. And I need to see . . . I need Drew."

"Drool?"

She shook her head, refusing to look at him. "Don't start that. You have no right. None." Magee was engaged to someone else, to her cousin. He had his purpose and now she needed to reconnect with hers. With her job, with her image, and with the Mr. Right who went so well with both.

Magee left her alone after that.

Once they reached the parking lot of the nature amphitheater and she saw the trailers and semi with *GetTV!* emblazoned across them, she released a sigh of relief. Civilization. Her sanity. The Charmed life that she'd made for herself was still there, waiting for her to step back inside it.

As Magee pulled in beside one of the trailers— thick utility cords already snaking from underneath— she caught sight of Drew. His hair gleamed golden in the sun. His khakis had a knife-edge pleat and she'd be able to see herself in the shine of his tasseled loafers.

He looked exactly, perfectly, like everything she'd ever wanted.

Her hand on the door, she turned to Magee. His hair was tangled by his own fingers. Either he needed to change his razor blades or he'd forgotten to shave. His T-shirt read *Recreational Gynecologist.*

She had to smile. "Thank you for at least *looking* like the wrong one."

"What?" He tilted his head.

Her fingers itched to smooth his glossy hair. "Never mind. Just one more thing—"

"Something *more*?" But a glint of good humor had returned to his eyes.

She nodded. "I believe you do care about me. And if that's true—help me out, okay? Could you . . . could you keep Aunt Vi and the other Charms away from here the next couple of days? Please?"

Her gaze flicked to Drew, then back to Magee's face.

He must have seen who she'd been looking at because the humor in his eyes hardened. "Ah. Still working so damn hard to be something you're not."

She flinched, the nasty crack like a slap. Her fingers tightened on the door handle and she wanted badly, so badly, to hurt him back. The Felicity Charm she'd created was all that she had, didn't he see that?

"Well, that makes us two of a kind, then, doesn't it, Magee? Since you're working so damn hard to be *someone* you're not."

From the startled look on his face, she knew it was a direct hit.

And she told herself it felt good to come out the winner.

With Ashley in his arms, Peter hadn't felt so certain that anything was right since he'd made the choice to return to his broken, lifeless body on that mountain almost three years before. Being with Ashley fulfilled that conviction he'd been unable to shake during his near-death experience. The golden light had been so tempting with its promise of boundless love, but Peter had known he had more to do on earth.

She stirred, her cheek nuzzling his bare chest. Then, with a contented sigh, she stacked her hands over his heart and propped her chin on them. "I was a little nervous," she said, a smile tweaking the corners of her mouth. "But I think we did fine."

Smiling back, he lifted his hand to stroke her hair. "Just fine. And if you were nervous, think how I felt having to explain exactly what you could, uh, expect." To tell the truth, sharing with the woman who was his friend and his love that sex would be different with a man who had an incomplete lower motor neuron injury had not been as difficult as he'd thought. Ashley was more resilient than even *he* had known.

"Oh, yeah," she said, a touch of wickedness lighting her eyes. "Finding out your erections last longer and that you can climax but not ejaculate was a heck of a thing for a girl to accept."

"You're laughing at me."

"Peter, think about it."

"That there's no end to my stamina?" he said, leering at her.

"Better than that . . . there's no wet spot."

He laughed, then pulled her up to kiss her pretty mouth. "God, I love you."

"And I love you," she whispered. "I loved Simon, too, so much, but this with you and me . . . this will be a partnership."

"It won't be easy," he warned. "There's complications. Complications like—"

"What the hell is going on?" said a shocked voice.

Over Ashley's bare shoulder, Peter saw one of those complications looming in the bedroom doorway. "—Magee," he finished.

"Magee," Ashley echoed, and rolled over to face the other man, pulling the covers to her collarbone.

Gripping the bars of the iron headboard behind him, Peter pulled himself to a sitting position. Magee was still in the doorway, staring at the scene on the bed in clear confusion.

"It's exactly what it looks like," Peter said.

Magee blinked again, then appeared to focus on Peter's face. "Is that right?" His gaze flicked to Ashley. "Is that right?" he said again.

"It's right," Ashley confirmed. Her hand found Peter's and she held on tight. "Peter and I, the two of us—the three of us, counting Anna P.—we're right."

Magee walked with zombie steps toward the bed. Ashley tensed, but Peter didn't think there was anything violent in the offing. He was proved correct when Magee dropped to the end of the mattress. Ashley curled her legs to give him more room.

"I don't understand," he said, his expression still dazed, even as he made himself at home on the bed. He turned his head toward Ashley. "We're still getting married, aren't we?"

Eighteen

Felicity settled back onto the narrow couch in her GetTV trailer. Outside, the crew scurried about, carrying equipment into the amphitheater that would be used for the next day's live shoot of her *All That's Cool Afternoon*. Inside, the small space was sardined with wardrobe, makeup, and files of information on the products she'd be selling during her hour and the ones she'd be previewing on commercials they'd tape to be aired later.

On the floor in front of her the products themselves were stacked high, from the Caruso sauces to the mountaineering wear. She picked up a clipboard and pen, ready to familiarize herself with the merchandise and work on her presentation of each item. No matter how much attention Felicity herself garnered in public, on the set it was the product that was the celebrity.

If she had a secret, it was that she always focused on the star quality of the merchandise. She had to be able to answer the questions Who, Where, When, Why, How, What—and most important of all—So what? What about each product could make it exciting, fun, and for tomorrow's sell in particular, what about purchasing it would make the customer feel "cool?"

As she worked alone in the trailer, she felt an upsurge of confidence. Bottom line, she was good at this. She understood the appeal of transforming oneself, and she knew how to feature a product so an item as ordinary as tomato sauce became someone's passport to an evening as a hot-looking, hot-cooking Latin lover.

Coming from the knowledge that something as small as a new lipstick could make a woman feel more beautiful, Felicity worked to present her products in a way that made a customer feel more sexy or more adventurous or more hip. Turning one of the Caruso bottles around in her hand, she studied the sauce and scribbled down notes.

> *Foolproof fascination—with the meal and with you.*
> *Tastes like you've had it—and yourself—on simmer*
>   *for days.*
> *A first-class pleasure feast.*

The lightweight mountaineering jacket required a different mind-set. This product didn't promise pleasure so much as excitement and a window into the world of extreme sports. She lifted the black and neon fabric, then stood to slip it on. In the full-length mirror on the door to the bathroom, she inspected the sleek fit.

Not only have the competitive edge, but wear the clothing that shows you do.
What do you need to take life to the extreme? How about the right jacket.

She needed some pithier phrases, too, she decided, jotting down *high voltage. High performance*. The image on one of the advertising posters in the Wild Side popped into her head, an image of Magee in this very article of clothing, hanging by the crimped fingers of one hand.

Raw power.

The two words brought to mind other images: His strong arms around her. His long, limber fingers touching her cheek with such heartaching tenderness. Lost in memories, she didn't hear the door to the trailer open. "Felicity," a hoarse voice said.

She whirled. It was Magee. And something had turned him from Raw Power to Raw . . . Confusion? He stumbled over a box on his way inside.

Her knees going soft in sudden fear, she stared at the numb expression on his face. "Is it . . . is it something about Ben?"

He shook his head, then dropped to the couch where she'd been sitting. "It's not Ben. It's Ashley and Peter."

Her voice rose. "Something happened to Ashley and Peter?"

"I found them in bed together. Ashley isn't going to marry me."

Felicity's heart made an odd jump in her chest, as if the anchor that had been weighing it down now was released, leaving it free. "I don't understand." Or maybe she did. Ashley and *Peter*. Some things that had happened over the last few days began to make sense.

"I don't understand, either." Magee shook his head, his expression still dazed. "I . . . I don't know what to do."

Concerned by the wooden tone in his voice, she crossed to the trailer's small refrigerator and pulled out a cold soda. The loud snap of the pop-top didn't cause him to blink. When she pressed the can into his hand, he didn't appear to notice.

There could only be one explanation for his behavior, she decided, and her heart plummeted from its high place. "You love her. You must really love her."

He looked up. "I told you I did. She was Simon's wife. She's my friend."

Wait, wait, wait. Magee appeared poleaxed that Ashley, his mere *friend,* had dumped him. "But are you . . . are you *in love* with her?"

He made an impatient gesture. "You're not listening. I don't know what to *do* now."

"It seems obvious to me, Magee," she said slowly. "You go back to your own life. The bar, the rock gym, the Wild Side. You forget about the job in L.A. You can start climbing again."

He shook his head. "I've lost my purpose."

Her chest ached. The purpose he'd thought his life had been saved for was gone.

"Simon said it was time to grow up," he said, staring off into the distance. "To stop climbing, to get a regular job. Maybe I should still do that. Take the job in L.A., figure out how to be an adult."

With two fingers, Felicity rubbed the headache starting to pulse between her brows. "Magee . . ."

She tried to imagine him somewhere other than Half Palm, out from behind the bar, off the boulders in the rock gym, on the tame side instead of the wild. It took some effort, but then she pictured him behind a desk, then in a house in a trendy suburb, with a Mercedes instead of that ugly heavy-metal machine he drove. Magee, becoming that hardworking, success-and stuff-oriented man she'd idealized as her Mr. Right.

Her heart soared upward again, making it hard to swallow. Magee as Mr. Right. It would be double-desserts. Cake served twice, and eating it twice, too.

And she knew exactly how to sell the idea to him.

A long-overdue change, she'd tell him.

You should live out Simon's legacy.

Turn your life around and you'll feel good about yourself.

In Magee's vulnerable state, America's Sweetheart of Sales couldn't fail. Hadn't he once said that she could make people believe she had exactly what they needed? If she made him believe she had the answer to what he should do with the rest of his life, then once he was in L.A., she could have him, too.

She didn't doubt it. Magnet to metal filings.

"Magee . . ." she whispered, taking the ignored soda out of his hand to put it on the window ledge behind his head. Her fingers drifted through his hair, and he closed his eyes.

"I know what you need . . ." she started.

"Do you?" His hands circled her waist and he pulled her between his knees, then pressed his cheek against her abdomen. "Tell me. For God's sake, tell me."

Opportunity wasn't just knocking, it was battering down her door, Felicity thought. Her fingers trembled as she stroked Magee's hair. *Say the words!* Moving to L.A. will make you brand new again. Do what Simon planned—*it will be your passport to fulfillment.*

You owe it to yourself.

Reach your full potential.

Her fingers tightened in Magee's hair, and he groaned, nuzzling against her. "You're right, Lissie. What I need right now is you." His hands came around to the buttons of her blouse.

She shivered, letting him do what he wanted. Their physical connection would only add to her selling points. *Included at no extra cost.*

He tugged the blouse from her skirt, then pushed back the edges to reach her bra. The front clasp parted at a snap of his fingers. Her heart might be aching for him, but her pulse started pounding, her body heating with that bad-girl passion that only Magee could bring out in her.

But they were in her trailer! She shouldn't take the chance of being found here with him.

He peeled the silky fabric of the bra from her skin. Goosebumps rushed over her skin as he stared at her breasts.

Custom designed for you.

His hands slid beneath her opened blouse and around her ribs, tugging her closer. He buried his head between her breasts, and she didn't think any more about denying him.

His hair was smooth and warm against her, his hands rough and firm on her bare back. "You smell so good," he said.

Without making a further move, he breathed her in.

And then she realized it wasn't a prelude, a prologue, foreplay. It was skin-to-skin, man-to-woman, authentic intimacy.

She froze, even as another of her sales catch phrases flitted through her mind, *Why forgo the pleasure?,* but this . . . tenderness was as compelling as the passion he usually demonstrated.

Her hands went to his hair again, and she stroked it, giving him her time, her touch, her comfort. Maybe she should talk now, bring up the move to L.A.

There's no reason to hesitate.

That catch phrase worked for both of them.

"Magee . . ."

His head turned to lick one nipple.

Heat burned away anything more than one-word thoughts. Okay. Now. Good.

He licked again, and her nipple contracted to a hard, pulsing point. His lips surrounded the aureole and he sucked it inside his mouth.

Felicity flinched against him, the so-good pleasure pulling at her womb. Her hands held his head closer to her breast, but he didn't respond with anything more than the gentle sucking. Her heart quivered, and she combed her fingers through his hair. When he moved to suck on her other nipple she relaxed into his embrace and into the slow twist of tenderness and arousal.

The feeling was glorious. Fulfilling. It was sex and comfort, excess and simplicity, Mary Magdalene and the Madonna all rolled together.

It was a feeling she'd never known before.

Oh, no. No.

She'd wanted to convince him to move to L.A. because she wanted her cake and to eat it, too. Mr. Right and the Thrillbanger all rolled into one. Who wouldn't want that?

But this went deeper. She'd fallen deeper. She'd fallen off the deep end, the highest cliff, she was in deep caca.

"Lissie." He looked up at her, his mouth wet. "It's L.A., isn't it? I should go to L.A."

Her heart pounded in her chest as she looked into that beautiful, dark, dangerous—oh, she'd been warned from the first!—face. But he was almost hers. She almost had him.

It was time for a few clinchers to close the deal. Yes, she could say. L.A. L.A. and me. *Take advantage of this special offer!*

It's a winning decision! Don't delay!

Backing up a step, she opened her mouth. "No."

No? No, what? What the heck was she talking about?

She pulled the edges of her blouse together. Fastened a button. "No" came out of her mouth again. Startled by it, she jumped back another few inches. Thinking it was his face distracting her, she directed her gaze out the tinted window behind him. "You can't come to L.A."

He blinked, then turned his head to see what she was looking at. "This is about *him*?"

Him? Him, who? She squinted, and saw Drew in the distance. "Oh, n—"

"I'm not slick enough for you, is that it?" Magee's voice went hard and cold. "Not good enough?"

Not good enough? She'd started out life as a dirt-poor desert ratette. "What are you talking about? It's L.A. You . . . you don't belong there."

"What about us?"

She froze. "Us?"

"In L.A. we could let this . . . this thing between us burn out naturally. Seems like a good idea."

Her mouth dropped. *Burn out naturally.* She took another giant step back. Even with those words echoing in her head, she was terrified she'd still try to persuade him to be her Mr. Right in L.A.—until his interest in her burned out, anyway. Her face heated. "An hour ago you were engaged to my cousin."

"But Lissie—"

"No buts, ifs, or ands," she said, her voice hoarse.

"We don't belong together and you don't belong in L.A. any more than . . . than I belong in Half Palm."

His eyes narrowed. "Ah. So that's what this is about."

"What? I don't know what you mean." The space inside the trailer shrank as Magee stood up.

"It's about that little fantasy-Felicity you've concocted. You have to keep a safe distance between you and Half Palm, your family, and me, don't you, dollface? You especially can't risk being with a man who really knows you because he might topple all those castles-in-the-air you've created."

Of course she couldn't take the chance of the world finding out about her Half Palm beginnings and the real Charm relatives! But that had nothing to do with Magee. "Look, is this so difficult to understand? The ratings prove that my viewers love my persona, which includes the fictionalized Charm family. That's just the way it is."

"And that's the love that matters to you, isn't it? The love of a bunch of anonymous, credit card-toting strangers."

"I don't have parents. I don't have a brother. So maybe strangers are all I have," she retorted, crossing her arms over her chest. "Unless you're going to tell me *you* love me?"

He was silent a moment. "Love you? I hope to God I'm not that stupid," he finally said, then brushed past her to slam out of the trailer.

She dropped onto the couch and buried her face in

her hands. How had this happened? More importantly, how could she have *let* this happen? She'd always believed that with smart choices and hard work she'd achieve her heart's desire.

But now . . . now her shopping cart was chock-full of unhappiness.

Lifetime guaranteed.

A siren sounded, loud enough to restart a cadaver's heart. Revolving red lights flashed. Magee fought the urge to raise his hands over his head, and instead grabbed for an empty plastic cup, shoving it beneath the spewing slot machine to catch the flood of tokens.

"Jackpot," he muttered, disgusted.

As the first cup reached overflowing, an empty one was offered up. He grabbed it without looking or thanking the source. Manna from heaven—not that he believed in such a place—had been raining down on him all night long.

Finally the damn machine stopped belching coins. It took longer for it to cease its caterwauling. The police lights continued to revolve with bloody regularity as he glanced over to see who'd come to his aid with plastic cups a second, then a third time.

"Peter," he said. Maybe his good fortune—which had been running like a Derby winner all evening—had finally run out. "I'm not looking for company."

The other man's gaze flicked to the overflowing cups, then back to his face. "What *are* you looking for? A small fortune?"

"Ash said the slots helped her forget," he muttered. "I thought I'd give it a try."

Peter's eyebrows rose. "Forget? That's not like you. You're more of the stewer type."

"Cut the psych shit, or get the hell away from me." Magee turned back to the machine. He fed it a dollar coin. The stupid thing started shrieking at him again. Tokens gushed.

Peter handed him another cup. "Looks like it's your lucky day."

His back teeth made an unpleasant grinding noise in his head. "What do you want?"

"For one thing, to see if you're okay. Someone came into the bar and said they'd spotted your Jeep in the Easy Money parking lot. Seemed like a strange choice."

"On the day a man's fiancée dumped him?" The slot machine died down, giving his sarcasm the quiet it deserved. "Doesn't seem that strange to me."

"Is that what's bothering you, Magee? That Ashley and I are together?"

"Yes. No. I don't know." He hesitated. "All of the above."

"I love Ash and Anna P.," Peter said.

He knew that. And they loved him back. Leaving him the only unhappy one. "Simon would want them taken care of."

Peter let a beat go by, then sighed. "Just so you know, I'm not going to take care of them like Simon would. I'm not Simon."

You're working so damn hard to be someone *you're not.*

"Is that what you thought I was doing, Pete? Trying to be Simon?" Felicity had said so.

"I think you've been trying to figure things out."

Magee turned to look at the other man. "Why the hell did we do it?" He'd resisted analyzing his actions all his life, but the truth seemed imperative now. "Why did we take those risks? How long did we think our luck could hold?"

"Some of the why was because it was fun. And then some of the why was those demons, pal. I was showing my father I could accomplish something that took more balls than passing a class in anatomy."

There was a weight on Magee's chest that made it hard for him to breathe. He hadn't climbed to prove anything to anyone!

Or had he? Magee remembered telling Felicity about walking that two-by-four.

"I did it to give fear a face," he heard himself say. To take that amorphous disquiet hanging over his family and turn it into a rock wall, a new route, a summit he could physically tackle. He'd told Felicity his childhood had been suburban-sitcom perfect, but he saw now how the sudden knowledge that it could be taken away—fathers died! mothers feared! brothers threatened!—had hit him hard.

Air whooshed out his lungs. "Are we head cases?"

Peter shrugged. "I don't know. You don't miss it at all?"

"I hate the fucking snow." Magee's answer was automatic—and the truth. "I don't want big mountains anymore. I've been through epics, accidents, and sufferfests on them and now they've lost their allure. But . . . but I miss the rock."

He realized that was true, too.

"You know anything about adaptive rock climbing?"

Magee raised a brow. "You're kidding. You want to go back up?"

Peter nodded. "With the right partner."

"You want to risk again?"

"I want to *dare*. There's a difference I don't think I can explain." Peter hesitated. "What do you think?"

Magee studied his old friend. He knew what was being asked. A paraplegic climber needed a strong partner, and a patient one. Someone who enjoyed the chess problem of rock climbing as much—more than—the athletic challenge.

"I don't know if I can trust my judgment anymore—or if you should. And you gotta know that my luck ran out on that last climb with Simon."

Peter slanted a look at the overflowing cups of tokens. "You sure about that?"

Magee stilled, looking down on the piles of tokens. He hadn't lost his luck after all? "But . . ." He shook his head, trying to fit this new piece into the puzzle. Was life truly that random? Could it be so purposeless, so meaningless, that the reason he was alive and Simon wasn't was something so trivial as chance?

A familiar figure hovering just out of earshot

caught his attention. Felicity's Hardy Boy, Drew, looking like something a debutante had dragged in from a charity luncheon. Linen slacks, light blue dress shirt open at the throat, a navy blue blazer. All that was missing was the yachtsman's cap or a polo mallet.

"What's he want?" he ground out.

Peter glanced over his shoulder, looked back at Magee. "You. He came to the bar and said he wanted to talk to you."

As Pretty Boy approached, Peter wheeled away. Magee set the cups of tokens aside and folded his arms over his chest.

"Good to see you again, Magee," Drew said, his palm outstretched. "I have a favor to ask."

Magee shook hands, then, glancing down as he shoved his fingers in the pockets of his faded jeans, he noted the slogan on his T-shirt. "I'm in a pisser of a mood, and frankly, Drew, I think my shirt says it all."

The other man's gaze dropped.

I can only please one person a day, today isn't your day and tomorrow doesn't look good either.

Amusement glinted in Drew's pale blue eyes as he raised a hand to smooth back the strands of his perfectly smooth hair. Magee stared him down, refusing to shake back the ragged stuff that was hanging over his own forehead.

"Still . . . I was hoping you could do something for Felicity."

Magee set his jaw. He *was* doing that, damn it. She wanted to walk out of his life and he was letting her.

That he'd suggested it be any different had been his surprise talking—shock—because his original plan for the future had been derailed. He'd always known what he and Felicity had was of the here-today-gone-tomorrow variety.

He'd counted on it.

Drew's eyebrows rose. "Is that a no?"

Magee shrugged. "Depends on what it is." So he was curious. Sue him.

"She told me about that tightroping you did at the rock gym."

"Yeah?"

"It's . . . impressive. I thought we might pump up the presentation of the Mountain Logic merchandise with a demonstration."

Magee frowned. "You want to tape some folks doing it at the rock gym? It's fine with me, though you'll have to check with my other partners, too."

"I want a live demonstration. At the amphitheater. With you on the rope."

"Is this Felicity's idea?" She hadn't appeared to like him doing it all that much the first time.

"This is between you and me."

Ah. "For Felicity . . . or should I say, Felicity's *show*."

Drew smiled, displaying a piano's worth of dazzling dental work. "You understand."

Oh, he did. He hadn't been challenged to a pissing contest in years, but nothing about them ever changed. This was between him and Drew and which one of them would look like a real man—the right man—in Felicity's eyes at the end of the day, the boulderer or the businessman.

He could tell Drew who she'd pick. Magee could also tell him he didn't want her—she was too shallow, too uptight, too ready to leave him and Half Palm behind.

But he had nothing else on his agenda, nothing else mapped out for the rest of his whole damn, meaningless life.

And he didn't want Drew to best him, either. "You're on."

It was a purpose—though not a noble one. And maybe it was nuts, but at least it was going to get him through another day.

Nineteen

Sitting across from Aunt Vi, Felicity drank her last cup of coffee in the old kitchen. She'd slept her last eight hours in her old bed the night before. It had been easy enough to dodge Drew—he'd actually disappeared on *her*—so she hadn't been forced to stay in the same Palm Springs hotel with the rest of the GetTV group.

If Drew asked about that, she'd give him some sort of excuse, but the day would be so busy she suspected it would slip right by him.

Though they hadn't seen hide nor hair of Ben yet, Felicity had to believe he'd turn up any minute. She did believe it. In an odd way she trusted Mr. Caruso. By the end of today, her life would be back to normal. The airing of her latest *All That's Cool Afternoon* would be a smooth-running success. She would escape Half Palm and the Charms for the second and final time in her life. She would make it through the day and back to L.A. without ever seeing Michael Magee again.

Aunt Vi got up to top off their mugs, then settled back into her chair, the movement setting the rickety table to wobbling. Felicity steadied it without thinking, then frowned. "Aunt Vi, you should buy yourself a new table." Not to mention a new housecoat and slippers. As a matter of fact, Felicity had sent her a beautiful set last Christmas.

"I'm comfortable with the things I have," Aunt Vi replied with a vague wave of her hand.

"But I send you money every month." And Felicity had, from the day her GetTV salary had covered more than just her necessities. Suspicions growing, her frown deepened. Those no-good Charms! "Aunt Vi, what have you done with it?"

She sipped at her coffee. "I'm saving it for a rainy day."

Felicity sighed. At least some other Charm hadn't bilked it out of her. But the table had two, if not three teetery legs! "Isn't today rainy?" she asked, lifting her mug and letting the table wiggle away.

"No." Aunt Vi glanced out the kitchen window. "Today is beautiful, and will be even more so as soon as my Ben is back."

What could Felicity say to that?

"Besides," Aunt Vi continued, "I'm saving it for you. I don't need anything more than I have."

Felicity's jaw dropped. That money was intended for her aunt! It was supposed to make Aunt Vi's life more comfortable . . . and Felicity more comfortable with absenting herself from it.

Blood money, a little voice inside her said. *Ransom.*

She jumped up to give Aunt Vi a brisk, brief hug. "I've got to get going. My car's all packed, and . . ." The sting of tears was beyond silly. "Don't forget to call that number I gave you the *instant* Ben walks through the door. GetTV's using one of the ranger station's landlines and my crew will get word to me."

"Will you have a chance to stop by Uncle Billy's shop on your way out of town?"

"No." She planned on risking speeding tickets. "Is that a problem?"

"He has your statue."

"My statue?" Her Joanie. Her mangled, busted Joanie. Why would Uncle Billy have it? But she didn't want the thing. She never wanted to see it again, because it reminded her of things she never wanted to think about again.

Of him.

"Maybe I'll win another one next year." She would, she decided, definitely. Another year of hard work, of buffing her image and polishing her performance, and she'd possess that untarnishable perfection she reached for.

Aunt Vi pulled her down for another hug. "You know we love you. Don't be a stranger."

Felicity left the room without saying that's exactly what she hoped to become to them.

A live show was chaos. A live show on-location was Chaos. A live show, on-location, with an audience was Utter Chaos.

Felicity would usually have fed off the energy of it,

however. But today, the manic scurrying of the crew and the excited buzz of the crowd the audience manager had found at Palm Desert's famous El Paseo shopping district and then bused in to fill the seats in the nature amphitheater only sucked away her spirit.

So she hid in her dressing trailer, foregoing her usual last check of the set. As for the audience—she didn't feel up to facing anyone, including the eye of the camera. Her hands trembled with stage fright as she shuffled through her note cards. And she nearly leaped out of her skin when there was a knock on her door—but it was only her assistant. Not with a message from Aunt Vi, but with the notice that it was near time for Felicity to get mic'd up.

Where was Ben?

The question screamed in her mind and was answered by every mob movie and episode of *The Sopranos* she'd ever managed not to click away from fast enough. Violent programming sent her channel-surfing, but even she could imagine a dozen gruesome endings for her goofy, good-hearted young cousin. Yet she had Mr. Caruso's word.

The crime boss of the California Mafia.

Her assistant knocked again, giving Felicity no more time to wallow in anxiety. She was hardly aware of threading through the cables, satellite dishes, and other GetTV trailers to arrive at the amphitheater's side entrance, but she relished the few more minutes of semi-privacy as a technician wired her with the microphone and also the IFB. The Interruptive Feedback Button fit snugly in her ear and gave Drew, as producer, an open line to communicate instructions during the show.

As the audience manager warmed up the crowd for her introduction, she whispered to her assistant, "I'm expecting a message on the landline. If it comes through, have Drew pass it on, all right?"

Until she knew that Ben was home, she wouldn't present a single Caruso product. It might mess with the schedule Drew had handed her the day before, but once she was on-air, no one could stop her from running the show as she liked.

Then she heard her name announced, and, waving and smiling, she high-heeled it across the amphitheater's stage to her stool and table full of products. During the trip across the short distance she absorbed as much as she could.

The set pretty much as it had looked the day before. Pacifying.

Large, enthusiastic audience. Gratifying.

And in that audience, standing out like crows in a wheat field, a sprinkling of hard-jawed, olive-skinned men in severely cut suits.

Terrifying.

Apparently Mr. Caruso was determined she keep to her end of their deal as well.

She collapsed onto her stool, grateful her knees no longer needed to hold her up.

"What's the matter?" Drew said in her ear. "You look like a rabbit. Lick your lips, then smile some more."

Felicity did a quick check of her appearance in the

three separate monitors set up in front of her, off-camera. One showed the full-frontal shot that was beamed into the viewers' living rooms, while the others showed her left and right profiles. Drew was right, and rabbit impersonations weren't going to win her another Joanie.

With a little bounce, she resettled herself on the stool, straightening her spine and squaring her shoulders. Then, touching her ear, she grinned at the audience. "My producer just told me I resemble a rabbit. Not a good thing in these wide-open spaces, wouldn't you agree?" She pretended to scan the bright blue sky above her for predators, noting but dismissing another cable that was strung between two of the one-hundred-foot-high boulders behind her that served as the walls of the amphitheater.

Most of the audience laughed.

Ignoring the serious Suits who didn't, she launched into a welcome for the live audience and a brief explanation to the at-home viewers about their location. "We've taken you to the ski slopes of Tahoe, the pier in Santa Barbara, and that memorable roller-coaster at the Magic Mountain theme park. But today we're at one of the most unique—and starkly beautiful—spots in Southern California."

Her eyes scanned the scenery around them. "I wish I could tell those of you at home how blue the sky is here. We're sitting snug, cupped in a bowl of mountains. The air is so clean and dry that the smallest detail is cleanly etched against the stark blue, almost like a movie backdrop. As a matter of fact, this area served as the location for many movies over the years, standing in for everything from the Sahara to a lush tropical isle. I think the audience with me today will agree that basking in the seventy-something-degree sunshine while not far away rises the snow-covered San Jacinto Mountain makes a special way to start the New Year."

The audience clapped, except for the goons.

"Get a move on," Drew directed in her ear.

It wasn't the message she was waiting on. So she smiled again, stalling. "They say you have to see the desert in spring to appreciate it, but winter is pretty wonderful as well. Now, bring me back here when it's a hundred and eleven in August, and you may hear an entirely different story."

The audience laughed and clapped again.

"In case you've forgotten"—Drew's voice was as dry as the air—"we're here to sell."

She darted a quick glance to the rear of the audience, where she could see him standing, wearing his headset and accompanying mic. He looked his usual put-together self, but she sensed his impatience.

"Read the prompter, Felicity. The revised schedule's on there. Start with the massage pens."

Revised schedule? Her gaze darted to the prompter, but the first product was the same from yesterday's schedule. With a tiny nod, she took a breath and picked up one of the vibrating pens that came with a diagram of stress points on the body. Her mouth opened and she launched into her sales pitch on automatic, her delivery smooth and her enthusiasm real-enough-sounding, even as her mind focused on the problem at hand. The Caruso products were to follow and there was still no word that Ben was safely home.

Her gaze found each of the mobsters in the audience. Sweat was glistening on their faces—she could have told them a business suit was a bad fashion choice for the desert outdoors—and a few of them were shifting in their chairs, apparently bored.

One shot her an evil look.

Her speech hitched a second, along with her breath. If she'd doubted their presence was meant to intimidate her, now she knew she was wrong. Oh, what to do?

If she introduced the products, then she lost her leverage for getting Ben back.

If she didn't introduce them, it would be one public, potentially damaging career move. Drew would think she'd lost her touch and her marbles. After all, she was the one who had waxed poetic on the sauces to begin with.

The sales period wound down for the massage pens and she was still unsure. She tried stalling with a few more comments about the desert until Drew growled in her ear again. "Get on with it, Felicity. Read the prompter."

She didn't need to read the prompter to know what was next. As she half-turned toward the table beside her, her eye caught a figure looming in the same side entrance to the amphitheater that she'd used. Her heart stuttered in her chest and her body froze.

Magee. Michael Magee, the man she'd planned on

never, ever seeing again. Out of his usual ratty jeans
and rude T-shirts and in a pair of shorts and shirt that
she recognized as Mountain Logic climbing gear.
There was a climber's harness buckled around his
hips and flexible rock shoes on his feet. He watched
her with his cool, gunslinger's stare.

And underneath that dark, judgmental gaze, she
was supposed to sell the Caruso products, and sell out
her family.

"The prompter," Drew growled again in her ear.

Her eyes still locked on Magee, she blindly reached
for one of the bottles of sauce. There was a high-
pitched whine in her ears, but she didn't think it was
coming through the IFB. It was her nerves, every last
one of them plucked and humming, thanks to
Magee's presence.

Trying to catch her breath, she turned to the audience. The Caruso cohorts were all sitting up straight.
The one who'd given her the evil look had lowered his
brows and folded his arms over his chest in a clear
posture of intimidation.

But Felicity refused to let herself be rattled. Holding the product toward the audience, she smiled and
spoke directly to the Evil Suit. "Here's something
new I've just uncovered—a hidden treasure—from a
local family who keeps several secrets."

"Felicity," Drew cut in. "Not that, read the
prompter."

She ignored him, focused as she was on Evil Suit,
who sat up even straighter as what she said appeared
to sink in. He half-rose out of his seat.

"As a matter of fact . . ." she continued.

"The prompter," Drew ordered again.

She ignored him again. ". . . I've known this family for years, but until just recently I didn't realize that—"

A hand swiped the bottle of sauce away from her. Felicity looked around, startled. Magee! Michael Magee, on her set, with her sauce, trying to stop her from doing what *she* wanted!

He leaned down to burn her ears with an angry whisper. "I'm going to be mad as hell if I was saved for this. If I find out my sole purpose in life is to keep you from pulling stupid stunts."

Stupid stunts! Felicity heard that echo and re-echo even as she finally paid attention to Drew's commands and glanced at the teleprompter. He *had* revised the schedule. The Mountain Logic clothing was up next, not the Caruso sauces. She made a quick apology to the audience—"This is why they call it live TV"—even as Drew spoke again in her ear.

"Your friend will demonstrate some climbing moves while you give the pitch."

Later on she'd figure out whose idea this was and why. For now, she dragged her professionalism back around her and flashed another smile for the audience. "World-famous climber Michael Magee is here to show us what the products from Mountain Logic are designed to do. While you might not aspire to extreme sports, you'll feel like an extreme athlete in this comfortable yet hip line of sportswear."

On one of the monitors, she saw the camera zoom

back to catch Magee leaping onto a sheer rock face behind her. He landed like a fly, his fingers wedging into an unseen fissure, his rock shoes balancing on an invisible ledge.

She had to keep her eyes on the audience after that. Not that she was afraid for Magee—Lord knows it was clear the man was made to crawl up perpendicular surfaces—but because watching him move with such power and grace made her remember too much about how they'd moved together.

It took him hardly any time to reach the top of the pillar of rock. There was another man up there— Gwen's brother from the rock gym?—to help him off with his harness. Then Magee stood alone, on top of the world, it seemed. She wanted him so badly she could cry.

Drew commanded again, "The prompter."

She read it silently first. *To show just how extreme you can get in Mountain Logic gear, Michael Magee will demonstrate a maneuver called tightroping a slack line.*

That cable she'd noticed when she'd walked onto the stage was no cable at all, she realized, but climbing rope. She glanced up at it, stretched high above her. Barefoot, Magee approached the ledge, then glanced down at her.

Her heart stumbled. Unable to look away, she remembered Gwen's brother taking off the climber's harness. Which meant Magee wasn't wearing a safety leash.

Her heart stumbled again and her mouth went desert-dry. What did he think he was doing? Talk about stupid stunts!

But she could see that reckless gleam in his eyes and she thought about how lost he'd seemed the day before without his "purpose" of taking care of Ashley and Anna P. It had never occurred to her that climbers had a death wish, but the idea suddenly had her around the throat and was squeezing.

She cupped her lapel mic, preparing to shout him out of this foolishness.

"Felicity." Drew's voice in her ear interrupted. "We've blocked off the entrance to the amphitheater and its parking lot, but I just got word that there's a group outside who want in. They say they're your family?"

Now?

Now?

It had to be Charms. Only Charms could mess up a simple instruction like "use the telephone" and show up at a time like this. She felt like screaming in frustration.

Well, let them cool their heels until she persuaded Magee not to take this tightrope walk.

"Felicity? Thumbs-up, we'll let them in. Thumbs-down, we won't."

With a grimace she glanced toward Drew at the rear of the audience, then back up at the eerie grin on Magee's face. She was really going to kill him this time if he didn't stop this nonsense *immediately*. But how?

Unless . . . It would stall him, she was sure of it.

Never looking away from Magee, she flashed Drew a thumbs-up.

She recognized when the newcomers entered at the rear of the amphitheater, because Magee blinked, his face showing sudden surprise. The rest of the audience was leaning forward in their seats, their eyes on him, and they must have seen the way his expression changed, too. Everyone's heads, including Felicity's, turned.

And there they were, the whole motley crew that was her family. Aunt Vi in another of her straight-from-the-seventies polyester pantsuits. Uncle Billy, in his grease-stained coveralls and gap-toothed smile. Ashley, Anna P. on her hip. Roberta, the old geezers, and the only well-dressed one of the bunch—her cousin the golf hustler—too far back for anyone to see, naturally.

But Ben? She glanced up at Magee and then back at the grouped Charms. No goofy towhead in sight. Her heart pounded.

Looking at Aunt Vi, she mouthed the question. "Where's Ben?"

"Surprise!" From the side entrance to the stage, a figure came running. Goofy, towheaded Ben had grown into a tall, goofy towhead in the last couple of years. Felicity had never seen a more precious sight.

Paralyzed by relief, she let him rush her, then tackle her with a one-armed bear hug that had her mic leaping in one direction and her IFB in the other. She didn't care. Instead, she hugged him back, her arms locking around his lanky form. "You idiot." She said it over and over.

He only laughed, then pulled away to look down into her face. "Unlucky idiot. Or maybe just lucky to have you in the family."

She almost *shh*ed him, but with her mic swinging on its wire somewhere at her feet, she didn't bother. A story explaining who Ben was and why he was here would occur to her any second.

And though Drew was probably going crazy, without her IFB in, she didn't know about it. So she took another minute to get a question answered. "What happened? What took you so long?"

He laughed again, like the darling doofus he was. "You can thank Uncle Billy for that. They had me out at some old place in the desert. On our way back, we ran into an area of road he'd salted. Four blown tires."

She gaped at him. "I swear I'll kill him with my two bare hands!"

"That's why he sent me up with a peace offering." From behind his back, Ben whipped something out.

Felicity stared at the blob of metal in her cousin's hand.

"Uncle Billy and Mom put it back together for you," Ben continued. "I heard it looked a little different before, but hey, I think they did good." He shoved it at her.

It took Felicity a moment, but then she realized what was in her hands—what Uncle Billy and Aunt Vi had done. They'd rebuilt her Joanie.

Apparently the statue hadn't broken cleanly in two, because when soldered back together she'd lost her elegant stance for a much less ladylike slouch.

Her scars and scrapes were still in evidence, but someone—Aunt Vi, it had to be—had glued a chartreuse pom-pom on top of her head as a hat-cum-coverup for the major damage that part of Joanie had sustained on her near-fall from the mountain.

Mountain . . . She looked up, but Magee was no longer there. She glanced toward the rest of the Charms and found him, leaning against the rock behind them, all dark hair and gunslinger glare. Her gaze moved back to the family, and by contrast, their love and pride in her shone from their eyes.

Her fingers squeezed the cool metal of the Joanie.

When he'd accused her of turning her back on her family, she'd told Magee the only people she had to love her were strangers. But looking out at the Charms, she had to take it back. Take it all back.

She'd been wrong. So wrong.

All this time, the Charms had loved her, even when she'd distanced herself from them. They'd loved her when she'd made up stories about them. They'd always loved her.

But she'd done the whole, dumb Dorothy thing, hadn't she? Gone to Oz looking for love, when all the time it was in her own back yard?

Cradling the Joanie against her, she smiled up at Ben. "You're right. They did do good. I love it just as it is."

As they'd loved her, just as she was. Orphaned or not, they'd always thought of her as one of their own.

Turning toward her family, she held up the Joanie. "It's wonderful!" More than wonderful, perfect. Oh, yes. Just like the Charms were perfect, scars, scrapes, pom-poms, and all.

Love could do that.

Then, realizing they hadn't heard her, she grabbed for her dangling mic and clipped it back into place. Beaming, she shook the Joanie in the air. "Thank you! Thank you, Uncle Billy and Aunt Vi!"

The collective gasp of the audience made it absolutely clear her secret was out. Uncle Billy wasn't a wine connoisseur. She supposed no one would believe Aunt Vi and the George Bernard Shaw Society now.

But so what? Who needed public adoration when Dorothy had Aunt Em and Felicity had Aunt Vi? With a wave of her free hand, she urged the Charm clan toward the stage. Then she turned to the camera and said, "I have some lovely people I'd like you to meet."

As they filed toward the stage, smiling, Felicity almost clicked her heels three times—but then stopped herself. She was already home.

Twenty

The second hour of Felicity's *All That's Cool Afternoon* went more smoothly than the first. The Charm relatives were given seats in the audience. She'd wasted so many minutes on her reunion that Drew had instructed her to move on from the Mountain Logic products to the others. Her sell of the Caruso sauces had sounded sincere.

The truth was, they tasted really good.

When Drew finally said in her ear, "We're out," she slumped onto her stool. Her assistant handed her a bottle of chilled water. Then, after a long, closed-eyes swallow, she took stock of her post-show surroundings.

Shooed along by staff members, the audience was heading out of the amphitheater toward the parking lot and waiting buses. Her Charm relatives, somewhere in the middle of the pack, appeared content to be herded along with the rest.

Drew stood in the middle of the clearing seats, huddling with the first cameraman. As for Magee, he'd disappeared after his aborted attempt to tightrope the slack line. But as she lifted her sweating bottle to take another swallow, he sauntered back onto the stage from the side entrance, his climbing harness in his hand.

His gaze brushed her face. "You surprised me, dollface."

She didn't know what to say. "I surprised a bunch of people, I think." Her staff, Drew, her viewers. Her job might be at stake.

Magee didn't say anything more, just studied her face as if he were trying to figure her out. She didn't know what her expression revealed, though she knew that after the stress of the day she was out of defenses. If he stood there much longer, she might lose all her pride and beg him to take her in his arms. Admitting who the real Charms were and accepting and appreciating what they'd always offered her hadn't changed anything about that other truth she'd finally admitted to herself as well.

She was in love with Magee.

She could only hope that the memory of his last words to her in the trailer—*Love you? I hope to God I'm not that stupid*—would stop her from making a fool of herself and blurting it out.

His eyes still on her, he stepped into the climbing harness.

She blinked. "What are you doing?"

"I agreed to tightrope. Drew wants to get it on tape."

For the teaser segments, she presumed, and noted that the first cameraman, Warren, was now in position. Drew stood at the rear of the amphitheater once more, watching. She gestured toward him, then looked back at Magee. "If you'd like, I can . . . I can talk him out of it."

A wry smile flickered over his mouth. "I just bet you can." Metal clicked against metal as he latched the harness around his hips. "But you know me—I'm big on following through with my promises."

Just one of the reasons she'd fallen in love with him. "You'll use the safety leash, though, right?"

He walked toward the rock pillar he'd free-climbed earlier. "Ready?" he asked Warren. At the other man's nod, he glanced over at Felicity. "I don't think so."

Her heart leaped as he leaped onto the perpendicular surface, about four feet off the ground. She rose from her stool, clutching her water bottle to her chest. "What do you mean, 'I don't think so'?"

He glanced down at her, then reached for another hold. "I mean, no, I'm not going to use a safety leash." With another stretch, he moved farther up the rock, farther away from her.

"Don't be crazy!"

"I feel a little crazy." He made a lateral move that widened his stance.

Twenty feet above the amphitheater's stage, his body hugging the rock, stuck to it with only finger pads and toes, he was grinning at her. That wild, reckless grin of his that was starting to scare her. "What are you doing, Magee?"

"Testing my theory, dollface. I told myself there was some purpose to what happened on that mountain eighteen months ago. But now I'm working on a new hypothesis."

Her stomach drew into a tight fist as he moved up. Shading her eyes, she stepped back to get a clearer view of him. "What hypothesis is that?" she called out. With the audience gone, her voice echoed against the surrounding rock walls.

"That there's no meaning whatsoever." He reached behind him to the chalk bag hanging from the harness at his back. "And that the better man died, while the Lucky Bastard lived."

Speechless, she stared at him as he groped for the chalk with his other hand. A scattering of dust fell from the lip of the bag, the afternoon light turning it golden, like an angel's dust.

But where were they? Where were the angels she'd met that night in the desert now?

Something touched her shoulder. Startled, she whirled to face Magee's old friend, Gwen's brother. "What is it—?" She didn't know his name.

"I'm Barry." His serious expression magnified her own anxiety. "There's another way to the top. It's a scramble, no climbing. Can you do it?"

"Of course I can do it." She glanced down at her tight skirt and high heels. "I *will* do it." As she followed Barry out of the amphitheater, she swiped one of the sample pairs of Mountain Logic rock shoes from the pile of products.

Once around the corner, she kicked off her heels and peeled down her pantyhose, then laced up the flat, rubber-soled rock shoes. They were a little big, but would have to do. Then she ran after Barry, and saw what he meant by "another way to the top." A series of various-sized boulders were tumbled behind the pillars that made up the amphitheater walls. While it looked a bit more than a "scramble" to her, she thought she could do it, if—

"Do you have a knife?" she asked Barry.

When he handed a pocketknife over, she used the blade to hack at the bottom of her skirt, turning the modest hemline into a mini. *Now* she could scramble. "Let's go."

It was harder than she thought. Air wheezed in and out of her lungs as she tried following each of Barry's steps. But with that image of Magee's reckless grin burning in her brain, she pressed upward, and then finally found herself standing on top of one of the pillars.

The wrong pillar, she realized, as Magee pulled himself over the top of the other, twenty-five feet and the tightrope away. Her head jerked toward Barry. "But—"

"We can't get to the other one like this," he said.

She looked back at Magee. He was frowning at her, giving her a dose of that dangerous, gunslinger stare. "I can't let you do this," she called across the chasm.

His expression eased and he laughed, his hands going to the latch of his harness. "How are you going to stop me?"

"By reminding you of . . . of what could happen." Her stomach twisted at the thought. "You should know life . . . life is beautiful, every minute precious."

His harness dropped to the ground and he made no sign that he'd heard her. "Magee! Magee, listen!"

He looked across that yawning distance.

"That night in the desert," she said. "I never told you . . ."

"Never told me what?" he asked, drawing closer to the edge.

Her heart stuttered. "I saw you. I saw you from outside my body, from above the both of us."

"You've been spending too much time around Peter." He bent over to unlace his shoes.

"I was dead, Michael. I know I was dead."

He stilled, then straightened, tossing the shoe in his hand to the ground. "You couldn't—"

"I did." She had tried to ignore and to pretend away the experience, because it was unnerving and . . . confusing, but it seemed to be clearing up in her mind even as she spoke. "I saw you pleading with me to live. I saw you kissing my hand and holding it against your cheek."

He looked angry now. "Then you were half-conscious."

"I wasn't. You know I wasn't. I was dead. And there was a warm, dazzling light opening behind me and as I turned toward it, two figures stepped out. They were familiar to me—I think they were my parents." Of course they were, she thought, suddenly remembering. They'd been wearing the same clothing as she'd seen in that photograph she'd found at Aunt Vi's.

"And then, Magee, I had a choice. I could go with them into that beautiful shining light, or I could . . . I could go back into my body." Heavenly love or earthly love. And she'd looked at that gorgeous stranger with tears in his eyes and that desperate note in his voice, and her selfish heart had opened up and taken him in. "There was nothing random about it, nothing random at all."

"If I follow that logic, dollface, then you're saying that Simon chose to die, that he chose to walk away into that bright light of yours and leave Ashley and Anna P. and me behind."

"No!" She shook her head, frustrated. "I'm not saying that. I'm not saying I have all the answers. But I know that when I opened my eyes, when I realized that I was *alive,* I saw the world as louder, brighter, sweeter, and I don't think you should take all that beauty for granted."

But he was already unlacing his other shoe. Panic caused her breath to stutter in her lungs and she couldn't think of another way to dissuade him. She didn't have anything else to offer up.

Except the one thing that would strip away her pride—and probably wouldn't stop him anyway.

He approached the rope strung between them. It was now or never, just like that moment of choice she'd made that night in the desert. But she'd been . . . she'd been promised earthly love! She'd chosen it, she'd chosen him, and he wasn't doing his part!

Earthly love, she thought again. And then it hit her, hit her hard. She'd been promised love on earth. And she had it, didn't she? She loved him. But she'd never been promised that Magee would love her back.

And he was inches away from walking across the air without a net.

"Michael! Michael, one more thing." There was nothing left to do but lead with risk and hope for reward.

With more than a trace of impatience, he looked up. "What now?"

"I'm in love with you." She smiled, even though she felt the sting of tears in her eyes. "Just so you know, I'm in love with you."

"Nice try, Lissie," he replied, shaking his head. "Opposites attract, I'll give you that. But love? I don't think so."

He didn't believe her! She'd laid bare her heart, let him see her naked emotion, and he thought it was just something she'd said to stop him. Tears stung again.

He pulled his shirt over his head and threw it down. "I have to do this."

What was she supposed to do now? She'd wanted to believe so much that fate or destiny or the angels had conspired to bring her a soul mate, her true Mr. Right. That's what she'd chosen that night in the desert.

She blinked and, in the dry air, found that her tears had evaporated. And then she found that her fears had evaporated, too. *Believe.* That's what she had to do. Have faith in something besides smart choices and hard work. Have faith in love. And hadn't the enduring love of the Charms shown her she could?

"I have to do this," he said again.

Felicity took a breath. "Yes, you do," she said
softly. "Yes, I think you do."

It wasn't a death wish, Magee told himself, shaking
his arms to relax the muscles. Despite what Felicity
thought, what Barry was thinking, if the expression on
his face was any judge, he wasn't doing this to cancel
out the life that Simon's heroic effort had granted him
eighteen months ago.

He was doing it because . . .

Hell, he was no better at navel-gazing now than
he'd ever been.

Closing his eyes, he took a deep breath. Then he
opened them, and keeping his chin lifted and his gaze
on the narrow strip that tied him to this earth, he
stepped out.

The rope sagged. It was tighter than when they
knotted it down at the rock gym, and he accommo-
dated the slight wobble with ease. He'd known
climbers who pushed things right to the brink, claiming then they saw God in every pitch, but Magee had
never believed a higher power would waste time with
some death-courting idiot unless it was to haul his ass
off to hell.

Magee continued walking across the rope, steady
and sure. A slight wind tickled his hair away from his
face, but it wasn't enough to distract him. He made it
past the halfway point and kept moving.

At the three-quarter mark, Magee was close to admitting he didn't have a clue why he was up on the

rope and what he hoped it would accomplish. Then, still several steps from the other side, he remembered that Simon used to term riskier moves as calling angels, and maybe, Magee thought, maybe that's what he was doing now.

Calling angels.

For the answer. Was his life a random chance, a happy un-accident? He took another step, and then another. Was he alive because his luck, after all, had held?

I told you. You're alive because it wasn't your time to cark it.

The Aussie voice was in Magee's brain and on the breeze blowing across his sweating face.

Shaking his head to dislodge it, he had to seesaw his arms to keep his balance. His stomach lurched.

His heart took the fall he was suddenly desperate not to make.

Fear welled, taking up the freed space inside his chest. He froze, as everything changed. Instead of daylight, it was darkness, below him, around him. Waiting for him. Was it death?

It's not living, which is what you've been doing the last eighteen months, mate. Step out, you dumb yobbo, step out and grab life around the neck.

But Magee couldn't move, not when his limbs felt so cold and clumsy and there was all that bleak darkness yawning beneath him.

"Magee."

Lissie's voice. He looked for it, for her, and his gaze found hers. Over the distance between them, their connection, that link he'd sensed so often, forged. How had he dismissed it before? How could he have thought it simple chemistry when now he could see it was so much more?

More than chance, it was something big, it was whatever forces that came together when two people—against the odds—fell in love.

Step out, you dumb yobbo, step out and grab life around the neck.

This time he obeyed, and holding fast to that line between himself and Felicity, he made the last steps. On solid ground, he grabbed the first thing his arms found—her.

He fell to the ground, taking her with him, and then held on tight.

Eyes wide open, he stared into the startling blue overhead. His heart had been restored to its original spot in his chest and was thumping like a drum, powerful enough to be the pulse of every living thing in the world. On his next breath, he inhaled clean air and the delicate scent of Felicity's shampoo.

"Louder, brighter, sweeter," he murmured. "I didn't understand."

She lifted her head, her blue eyes darker than the sky, and deeper. "I know."

The moment, that moment, *this* moment, seemed to shimmer with magic. "On Denali eighteen months ago, there came a point where I thought the remainder of my life had been pared to a handful of minutes. But then I was given a gift. Instead of those few minutes left, I had millions of them, but I didn't want them if the cost was Simon's death."

"You know it wasn't."

"Not until today." He traced her mouth with his forefinger, because he wanted to, and because he could. "My mother accused me a few months back of having a bad case of survivor's guilt. I think maybe she was right, and that I've had it for a long, long time. Why Simon and not me? Why was my father alive and well when my brother's had been murdered?"

"And you have the answers now?"

He sat up, taking her with him. She was such a little thing that he easily lifted her onto his lap and held her there, his chin on the top of her head as he gazed out over the vast desert surrounding them. "No, just more questions."

Had Felicity truly seen angels? Was that voice he'd been hearing Simon's, or just a figment of his imagination—or his common sense?

He turned his face to caress the top of her head with his cheek. "The questions might be the best gift of all, though. Because now I'll have to ask myself, every day, have I done the best I could? Have I made the most of my time?"

A breeze gusted, tossing her feathery hair into his face. He stroked it back down, combing it with his fingers. "But now I have a question for you."

"What's that?" She half-turned to him.

"Are you really in love with me?"

She stiffened, and tried turning away.

He caught her chin in his hand. "Are you in love with me, Lissie?"

"Opposites attract, but . . ."

He winced, remembering how he'd thrown her declaration back in her face. He hadn't been doing the best he could, then. He hadn't made the most of *that* moment. "I'm sorry, dollface. I shouldn't have said that. I should have said instead . . ."

"What?" she whispered.

And in that instant it was her vulnerability that Charmed him. Other times it had been her confidence, her incredible passion, her ability to smooth-talk the world at large, her intention to leave her family behind that had materialized into her fierce protection of them instead. But Magee's heart flipped over this glimpse of the uncertain, unsure Felicity who had once been an orphaned little girl creating a fiction for herself in order to feel loved.

She'd made herself into a hell of a woman.

His heartbeat speeded up and his mouth dried, overcome with gratitude. "Thank you," he croaked out. She'd careened into the darkness he'd considered "living" and awakened him to beauty, passion, and . . .

But he hadn't said that word yet, had he?

"I'm in love with you, too," he said. "I love you so much."

And then she threw herself against him and he fell over, Felicity landing on top of him. He laughed, and with the earth at his back and the sun on his face, Michael Magee held on tight, preparing for the biggest thrill of his life.

Epilogue

From the GetTV web site:

> GetTV is happy to announce that our own
> award-winning Felicity Charm married rock
> climber and businessman Michael Magee in a
> small beachside ceremony on Kaui, February
> 14. Follow the links below to exclusive honey-
> moon photos of the newlyweds swimming, sun-
> bathing, and, of course, shopping!
>
> Felicity will return on-air in April, once she and
> her husband settle into their new home, which
> Felicity claims is exactly equidistant from each
> of their former residences. "When opposites
> attract," she told us, "it's natural to meet half-
> way!"

From the back of an oversized postcard tacked
to the bulletin board at the Bivy, in Half Palm, California:

Aloha, the Bivy! We were shopping (can you believe it?) and Felicity found some joint where you can make postcards from your own photos. So here we are in that famous sacred pool (men, you'll remember it from the Sheryl Crow music video of a few years back). My bride climbed to the top of the cliff happily enough, but then refused to jump in. So . . . oops! . . . I grabbed her by accident and took her down with me (which explains how I ended up in a shopping center, it was the only way to get her talking to me again).

Tomorrow we have a long hike planned. Must say I think marriage is agreeing with both of us. Until we see you all—carpe diem! (And to whoever gave us the his and hers *Carpe Genitalia* T-shirts—I assure you, we're doing plenty of that, too.)

—Magee

There's good cheer
and lots of cuddling by the fire
for readers of these great new
Avon Romances coming in December!

My Own Private Hero by Julianne MacLean
An Avon Romantic Treasure

To avoid the scandal and heartbreak she's seen her sisters go
through for love, Adele Wilson agrees to marry the first landed
gentleman her mother puts in front of her. Her strategy seems to
work, until, on the way to seal the deal, she is overtaken by
Damien Renshaw, Baron Alcester, and her plan suddenly falls by
the wayside of desire . . .

Wanted: One Special Kiss by Judi McCoy
An Avon Contemporary Romance

Lila has traveled far from home with only a vague plan to make her
dreams come true. Instead she finds herself in a small coastal Virginia
town, taking care of adorable twin boys for an overworked physician
father whose charm seems to be pulling Lila in. Falling in love was
not the idea, but once this attraction gets sparked, even the best laid
plans don't have a chance!

Must Have Been the Moonlight by Melody Thomas
An Avon Romance

Michael Fallon is the most exciting man Brianna has ever known—
and now he's her rescuer! But when Michael unexpectedly inherits
the family dukedom, the marriage of convenience Michael proposes
is anything but, and Brianna suddenly finds herself falling in love with
the very man she vowed never to trust with her heart.

Her Scandalous Affair by Candice Hern
An Avon Romance

Richard, Viscount Mallory, is stunned when he sees a family heir-
loom on the bodice of a woman he's only just met. The Lover's
Knot, as the broach is called, has been the Mallory obsession since
it was stolen fifty years ago. Now Richard is determined to know
how Lady Isabel acquired it, and if a few kisses will do the trick,
then he's up to the challenge . . .

Have you ever dreamed of writing a romance?

And have you ever wanted
to get a romance published?

Perhaps you have always wondered how to
become an Avon romance writer?
We are now seeking the best and brightest undiscovered
voices. We invite you to send us your query letter to
avonromance@harpercollins.com

What do you need to do?

Please send no more than two pages telling us
about your book. We'd like to know its setting—is it
contemporary or historical—and a bit about the hero,
heroine, and what happens to them.

Then, if it is right for Avon we'll ask to see part of the
manuscript. Remember, it's important that you have
material to send, in case we want to see your story quickly.

Of course, there are no guarantees of publication,
but you never know unless you try!

We know there is new talent just waiting
to be found! Don't hesitate . . . send us
your query letter today.

The Editors
Avon Romance